THE
MOON
RIDERS

THE MOON RIDERS

THERESA TOMLINSON

eos

An Imprint of HarperCollins*Publishers*

Eos is an imprint of HarperCollins Publishers.

The Moon Riders
Library of Congress Cataloging-in-Publication Data
Tomlinson, Theresa.
The moon riders / Theresa Tomlinson.— 1st American ed.
   p.   cm.
Summary: When thirteen-year-old Myrina of the Mazagardi tribe
joins the Moon Riders, a revered band of warrior women, she
becomes caught up in the life of the Trojan princess Cassandra and
the epic, ten-year Trojan War.
ISBN-10: 0-06-084736-0 (trade bdg.)
ISBN-13: 978-0-06-084736-4 (trade bdg.)
ISBN-10: 0-06-084737-9 (lib. bdg.)
ISBN-13: 978-0-06-084737-1 (lib. bdg.)
1. Amazons—Juvenile fiction. [1. Amazons—Fiction.
2. Cassandra (Legendary character)—Fiction. 3. Trojan War—
Fiction. 4. Troy (Extinct city)—Fiction. 5. Mythology, Greek—
Fiction.] I. Title.
PZ7.T5977Mo 2006   2006000790
[Fic]—dc22   CIP
                                                                      AC
Typography by Hilary Zarycky
1 2 3 4 5 6 7 8 9 10
❖
First American Edition
First published in 2003 in the United Kingdom by Corgi Books, an
imprint of Random House Children's Books

In memory of my great-grandmother Miriam Beer

TABLE OF CONTENTS

PART TWO: THE SNAKE LADY

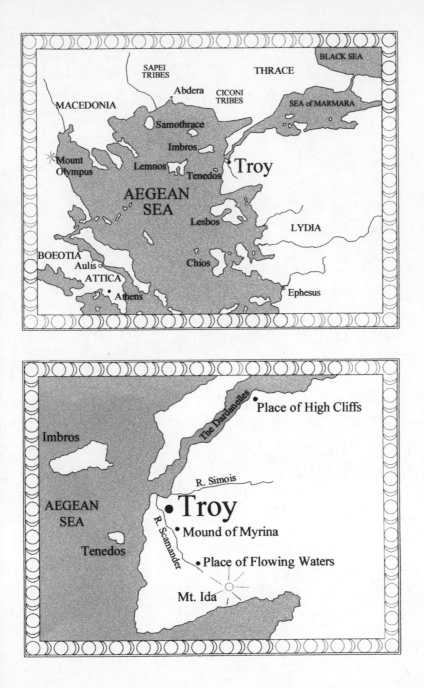

Part One

THE LITTLE SNAKE

CHAPTER ONE

The Dancer

T HE NIGHT WAS cool beside the Lake of Kus. The mother and grandmother sat together outside their round tent, soft woven rugs fastened about their shoulders. They beat a steady rhythm on small drums and sang. Aben leaned close to the fire, the muscles in his cheeks taut, as he strummed a simple melody on his oud, the music thrumming over rocks and grassland.

Myrina, carefully dressed in bangles, beads, trousers, and layers of smocks, danced barefoot about the edge of the fire. She was warm, the dancing saw to that. Her hands and arms twisted, sinuous as snakes; her hips swung back and forth in time with the ancient music of her tribe. She took her final pose with a flourish.

Gul's voice dropped. "Is my daughter ready?" she whispered.

Grandmother Hati smiled broadly. "Aye. I'm sure of

3

it." She turned to the young girl, her face suddenly solemn with the importance of her words. "Myrina, my daughter's daughter! When we go to the Spring Celebrations, I feel sure that Atisha the Old Woman shall take you with her!"

"Thank you, grandmother." Myrina spoke with quiet satisfaction.

Soon the tribes would meet at the place of Flowing Waters; the sacred place at the foot of Mount Ida, not far from the high-walled city of Troy. The joyful Spring Celebrations and shrewd horse dealing that took place there was always exciting, but this year would be better than ever. She, Myrina, who was named after one of the most famous dancers of the past, would leave her family and become one of the honored priestesses of Earth Mother Maa, known as the Moon Riders.

Myrina could not settle to sleep that night, so she slipped out to the roped horse corral. Isatis, the eight-year-old blue-black mare, picked up her scent and, leaving the other horses, she came at once to her mistress's side, whinnying gently.

"I'm to join the Moon Riders," Myrina whispered, stroking the smooth short hairs on the horse's neck. "And you will be my steed."

Myrina was both terrified and excited at the thought of leaving her parents' home tent. She would follow in the footsteps of her mother, grandmother, and Reseda, her older sister.

Reseda was now due to return home after spending seven years traveling from place to place with the Moon Riders, performing sacred dances and songs for those who honored the Great Mother, Maa. Myrina would take her sister's place.

She'd learned to ride, as did all the Mazagardi tribe, when she was just a baby, and traveled constantly from camp to camp, with their herd of goats, sheep, and horses. But she'd never before been away from her family and tribe; and that thought brought a touch of fear with it.

She would have to leave her friend Tomi, who'd ridden at her side since they were children learning to hunt together, sending sharp, light arrows straight and fast toward their prey. In the evenings by the campfire they would lean together for warmth, but now that Tomi had seen fourteen winters he too must leave the tribe for months at a time, buying foals and selling horses with the other young men. Thank goodness at least Isatis would be going with her.

Isatis had been hers from the day that she was born. Myrina was only five when she'd wandered away from the tents and found her father crouched with concern over his favorite horse, Midnight. The pregnant mare had moved away from the rest of the herd to the far edge of the camp. She lay very still beneath an olive tree, her lolling tongue turned gray and her swollen stomach drenched with cold sweat.

Myrina's father had turned to his little daughter in desperation, for all the adults were out of calling distance. He made her help him with the difficult birth and at last a small, stick-legged creature was born into Myrina's arms, half covered in wet membrane.

"If this foal lives, she shall be yours," her father had promised.

Both Isatis and Midnight had lived and Myrina had loved the young blue-black mare ever since.

Seven days before they were to move on for the Spring Celebrations, Myrina sat outside the tent, trying to keep still while her grandmother pricked her skin with a sharp bone needle.

"Do not scratch!" Gul spoke sharply, slapping her daughter's hand away from the nose ring that had also been snapped, red hot and searing, into place.

"It itches like a scorpion's sting," Myrina complained, "and so does this."

"Keep still! Eyes shut!" Hati warned. "The more you wriggle the more it will hurt! Shut your eyes . . . think creature!"

Myrina squeezed her eyelids together, then slowly lowered her shoulders, trying to ease the clenched muscles and think creature. She must make herself believe that she was moving steadily through the grass on her belly, swaying from side to side, a warm wind blowing into her face. It was just possible, if she really relaxed, to lift her thoughts and send them far away from the sharp pricking of the needle.

Hati was skilled at making body pictures and she worked fast, rubbing soot mixed with herb juices and honey into the punctured skin, creating her marks. All young girls destined to become Moon Riders were decorated with body pictures; the work began on their eighth birthday. For the last five years, Hati had added a new picture each spring to Myrina's fast-growing collection. A leaping deer with curling antlers stood out clear blue-black on each foot, bestowing on her the suppleness and grace of the animal. Leaves and flowers rained down from her shoulders, sprinkling the tops of her arms, symbolizing the energy of plant growth. A sharp arrowhead was etched on each cheekbone, warning anyone who came close of hidden strength. Hati herself had scorpions patterning her cheeks and arm, though the dyes were faded now and hidden away between wrinkles. Gul bore the rose flowers of her name—a gentler symbol for a gentle nature.

Now on this special day, Myrina was being decorated

with the last and most important body picture of all, her own chosen symbol, covering her right forearm.

"Almost done," Gul soothed, looking over her mother's shoulder. "I will fetch the milk. The picture is so right; it's you, Myrina."

At last Hati put down her needle and picked up the bowl of precious mare's milk mixed with honey that Gul had brought. She reverently poured a little of it onto the earth as an offering to Maa, then gave the rest to Myrina.

Eyes still closed, Myrina sipped the warm strong-tasting milk with relief. The sharp pains were over and her body picture had taken shape.

They took the bowl away from her, and both Gul and Hati one after the other took Myrina's small hand, kissed it gently and pressed it to their cheeks. "May your picture-magic give you the strength and grace of its images," they whispered. Then Hati sat back and stretched her spine. "Open your eyes," she ordered.

Myrina opened them nervously, glancing down. The skin was red and swollen, but she could see the picture clearly. An undulating snake rippled down her forearm, resting its patterned head on her thumb. Its curling tail just touched her elbow.

"Thank you, Grandmother," she said quietly. "I think it *is* me!"

Gul suddenly caught her breath and pointed beyond

them to a pile of rocks.

"What is it?" Hati asked.

Gul still couldn't speak, but only point.

Myrina turned to look toward the rocks, then she saw it, too. A golden brown viper was weaving its snaky way out into the sunshine, heading toward her feet.

All three women froze for a moment, then in a flash Hati snatched up her stick, raising it above her head.

"Do not strike!" Myrina whispered. "It will not harm me."

The snake stopped and reared up, looking directly at Myrina, then it dipped its head gracefully and turned away. Hati laughed and lowered her stick. "No, I'm sure you are right, though it may not recognize us as friends of the young snake lady!"

The creature slunk smoothly away into the rock shadows once more.

Gul breathed freely again. "Is it a sign? It must be! What can it mean?"

"I don't know." Hati smiled with determination. "But it can only be good. I'm sure of that."

CHAPTER TWO

A Warrior for a Grandmother

OVER THE NEXT few days the swelling and soreness vanished from Myrina's arm, so that her snake-symbol looked very lifelike. Among the Mazagardi there was much talk of the coming Celebrations at the Place of Flowing Waters. All the nomadic tribes who honored Earth Mother, Maa, would gather to rejoice in the coming of Spring; also, they would be presenting their daughters to Atisha, the leader of the Moon Riders, and hoping that she would accept them as priestesses. The Mazagardi tribe had a reputation for providing the best dancers and the best warrior women, too.

"I hear that King Priam wants to buy horses," Gul told Aben. "They say he's richer than ever, now that he's taxing the trading boats that pass through the Hellespont. He makes Achaeans pay twice what he charges our tribes and his Hittite allies."

Aben smiled. "This wealth may help in our dealings with

him, but I swear the man's hoarding trouble for himself!"

"What sort of trouble?" Myrina was curious.

Her father was thoughtful. "The Achaean kingdoms need tin to make their bronze weapons and this new metal they call iron. Their ships bring it from the north, passing through the Hellespont; there's no other way. I'm sure Agamemnon of Mycenae and Menelaus of Sparta will not tolerate Priam's soaring charges forever, and I fear for us all if those two brothers run out of patience."

Myrina nodded. They all feared the fierce Achaean raiding gangs that came north from time to time, plundering gold, murdering the men, and taking women as slaves. She came from many generations of brave warrior women who were always ready to take up arms to defend those they loved. "I'll fight Achaeans if they come raiding," she insisted.

Both parents smiled at her fierceness.

"Well . . . Grandmother turned warrior! She rode with the Moon Riders through Thrace to challenge Theseus, didn't she?"

Gul nodded. "Yes. Hippolyta led them to Athens to rescue Antiope whom Theseus had stolen away."

"So brave of them." Myrina sighed.

Gul's face was full of doubt. "Brave but maybe foolish. The fight cost Hippolyta her life, along with many others. And as Hati will tell you, when it came to it Antiope didn't wish to return home."

Myrina frowned. "She wanted to stay with the Achaeans?"

"Not *wanted*, exactly, but that was what she chose. She'd just given birth to Theseus's son."

"I can't believe it!" Myrina argued. "He forced her to be his slave! She can't have wanted to stay with him!"

Gul shrugged her shoulders.

"War brings strange situations." Aben spoke with his usual tolerance. "We can't know the terrible misery there must be for such as Antiope."

But Myrina was enthralled by the boldness of the adventure. "When the Moon Riders rode to Athens, the Achaeans feared them and called them Amazons!" she recalled, her voice shaking with pride.

Gul could only whisper her doubts. "So many died."

"If Grandmother turned warrior, then so can I!" Myrina insisted.

"What's that?" Hati demanded, dipping her head as she came in through the open tent flaps.

"We are just remembering some of your wilder adventures, Mother," Gul said, smiling again.

As the moon waned, the tribe began to pack up their goods, ready to move on to Mount Ida and the Place of Flowing Waters. Myrina's sister would return to the

Mazagardi there and choose herself a husband.

The night before their move, Myrina sat on a cushion in the tent, fingering her new traveling goods. Tomi came to sit with her.

"I can't wait to use them," Myrina whispered.

There was a carved-horn drinking cup in a felt holder and a strong leather bag containing a flat round of polished wood with three separate wooden legs that would screw into place to make a small camp table. Supple deerskin riding boots stood side by side next to her lightweight bow made of horn and horse sinews, its quiver full of sharp new arrows.

Tomi stroked the polished leather quiver. "Think of me when you hunt with the magical Moon-maidens," he whispered.

Myrina looked up at him, feeling very sad that they would not hunt together again. "When I return you'll maybe have a wife," she said.

"Maybe not." Tomi stared down at the arrows.

"If you wait," she told him, suddenly shy, "if you wait and refuse all offers, then I'll choose you for my husband when I return in seven years' time."

He smiled at that and bent close so that their lips touched gently. They both laughed nervously as they heard Tomi's father calling him to feed and water the horses.

He got up obediently. "Father always had good

timing." He raised his eyebrows. "But I think I can manage to wait for seven years to marry an honored and magical Moon Rider."

He bowed formally and went outside.

Myrina smiled to herself and reached for the delicately wrought silver mirror, patterned about the edges with twisting snakes, two fork-tongued heads crossing at the top. The mirror was the most precious symbol of those who rode with the Old Woman; so Aben had worked long and hard to produce a fine, magical mirror for his youngest daughter. She'd carry it always, swinging from her belt. When her years as a Moon-maiden were over, the mirror would be melted down and shaped into a marriage bangle.

"It's beautiful," she murmured. "But I've never been one for sitting admiring myself!"

Gul came in through the tent flaps, overhearing her daughter's words. "There's more to a Moon Rider's mirror than pouting your lips at it," she said. "Isn't that right, Mother?"

"Oh yes." Hati followed her daughter into the tent, smiling at her words.

"What more?" Myrina demanded.

Hati and Gul chuckled secretively, but they wouldn't reply.

"Atisha will tell, when the time is right," said Gul.

And though Myrina begged again, they clamped their lips tight and would say no more. She watched her mother rolling up the felt flooring, knowing somewhere deep down that a time would come for weeping, but the moment was not here yet: this moment contained nothing but burning eagerness.

"I wish I could see Reseda for longer," she said, a touch of regret creeping into her voice.

"Seven days will have to be enough."

"I want to dance at her wedding."

Gul clicked her tongue. "An important woman like Atisha cannot be kept waiting while a girl makes up her mind which man she wants. Reseda must not be rushed in her choice, so you'll go off with the Moon Riders, and you'll be happy."

"Yes I will." Myrina was easily persuaded of that.

The Mazagardi were up before sunrise packing away their tents. All the tribe members performed their own tasks well, even the tiniest of children. They had done it so often that there were no arguments and little need to speak. The whole tribe mounted their steeds and moved off as they did at every new moon.

Myrina and Tomi rode in unusual silence side by side. The Mazagardi traveled fast, fording the River Scamander. The dreary days of the Snow Months were over and they were eager for the return of the sun.

Both warm and cold springs issued from high rocks at the Place of Flowing Waters. Tall shady trees grew alongside the riverbanks and fresh shooting grass provided rich grazing for goats and horses.

"Why do we not stay here forever?" Myrina had once asked her grandmother, when she'd been very young.

Hati had laughed. "I wish we could, my honey-child. This place is perfect, but it wouldn't stay perfect for long if we lived here. The waters would run dry, the grazing would be used up and the ground poisoned with our mess; we'd destroy what gives us so much pleasure."

"So we've got to leave it alone to have a rest before we come back again!" Myrina had tried hard to understand.

Hati had smiled and touched her cheek. "You are learning fast, little one."

CHAPTER THREE

The Place of Flowing Waters

THE SUN WAS sinking in the sky as they arrived at the meeting place. The setting up of the new camp was noisy, for a small city of tents had already established itself. Greetings were bellowed across the water, news gabbled of famines, wars, plagues, and fighting, good trading and bad deals.

"They say that Priam is coming here tonight; his tent is set up and waiting," Aben told Gul, bustling in and out of the family's tent flaps. His news made her pause as she unrolled the felt flooring in front of the hearth stone. "I've been thinking of offering him our yearling gray mares," he continued.

Gul nodded. Aben enjoyed nothing better than a good bargaining session. His wife recognized the light of battle gleaming there in his eyes; his weapons would be determination and clever argument, and pride in the beautiful silver-colored horses that he'd been carefully breeding for the last five years.

"Priam?" Hati was a touch disapproving. "Those Trojans give scant respect to Maa; Apollo and the Owl Lady are more their style."

"What folk *say* they believe can be very different to what they really believe." Aben winked at her.

"Aye, I should know that," Hati agreed, remembering her own days as a priestess. "Many sing praise to Zeus and Athene, but quietly send for the Moon Riders when rain is needed or a touch of sun for their crops."

The following morning Aben was up early, combing the manes of his most valued mares. "Come with me, wife," he coaxed. "Come with me to Priam's tent. The sight of fine women riders might stir his enthusiasm for our horses."

Gul shook her head. "Trojans disapprove of women riders, but maybe you will take Myrina; a skilled young girl should not give offense."

"Aye, you're right." Aben sighed. "Trojans, like Achaeans, keep their women safe at home, though I for one can't understand such foolishness; those whose women ride and fight have twice as many warriors."

Dressed in her finest linen trousers and smock, Myrina rode for Priam and his attendants on one of the silver-gray mares. She trotted, cantered, and galloped, finishing with a spectacular display of bareback dancing, at which she'd been skilled from an early age. Priam was impressed and bought six mares, willingly paying the high prices that Aben asked. Afterward the King of Troy invited them into his huge tent to drink delicate rose-scented tea.

Myrina stared about her; she'd never been in so luxurious a place before. Silken cushions were piled high on long low seats carved with curling patterns and painted in gold leaf. The carpets were so thick and soft that Myrina wanted to fling herself down and roll about. "If this is his tent, what must his palace be like?" she wondered.

A thin girl with dark hair, who seemed a little older than Myrina, poured tea from a silver jug. Myrina caught her breath for a moment as she looked at her. It was the young woman's eyes that made her feel so discomforted: one blue as the Aegean Sea, the other green as fresh grass, giving her a strange, unsettling look. A delicate golden-rayed sun adorned the circlet about her brow, pale and subtle beside the stunning saffron dye of her gown. Myrina found it difficult not to stare.

A younger girl of about eleven summers helped to serve the tea. She was just as beautifully clothed, but in silver, with a pearly crescent moon on her brow instead of the sun.

"I am Cassandra, daughter of Priam," the older girl said. "I have never seen anyone dance on a horse like you."

Myrina was pleased with such open admiration but still felt a little uncomfortable. She longed to stare directly into the mismatched eyes, though she knew that to do so would be a deep discourtesy. Priam was known to have many children, so Myrina assumed the younger girl must be another princess of Troy.

"I learned to ride when I was small," Myrina said, keeping her eyes lowered.

A moment of silence followed, but her curiosity grew so that she must glance up again.

"You may look at me, if I may look at you," Cassandra said, faintly amused. "I have never seen a girl with arrows etched on her cheeks!"

Myrina smiled. "We are both different," she acknowledged. "But you could learn horse skills, if you were willing to put in the work. You are not too old, I think!"

Suddenly tears spilled down Cassandra's cheeks. Myrina was horrified, fearing she'd given offense, but Cassandra quickly dashed the tears away. "I often cry. It means nothing," she said. "I would never be allowed to ride, though I long to try."

Myrina remembered what her father had told her about the way the Trojans protected their women. What were they afraid of? Might their women ride away and never come back if they learned horse skills?

The younger girl twined her arm around the princess. "Don't cry again," she begged.

Cassandra changed at once, smiling at the child, tolerant of the hero-worship that shone from her eyes. "This is my little friend Iphigenia, daughter of King Agamemnon. His queen Clytemnestra is visiting us and we girls look after each other while the queen goes shopping."

"Uncle Menelaus is here, too." Iphigenia yawned. "He talks of nothing but trade and ships."

Myrina was awed. "The great Queen Clytemnestra comes to Troy to do her shopping?" Agamemnon, King of Mycenae, was the powerful overlord of the Achaean lands to the southwest. All the smaller kingdoms bowed to his rule.

"Father must stay at home to keep his kingdom safe, but Mother buys her clothes in Troy." Iphigenia spoke with childlike honesty. "She buys mine, too."

She let go of Cassandra's hand for a moment and twirled around so that her beautiful silken skirt swung out, ringing the tiny bells with which it had been embroidered.

Cassandra explained. "Troy is full of textile slaves; spinners, weavers, and dyers. Many a wealthy visitor comes to Troy looking to adorn herself."

"Aunt Helen cannot come," Iphigenia said. "She must

mind Sparta while Uncle Menelaus is away, but she would like to visit. Nobody loves clothes like my aunt Helen."

Cassandra looked a little bored at the way the conversation was going and Myrina sensed that dresses and adornment were of little interest to the princess, though she herself was so beautifully attired.

Meanwhile, Aben talked with Priam and was introduced to a handsome man, who kept glancing across at Myrina with open admiration.

"Who is he?" Myrina dared to ask at last.

Cassandra's mouth took on an angry twist. "He is my long-lost brother Paris," she said.

Myrina was surprised at the bitterness in her voice. "He is . . . good to look at," she whispered politely.

"Oh yes," the princess agreed. "Everyone thinks so. But . . . he was sent away at birth, for the omens foretold he'd bring destruction to Troy."

Myrina was puzzled. The tribes knew little of omens; but to send a newborn babe away from his family seemed to her very sad.

"He lived on the slopes of Mount Ida, raised by shepherds," Cassandra continued. "He was never supposed to return to Troy and I felt sorry for him then!"

"You are not sorry for him anymore?" she asked.

Myrina couldn't understand why the princess would hate her brother now.

Cassandra shook her head fiercely, her mouth still grim. "Four years ago he returned to Troy and beat our strongest men at the summer games. When he revealed his identity Father relented and swore that he could not live apart from such a strong and handsome son. Since then he is Father's favorite and cannot put a foot wrong. He went to fight for the Hittite king and returned with gold and slaves for our weaving sheds; now, everyone adores him and the omens are forgotten."

"But not by you?" Myrina spoke warily, thinking that she'd not like to fall into disfavor with this changeable princess.

Cassandra shrugged and suddenly her strange eyes seemed to lose focus, as though she were watching something far away in the distance. "His presence fills me with fear," she whispered. "I can't explain why. I know they think I am jealous; and as I'm only a girl, they take heed of nought that I say!"

CHAPTER FOUR

The Windy City

MYRINA LISTENED TO Cassandra with some sympathy. Both the Achaeans and the Trojans were known to give scant respect to their women's wishes and used them mainly as marriage pawns, selling them off as brides to the highest bidder. She could see that their pampered, restricted lives were not much to be envied.

It was clear that Iphigenia loved Cassandra. The young girl smiled up at the older one, clinging trustingly to her hand. Myrina was touched by the simple need for love that she saw in the child.

"Snaky Lady!" Iphigenia exclaimed in a hushed voice, pointing to the twisting body picture that adorned Myrina's right arm.

All at once the dashing Prince Paris strode across and bowed to the three girls. "You are as daring a rider as any lad I've seen," he flattered Myrina, his blue eyes regarding her boldly.

She nodded with dignity, but there was something in his praise and in his stare that made her feel uncomfortable. Paris turned to whisper in his father's ear.

Priam smiled tolerantly and spoke to Aben. "My son begs me take your skillful young rider back to Troy along with the horses."

Aben answered anxiously, "I do not wish to offend, but Myrina is promised to the Moon-maidens; if the Old Woman accepts her, she must leave with them after the full moon."

Priam looked surprised. "I would pay highly for such a child: she'd entertain my court and delight my wives. You may name your price."

Aben was clearly troubled. Myrina caught her breath for a moment; her father must fear he'd lose the excellent horse sale he'd just won if he did not accept Priam's offer! She needn't have worried, for Aben would not be moved. "Myrina is the delight of my life," he told them firmly. "I would dearly like to keep her with *me*, but she's promised to the Old Woman."

A flash of annoyance flickered in Priam's eyes but Cassandra intervened. "Father, we would not have her come unwillingly to Troy."

Myrina feared they'd seem ungracious. "Would you like me to come to Troy to give one performance there, before I go away?"

Cassandra was suddenly radiant. Priam nodded, honor satisfied by this concession, bowing courteously. "We would be honored," he said. Paris looked displeased, but said nothing.

Aben sighed with relief.

The next morning Myrina rode Isatis toward Troy, along with her family, following in the wake of Priam's royal procession. Even Hati came, staring about her with curiosity, despite her disapproval of Trojans. She turned to point out a mound that they passed. "The tomb of Dancing Myrina," she told them. "Ancient leader of the Moon-maidens."

"The one I'm named for?" Myrina asked.

"The very one," Hati agreed.

The golden limestone walls of Troy, built snugly into the sloping edge of the plateau, rose above them as they moved on at a steady pace.

"You'd think the Great Mother had built those walls," Hati acknowledged. She was impressed, though she tried to hide it.

Myrina had a moment of fear about the performance she'd promised, but then leaned forward to stroke her mare's glossy neck. On Isatis's back she could do any-thing.

They passed through the sprawling lower town, filled with small huts and noisy traders. A babble of different languages filled the air so that the only words that made sense were in the Luvvian tongue that Hati had taught her. Dyers bent over huge vats, their arms and faces spattered with the colors they produced. Two springs of water, one cold, one steaming hot, gushed into pools where women washed and scrubbed, wading knee deep in the water; long gowns hitched up and fastened at the back.

The procession moved on through the Southern Gate into the citadel, which was fronted by six statues depicting the Trojans' gods. First and foremost was the sun god, Apollo, with the strange beaked Owl Lady next to him.

"How can anyone worship a carved image when they've the moon and sun to honor?" asked Hati.

They passed low sheds where weaving women toiled, their heads bent over their work, ankles roped. Myrina frowned at the sight and remembered how Cassandra had told her that Paris had brought back slaves from the Hittite wars.

They rode onward up the paved slope to high terraces of wonderful buildings. Each one seemed a palace to Myrina. The higher they went the sharper the breeze blew, and Myrina soon understood why Troy was known as the Windy City.

Cassandra, who had been carried in a litter at the front of the procession, alighted and came pushing through the servants to find Myrina. Iphigenia trailed in her wake and now another young woman walked at her side.

"Father begs you perform for us tonight, before our feast," the princess said. "It is the last night of Lord Menelaus's stay, and Iphigenia and her mother must set sail with him tomorrow to the Achaean lands. Father is anxious to find an entertainment that will please him."

"I'm honored," Myrina agreed uncertainly.

"You are all invited to join us at the feast." Cassandra waved her hand to include all Myrina's family. "This is my dear friend Chryseis, daughter of our most respected priest of Apollo, Chryse. She will show you to the guesthouse. Please ask for anything you need. I must go to help Iphigenia pack her new clothes."

Myrina forgot her apprehension as she watched them go. Iphigenia still clung to Cassandra's skirts. How bitterly the child would miss the Trojan princess when she sailed back to Mycenae in the morning.

Chryseis had a calm and serious manner; her saffron-dyed gown was plain, her brow decorated with the golden-rayed sun. Her quiet confidence confirmed that she was a young woman of high status. She clapped her hands to call the grooms to take the horses, then led Myrina and her family through a finely carved doorway.

They were shown into two rooms, with low beds covered with straw-stuffed mattresses and soft down cushions.

"One for the honored parents and another for the performer and her grandmother," Chryseis told them. "I shall have fruit and wine brought to you."

The walls were hung with brightly patterned rugs; none of them had ever been in such a room before.

"Where am I to perform?" Myrina asked.

"In the courtyard," Chryseis told her. "I will come back when you've rested and take you there." She glanced at Myrina's trousers, covered by a short smock. "We have beautiful gowns; you may take your choice."

Myrina shook her head. "If the king wishes me to dance on horseback, then I must wear my trousers!"

Chryseis's face brightened, making her look suddenly younger. "Dance on horseback? I have heard of such a thing but never seen it. I look forward to this evening very much." With that she bowed her head courteously and left them.

"Did you see the sun on her brow?" said Hati. "Chryseis is not destined for the marriage market; she's a priestess of Apollo and following in her father's tradition."

"Cassandra has the same sun on her brow!" Myrina said. "Is she a priestess, too?"

Hati nodded. "Some of them escape marriage that way."

"And what of little Iphigenia? She has a silver crescent on her brow."

"That is the mark of Artemis," Hati told her. "The huntress goddess who favors the moon."

"That's not so very different from us," Myrina murmured. "We give honor to the moon."

"We do indeed!" Hati shrugged.

"Are you going to have a rest, Grandmother?" Myrina asked.

"Certainly not!" Hati pulled a face. "I'm going outside to get a good look at this place while I've got the chance."

Myrina nodded. "Then I'll come with you," she said.

CHAPTER FIVE

An Invitation to Sparta

M YRINA AND HATI wandered through the
wide upper streets, down graceful stair-
cases, past stately houses decorated with
carvings and marble. They turned whichever way their
fancy took them, until at last they passed through the
Eastern Gate, where two huge wooden doors stood open,
leading to the busy narrow streets of the outer town.
Here they found themselves on high ground.

Hati examined the strong wooden doors and the thick
sloping lower parts of the walls with approval. "You'd
have a job to get in here if the Trojans didn't want you."
She laughed. "These walls curl around the hill like a giant
snail's shell."

They walked past stalls piled with mackerel, oysters,
and sea urchins. Sea urchins' eggs were offered to them
as a delicacy, which Hati ate with relish. Gray pots stood
row on row, alongside bales of wool and yarn and fine

linen dyed in expensive Syrian purple. The scent of coriander and cumin filled the air and again they were surrounded by the confusing babble of different tongues. The shopkeepers held up strong vessels of copper and bronze, crying their wares. It was a very busy, noisy place, and at last Hati was satisfied with what she'd seen.

"I'll go back to rest on that soft bed, after all," she said.

After they'd rested, Gul came to help Myrina dress, braiding her hair and fastening patterned scarves and girdles across her chest and hips.

"She must look beautiful," Hati insisted. "I'll have nobody look down on my granddaughter."

Isatis wasn't awed, even though her mistress was. Luxurious scents of food, wine and perfume drifted into the courtyard, where a statue of Apollo stood in the center. Priam, his eldest son, Hector, and Prince Paris sat with Menelaus under a canopy, nibbling at fruit and sweetmeats. Clytemnestra sheltered beneath a separate awning with Hecuba, Priam's chief wife, Iphigenia, and Cassandra at their side. Myrina was amazed at the richness of their clothes—even slaves and servants were beautifully dressed. She was used to getting better attention from her audience and felt disconcerted.

Hati helped her onto Isatis's back. "Do they want to watch me ride?" Myrina complained. "Or do they simply want to talk and gobble food?"

"You will make them watch you!" Hati said. Then she picked up her drum and beat a sudden loud drum roll, which shocked and silenced the crowd. Myrina rode forward with an angry burst of determination. She threw herself into the performance trotting, galloping, twisting, and turning while Hati beat time on the drum. Waves of applause greeted her as she swung backward and sideways, so that girl and horse seemed to move as one. She finished with a handstand, causing her audience to gasp with admiration then burst into wild shouts and whoops of appreciation.

Priam and his court rose to their feet, cheering. The king turned to beckon Aben forward. "Come and sit at my table," he ordered, leading the way into the banqueting hall. "You must be descended from centaurs, to produce such a child."

Seated at the women's table, Gul kept turning her head, keeping a strict eye on what her husband was up to. "Stop it!" Hati told her. "Who wants to sit with the men anyway?"

Myrina was so relieved to have finished her performance that she felt drunk with joy, even though no wine had touched her lips. The walls of the hall gleamed with burnished metal shields and gentle music came from the flutes and lyres of slave girls. As the meal progressed, the slaves carefully mixed wine with water and served it to the guests.

Cassandra came to congratulate Myrina. "Menelaus was stunned," she told her. "And even Queen Clytemnestra was impressed. My father is in such a good mood that I knew I could ask him for anything."

"So what did you ask?"

"I begged that I might come to see your springtime dances at the full of the moon. And he has agreed! Chryseis will come with me."

Myrina was pleased but surprised that a Trojan princess should so much desire to see the Celebrations of Mother Maa.

"Where is the princess Iphigenia?" Myrina asked, noticing that Cassandra's devoted shadow was missing.

"Fast asleep, curled up on my couch," she smiled.

Suddenly there were voices raised on the high table and chatter ceased.

"Oh no," Cassandra whispered. "Has Paris upset Menelaus again?"

All eyes were turned to the smaller, middle-aged brother of Agamemnon. Menelaus, King of Sparta, was not quite as important as his elder brother, but still a powerful man to offend.

"No, no." Paris was shaking his head and smiling, oozing charm. "I am sure that your wife is beautiful, very beautiful—as is her lovely elder sister." He bowed to Clytemnestra, who was not impressed at being called the elder sister.

"No. That is not enough!" Menelaus thumped the table, still angry, his face rosy with wine. "She's not just beautiful. My Helen is the most beautiful woman in the world. Ask her sister, ask Clytemnestra."

Clytemnestra shook her head, weary of hearing Helen's praise.

"How I long to see such beauty." Paris was silver-tongued again, not at all put off by the dispute, though his father was anxiously trying to catch his eye.

Menelaus leaned forward and grabbed Paris by the arm. "Then come," he cried. "Be my guest and stay a while in Sparta. Then you may judge Helen's beauty for yourself. No! No! I shall be offended if you refuse."

Paris hesitated, looking at his father. Priam gave a brief nod. "I should be most honored to come with you," Paris agreed.

The amicable solution brought relief and the sound of cheerful conversation was quickly restored, but Myrina glanced at Cassandra and saw that her cheeks had turned deathly white. "What is it, princess?" she asked.

Tears spilled down Cassandra's cheeks. Myrina stared at her uncomfortably. This princess was truly quick to weep.

"The smell! So foul!" Cassandra clapped her hand over her mouth and nose in distress. "It stinks in here . . . smells like a slaughterhouse!"

Myrina was fearful that the princess might faint or vomit. All she could smell was the delicious food and sweet perfumes.

Cassandra keeled forward, blood suddenly pouring from her nose, splashing down in great dark drips to stain her lovely gown.

"Let me help," Myrina begged, ready to pinch the bridge of her nose as Hati had taught her.

But just then a tousle-haired Iphigenia came toward them, rubbing the sleep from her eyes. "I wondered where you'd gone," she cried, grabbing hold of Cassandra's arm. "Ah . . . you are bleeding!"

At once Cassandra sat up, wiping the blood away. "It's nothing," she reassured the child. "Just a silly nosebleed. There . . . it's gone!"

Myrina was amazed. The bleeding had stopped as soon as the words were spoken and Cassandra was smiling again. "Come here." She made space for Iphigenia to sit beside her, putting her arm around the younger girl. "Now we must talk. You know that we must say good-bye in the morning, don't you?"

Iphigenia nodded, her eyes full of sadness at the thought.

"Remember this," Cassandra told her, solemnly taking hold of both her hands. "Though we are apart, I will always be your friend. I will always be thinking of you, so that you will never truly be alone. Do you understand that?"

Iphigenia nodded again. "Never alone," she whispered.

Watching it, Myrina felt a great lump well in her throat. Cassandra was a peculiar young woman, but she was also full of kindness and seemed to sense others' emotions and feel them deeply. For a moment Myrina regretted that she must leave to join the Moon Riders; a longer stay in Troy might have been interesting.

CHAPTER SIX

The Night of the Old Woman

I N THE MORNING a great procession set out
through the Southern Gate, heading down to the
Bay of Troy. Menelaus's ships had arrived from
Besika Bay, a little to the south, where they'd been
anchored. They were rowed into the shallow harbor,
ready to take the Spartans aboard and set off home across
the deep blue Aegean Sea. Paris rode beside Priam at the
head of the procession. He'd travel in his own fine fleet
of ships that his father had built for him. First he'd take
Clytemnestra safely home to Mycenae; then travel on to
Sparta as Menelaus's guest.

Myrina and her family rode at the back of the procession, but soon turned away to the east to head back to the
Place of Flowing Waters.

As they reached the higher land, Myrina looked back
and saw the high-prowed ships setting off. The sea was
calm but beaten white by the precise lift and dip of each

set of fifty oars moving in perfect time. As they watched, the oars were hauled in and sails set; the wind was blowing in Menelaus's favor.

They arrived back at the spring gathering before the sun went down, and found Tomi faithfully guarding their home tent.

Aben was still excited by the honor of sitting at Priam's table and full of knowing gossip. "That was no trading visit," he told Gul. "What an excuse, Menelaus bringing his sister-in-law to buy her clothes? I swear by Maa, there's more to it than that."

"What's the truth then?" Gul begged.

"He was sent by Agamemnon to cajole Priam into removing the heavy taxes on Achaean ships."

"And was he successful?"

Aben was thoughtful. "Hard to tell. Priam is all courtesy and concession, but underneath I sense a stubbornness, an iron will."

"What will come of it?"

Aben shook his head.

Though she saw her parents' concern at the doings in Troy, Myrina could think of nothing but the exciting new turn her life was taking. The next few days passed quickly and one afternoon, a few days before the full moon, Grandmother Hati came into the tent in a hurry. "They're coming," she whispered, her voice shaking with excitement. "The lookouts have seen the dust rising in the south. The Moon Riders come for you, Myrina!"

Sounds of distant clapping and hooting from outside told them that the Old Woman with her train of traveling dancers would soon arrive.

Myrina got up and her stomach lurched; suddenly she felt that she couldn't bear to leave her family. How would she manage without their care?

First Gul then Hati went to kiss Myrina, fiercely. "I'm not going yet!" she cried. "Mind my nose. I'm going to scratch! I'm going to scratch!"

"No, you are not." Hati held her granddaughter's hands. Her voice was low and serious. "You are Myrina, sister of Reseda, daughter of Gul, granddaughter of Hati. You are thirteen years old and a woman—pain means spit to you!"

Her grandmother spat energetically onto the flattened earth outside the tent.

"Weariness means spit to you!" And again the spittle went flying outside. "You are the flower of our rocky pathways. You are the pride of our tribe. You are a dancer!"

"She is a dancer!" Gul echoed with joy.

Myrina smiled fiercely at them, her doubts fled, and her belly filled with pride. She ignored the burning desire to scratch and instead gracefully raised her arms, twisting and turning her hands as she'd been taught, shaking her hips, so that tiny tremors went running through the lower part of her body, setting all her trinkets tinkling.

"Remember this!" Her grandmother's voice dropped low and Myrina stilled her movements, recognizing the importance of what was to come. "Such a one would never scratch!"

They went out with Aben to welcome the Old Woman. Now as darkness began to gather about the tents and horse enclosures, the tribes lit torches to welcome the priestesses. At last, a party of strong-armed young women emerged from the rising dust. They were about sixty strong, all on horseback, their eyes and body pictures gleaming in the torchlight. Long hair of many different hues streamed wildly behind them as they cantered through cheering, saluting crowds. Atisha, their leader, rode at the front, her mount the only stallion in the Moon Rider's herd.

The gathering was filled with wild excitement. The priestesses only stayed for seven nights, but it was seven nights that the tribes dreamed of all through the hot dry summer and the bitter winter.

The young women dismounted and fed and watered their horses, then set up their tents, aided by the young lookouts. Only Reseda, laden with jewels and gifts, was returning to her family this year. She left her companions to greet her family noisily, hugging each family member in turn. Shrieking excitedly, she showed off the wonderful collection of goods she'd amassed as her dowry. Gifts to the Moon-maidens brought luck and long life so no young woman left the service of Maa without a collection of valuable goods that added to her desirability as a wife and gave power in her choosing of a husband.

The Mazagardi traditionally gave the Moon-maidens their finest dancers, all trained by their mothers, who'd been dancers with the Moon Riders themselves. Respect between the tribe and the dancers was mutual.

Hati went to hug her old friend Atisha and share a pipe of tobacco. After they'd all washed and eaten, Hati begged Atisha to tell them a story. The Old Woman was willing and called for her special folding chair that elevated her a little, for she was small and thin in stature, though her turban stuck with peacock feathers gave the impression of height, and her loose, swirling robes gave the feeling of width.

Two of the older Moon Riders lifted deer's horn pipes to their lips and the deep thrumming notes brought everyone gathering about them.

A hush fell and Atisha threw a handful of incense grains into the fire, so that plumes of scented smoke rose and floated in the air. A touch of magic drifted in the smoke and the atmosphere changed. Suddenly the worn, wrinkled face of Atisha was alive with mischief, her glance traveling quickly around the eager faces, her memory sharp. "This is the story of the beautiful dancing maiden Hati and the stupid robber."

There was a ripple of amusement from the Mazagardi. Hati beamed with pride. "You'd better get it right, Old One," she warned.

"Oh, it will be true." Atisha cackled. "Though the truth may be of dreams, rather than bright day. Now then, this young Hati was a wonderful dancer and her favorite performance consisted of a fierce stick dance in which she swung and swished a silver dancing cane."

Atisha's voice rose and fell, cleverly taking the parts of the characters in the story. She told how the stupid robber had been seen emerging from his neighbors' tent, stuffing stolen goods down inside his tunic. Though he was a fat man, the stolen goods made him look even fatter and only stayed in place because he had a good strong belt. Hati had said nothing but kept her eye on the man, and later that night when she performed her amazing stick dance, she saw that the robber stood at the front of the crowd, his belly still bulging. She twirled and whirled and swung her stick so that the audience was enraptured by her skill and the robber more dazed than any. Then suddenly, with a powerful flick, she swung the tip of her dancing stick so that it sliced away the strong clasp that held the man's belt in place. Of course all the stolen goods came tumbling down, rolling all over the dancing space, with everyone there to witness the stupid robber's disgrace.

Whoops of appreciation followed the telling and Myrina leaned close to her grandmother's ear. "Was it the truth?"

Hati laughed. "It was the truth and a little bit more than the truth," she said.

Atisha got up from her chair wearily. "And now it is time for us all to go to bed," she told them.

CHAPTER SEVEN

Dancing for the Moon

ESPITE THEIR EXHAUSTION, Myrina and Reseda whispered together through the night. The elder sister stroked the carefully wrought silver snake pattern that coiled about the edge of Myrina's mirror. "Aye, this will work well," she whispered. "I shall be sorry to see my own mirror gone."

Myrina nodded with sympathy. Tomorrow Reseda must hand back her own deer-patterned mirror to Aben and watch him melt it down, making the gleaming liquid metal into a marriage bangle instead. Myrina knew that she too would grieve on the day she had to hand back her fine snaky mirror.

"Father polished it for months," she told Reseda. "Though I still don't understand why it's so important."

Like the other women, Reseda would not spill the secret. "Atisha will teach you," she said.

"What is it that she teaches? I can ride and dance already!"

"Only the Old Woman can tell you." She shook her head. Then she laughed mischievously. "But you and I have been closer than you knew, little viper girl!"

"The golden brown viper?" Myrina murmured in surprise, remembering the day that her snake picture was made. "Hati has told you!"

Reseda just smiled.

On the evening of the full moon, horses and armed Trojan guards arrived, carrying a richly decorated, closed litter. It seemed that Cassandra had been serious in her intention to see the sacred Celebrations of the nomadic tribes, and once again King Priam's tent was raised by the Flowing Waters.

As the Celebrations were about to begin, Myrina turned around to scan the gathering crowd and saw that Cassandra and her companion Chryseis were settled beneath a rich awning at the back, but well placed and raised a little to give them a good view.

"Now," Atisha announced. "Before the Moon-maidens dance to bring us the strength of the growing sun and the gentle timekeeping of the moon, I think you have something for me!"

A ripple of pride passed through the Mazagardi at Atisha's request; heads turned to Myrina. She rose to her feet with a thudding heart, realizing that the "something" that Atisha wanted was her!

The moment had come at last. Gul and Hati led Myrina forward. Two flaming torches had been set up in the cleared space beside the fire. Myrina stood between them, taking a pose, her heart thumping. What if she faltered in the dance? What if Atisha refused her? Her family and tribe would be ashamed. But there was no more time to build up fear, for Mother and Grandmother took up their drums and Aben began to strum on his oud.

Myrina moved a little shakily but she caught sight of Tomi's face, his eyes wide with admiration. Then, as the familiar rhythms lifted and carried her, she began to enjoy the dance, forgetting the importance of the occasion, carried along by the enthusiasm of the huge crowd that surrounded her. She twirled wildly, jumped, and swayed, cheered by the tinkling of her ornaments, and the high-pitched tongue-trilling that came from Reseda and her friends. Then as the dance progressed toward the end, loud whoops and cries rewarded her.

Atisha nodded her head until the tall feathers in her headdress shook. She pointed at Myrina. "Yes," she said. "You dance like a gazelle. Tomorrow, you come with me. Now we will perform the sacred dances of the night."

The atmosphere changed from celebration to concentration for the serious work of the evening. The priestesses took up their positions for the ritual rain-bringing dance. The movements were wild and fast, the young women rushing back and forth, throwing their silver dancing sticks toward the sky, then catching them deftly while the tribesmen and -women clapped and stamped their feet. The lively sun dance followed, while the watchers sang enthusiastically, dipping their heads up and down in time with the music. As the sun dance came to an end, all went quiet. There was no applause; these dances were a solemn duty not an entertainment.

Atisha rose from her chair and walked slowly into the center of the ring of dancers. She turned, seeking Hati, and beckoned her into the ring. Hati came, swaying gracefully, aware of the distinction meted out to her. She joined Atisha in the most sacred dance of all, performed to honor the moon-aspect of the Great Mother, Maa. For how could the tribes live without the moon's waxing and waning as the year turned, regulating their fertility and child bearing, year in, year out?

The two old women moved slowly, twisting and turning their arms, following the ancient intricate pattern of the dance. Even the Moon Riders were still and quiet now. Myrina stood watching, entranced; a shiver ran down her spine as a breeze sprang up, turning her hands and face cool. The dance was not long, but the atmosphere changed swiftly, bringing to everyone present a gentle desire for sleep and rest. The Moon Riders rang light-toned silver bells as the two old women took their final pose.

"And now to sleep," Atisha announced.

Obediently everyone turned and quietly headed back toward their tents. Myrina floated along in a dream, but something made her turn to look toward King Priam's pavilion. Bright eyes gleamed in the moonlight and she saw Cassandra. The princess looked longingly back at her, raising one hand in silent greeting, thick dark hair blowing back, making her face look thinner than ever, as Chryseis led her away.

"King Priam's daughter could not take her eyes from you tonight," Reseda whispered as they settled down to sleep. "She'd change places with you if she could."

Myrina smiled. "I would not change places with her for all her wealth," she murmured. "She will never be able to choose which man she wants."

"No." Reseda shuddered at the thought.

"So, who will you choose for husband?"

Reseda shook her head and shrugged her shoulders.

"Beno grows very tall and good to look at," Myrina insisted. "Don't choose Tomi; he's saving himself for me. Don't let anyone else choose Tomi either!"

Reseda laughed. "He's far too young for me."

"Beno makes me laugh," Myrina insisted. "If you chose Beno you'd never be miserable; I'm sure of that. Joda is

Father's favorite since he went riding off to sell the horses last summer and came back with more silver than we've ever seen."

Reseda smiled. "It seems you've been sizing up my prospects very well. Perhaps I should let you choose for me!"

"I wouldn't know which." Myrina frowned. "I'd like them all for my brother-in-law. Just remember to save Tomi for me!"

Reseda hugged her sister in the dark. "Your seven years as a dancer will soon slip by," she whispered. "Then we'll be together again and you shall make your choice."

Light fingers of dawn lifted darkness from the grassy plain, turning night shadows to delicate greens and golds. The Moon Riders were already up, feeding and watering their horses. Grandmother Hati shook Myrina awake, while Gul prepared fresh cakes of unleavened bread. "Open your eyes, child! The day has come. Atisha waits for you! But first you must eat."

Myrina growled and rubbed her eyes.

"Open your eyes, Moon-maiden, and greet the sun."

Myrina suddenly woke with a jolt, remembering the importance of the day. "My smocks and mirror?"

"All your finery is ready, my little cistus flower. Get up and dress, then you must eat something."

"I can't possibly eat!"

"Very well!" Hati clicked her tongue in disapproval. "Just get up then!"

Atisha was impatient to be off, and none of the tribes wished to offend so important a servant of the goddess. Myrina was hurriedly dressed, her precious silver mirror in its patterned leather bag slotted securely onto her belt. The other Moon Riders were chattering and laughing, pushing and shoving, as they folded their tents and awnings and tied them up in woven baskets to fasten onto sleds.

As Myrina swung herself up onto Isatis, she thought that she saw a young woman she knew staring at her from beside the baggage mules, but when she turned to look properly the girl had gone.

"Who was that?" she muttered. It seemed to her that she'd caught sight of someone she should know well, but couldn't even think of a name. She frowned for a moment but then became distracted by fears that she'd forgotten to bring out all of her traveling goods. "My bowls and table?"

"All here, on Isatis's back," Gul soothed, pointing to the bags and belongings that swung from the hooks. "You have everything a priestess can need."

"Blessings on you, daughter!" Aben kissed her hand.

"Are we off already?" Myrina panicked.

"Yes." Hati smiled and grabbed hold of her granddaughter's foot for a moment. "Remember . . . never scratch, and ripple, ripple like a snake!"

Gul covered up her mouth to hide the sudden trembling that came; she couldn't manage to say good-bye.

Tomi lifted his hand in salute. He also said nothing, but the intensity of his look told Myrina that he had not forgotten their agreement.

"Forward, my Moon Riders," Atisha ordered, and the startling caravan of tattooed young women moved off, heads held high, strung bows with full quivers strapped to their thighs. Myrina glanced back just once, as their pace quickened, but then she turned her face determinedly forward, toward the high plateau that lay ahead.

"Don't look back, never look back," she whispered.

CHAPTER EIGHT

Away with the Moon Riders

THE MOON RIDERS rode all through the morning. They passed the lofty towers of Troy in the distance and kept to the faster high ground north of the city. As the sun rose to the highest point in the sky, they reached a group of tall cedars by a stream and Atisha called a halt. The young women dismounted and fastened their horses to the lower branches of the trees. Each priestess seemed to be skillfully performing tasks, knowing exactly what to do, laughing and shouting at one another all the time. Some made a fire, others fed the horses and rubbed them down; Myrina walked among them, feeling uncertain.

"Don't stand there like a lost dog," Atisha told her. "Take the fresh bread your mother gave us and hand it around. We'll have an awning for shade. Penthesilea, can you see to it?"

One of the tallest young women, with a leaping panther

as her body picture, strode over to the baggage mules. She began pulling apart the laced woven containers for the awnings, but though she was strongly built and looked quite fearless, she suddenly sprang back from the baggage, pulling a sharp knife from her belt.

At once the others sensed her disquiet.

"What is it?" Atisha asked.

Penthesilea looked closely at the baggage again, poking at it with her knife.

The baggage moved and a small voice cried, "No . . . no!"

"Ha!" Penthesilea laughed. "Come, see for yourself," she insisted, lowering her knife.

Atisha moved swiftly toward the sled and everyone gasped for they could all see that it moved again as she approached.

"Snake?" a young priestess warned.

Penthesilea shook her head. "Too big for a snake, more a stowaway," she said.

With one fast movement Atisha ripped open the roll of tent felt, and out of the pack tumbled the girl that Myrina thought she had recognized just before they'd set off. Myrina knew her now, even though she was dressed in the rough trousers and tunic of a nomadic daughter of the tribes; this was Priam's daughter.

"Cassandra!" Myrina cried. "Princess!"

"Is this right?" Atisha asked.

Cassandra scrambled to her feet, looking very miserable, but she nodded. Some of the Moon Riders laughed with relief and some even clapped, but then they fell silent as they saw that Atisha's face was grim.

"Why have you done this, Princess?" the Old Woman asked quietly.

Cassandra's usually pale face flushed but she answered with determination, her fists clenched tightly. "Because I wish to join your band of Moon-maidens. I never saw anything so beautiful as the dances you performed last night!"

The watching young women looked at one another with a touch of surprise and pleasure.

Atisha sighed and shook her head. "That sounds very fine, but what does your father say? You creep away with us like a thief! Does your father know?"

Cassandra flinched. She looked very young in the rough dress and all the quiet confidence that she'd shown as her father's hostess seemed to have seeped away. "He knows nothing," she said.

Atisha cleared her throat and spat while all the watching Moon Riders stood still and tense, understanding now that perhaps the princess had placed them in danger. Though none were more capable of defending themselves than these warrior-trained priestesses, still, if

Priam followed with his heavily armed guards, nobody would come out of the struggle well.

At last Atisha spoke. "Can you dance?"

Cassandra shook her head.

"Can you ride or hunt?"

There came no reply at all.

"How old are you?"

"Fifteen," she whispered.

"Old enough for a Trojan princess to be married. Your father will wish to see you wed."

"No." Cassandra spoke out firmly at this, some of her royal confidence returning. "I was promised to Apollo as a tiny child. I was to be his priestess and live in the temple and never be a wife. They fear me in Troy or think me mad—nobody will miss me there. Well, nobody but my friend Chryseis."

Atisha was silenced for a moment; she scrutinized the young girl's face with intensity. "Such eyes," she muttered.

Cassandra seized her chance. "I turn away from the sun god, aye and all the other Trojan gods. I wish to honor the Great Mother, like you! This is right for me—I know it is!"

Though she was so small and slender, still her voice was full of passion. At last Atisha's sharp expression softened. She stepped forward and kissed Cassandra's brow so that the girl's face brightened with hope.

"Wait here a moment," the Old Woman ordered, then she walked away from them to the shade of the cedar trees, pulling out her mirror as she went. The Moon Riders stood still in silent respect while their leader seemed to study herself in her mirror.

After a few moments Atisha came striding back. "You must return with me, Princess, but I shall speak to your father on your behalf."

Cassandra nodded obediently, glad at least that she was not simply to be returned.

"We'll meet him on the way, for news of your disappearance has reached him as I feared." Atisha spoke quickly, beckoning Penthesilea to bring her horse. "He follows fast, his chariot pulled by silver-maned horses!"

Myrina frowned. How could the Old Woman know such a thing?

"Must we return at once?" Penthesilea asked, her voice full of resentment.

"Yes, at once," Atisha insisted. "No time for food or rest."

The priestesses swore and cursed as they turned to remount their steeds, and Myrina's heart sank. The last thing she wanted to do was turn back the way she'd come.

"You ride with me," Atisha told Cassandra sharply. "Give me your foot! Now, swing yourself up!" As the princess obeyed, flinging her leg awkwardly across the tall stallion's back, the Old Woman pushed her into place, then sprang up quickly behind her. "I pray that Maa will smile on us and our explanations," she said.

Myrina wearily climbed back onto Isatis, feeling nothing but irritation for the pathetic Princess of Troy. She'd been working all her life to learn the skills needed to become a Moon Rider. Why should this princess think she could join the priestesses without either work or skills? And now if they were forced to return she must risk seeing her family or Tomi again: a second leave-taking would be just too much to bear.

She couldn't quite understand how, but Atisha's prediction proved to be exactly right. They'd not ridden far before a cloud of dust in the distance warned of the approach of fast-running horses. Priam's party was small but Myrina recognized at once the six fleet-footed mares that her father had sold to the Trojan king, pulling three light battle chariots.

As soon as the Moon Riders were sighted the sound of Trojan horns rang out and both parties slowed their pace, meeting with some semblance of dignity. Priam rode with his eldest son, Hector, driving his chariot and four other armed warriors in attendance, speed their priority. The sight of his daughter returning to him on the Old

Woman's horse clearly brought some reassurance and the king greeted Atisha with a quick nod of the head. He gestured to one of the warriors, who leaped from his chariot to lift Cassandra down.

"Leave me!" Cassandra said. "I shall get down myself when I am ready!"

Priam dismounted and approached Atisha. "I assume that you did not knowingly take my daughter," he blustered.

"I did not," she agreed calmly. "But you and I must talk, for the princess wishes to come with us."

"I'll not hear of such a thing." Priam clenched his fist.

"Let us set up an awning and rest and take a drink together." Atisha's steady courtesy was determined.

"I have no time for tea parties!" Priam shouted. "I shall take my daughter and go!"

A moment of tension followed, as Penthesilea and many of the women let their hands creep onto the handles of the sharp knives they kept sheathed in their belts, while the Trojan warriors gripped their sword pommels.

"Are we to battle to the death over a wayward child?" Atisha asked.

Priam hesitated, then bowed in agreement. Though the Moon Riders' strange barbarian religion meant little to him, he knew that Atisha was held in great respect by the nomadic tribes of the north and he did not wish to make more enemies for himself. Acting as host to Menelaus had been a most nerve-racking experience. "We shall talk!"

CHAPTER NINE

The Time for Weeping

PENTHESILEA QUICKLY FIXED up an awning and the Moon Riders put away their weapons and offered figs and wine instead, which the Trojan warriors gladly accepted. Priam and Atisha talked together, first with anger, then with more calm. Cassandra wandered a little way off, looking very unhappy. Myrina watched her, seeing that her clasped hands would not stop trembling, though her face bore a brave scowl.

Myrina's own confidence in this new way of life was waning fast and the princess's actions were making it worse. At the same time she knew that Cassandra had risked much to reject her luxurious palace life. A touch of respect came with that recognition. She must be the only person there whom Cassandra knew, so she took her own drinking beaker from her baggage, filled it with wine and went after the princess. "Here, drink this," she commanded.

Cassandra looked at her with gratitude. She obediently

took the beaker and sipped the spiced wine, though her hands still shook.

"If they force me to return I shall kill myself," Cassandra said quietly.

"If you come back with me," Myrina told her, "then maybe you will hear what's being said."

They both went back and sat as close as they dared to Atisha. Priam acknowledged his daughter only with an angry glance, but he did not seem to be quite as furious as they might have feared. He and the Old Woman were deep in conversation, though the king now shook his head.

"It is for seven years," Atisha explained patiently. "Seven years and then my dancers return to their homes, full of strength and wisdom."

"They all return?"

Atisha looked across at the girl with the leaping panther on her arm. "Except for Penthesilea," she said. "Her courage is great and though she's still young she grows in wisdom, but—Penthesilea cannot return to her own people. Each leader must choose a young priestess to train to take her place eventually and I have chosen Penthesilea to follow me."

A touch of curiosity lit the old king's eyes for a moment but then the immediate problem of his daughter overwhelmed him. He shook his head. "Seven years . . . I cannot spare my daughter for seven years—besides she's promised to Apollo," he muttered. "Those who honor the sun god will whisper that Priam is disloyal to the Trojan gods."

Atisha bowed her head in understanding. "But should the princess ride with us, then you would have our loyalty," she assured him. "We would bring sun and rain for your crops, or rally fierce riders from the tribes, willing to come to your defense, should ever need arise."

Priam's lifted his eyes with new interest. Perhaps his daughter's rebellion could bring him new and different allies. He'd never looked for support from this strange source, never even thought of it, but he knew that the Moon Riders had fought many battles in the past. They were feared by the Achaeans who called them Amazon Warriors.

Prince Hector sat dutifully beside his father, waiting patiently for his decision. He glanced over at Cassandra now and then, smiling sadly at her and shaking his head.

"Your elder brother is not like Prince Paris," Myrina whispered.

"No indeed," Cassandra agreed. "He is a fierce warrior and a strict brother but still, he's always kind to me."

"Won't you be sorry to leave your family and your lovely palace?"

Cassandra looked at her with the touch of a smile. "You

have left *your* family and *your* tribe."

"Yes," Myrina had to agree. "But not a palace! And what about your friend Chryseis? Will she not miss you? Will your father punish her for returning to Troy without you?"

Cassandra shook her head. "He dare not punish the daughter of Chryse, chief priest of Apollo of Tenedos. I care nothing for the palace and Chryseis understands what I do."

Suddenly Priam was reaching out his hand to Atisha. Myrina could feel the terrible tension in the girl beside her. Priam looked over at his daughter, his eyes filling with tears. "Go with the Old Woman," he told her. "But return to visit me each spring. If at any time I need you, you will come back to Troy."

"Yes, Father." Cassandra went to him, throwing her arms about him. "Thank you, Father." Her voice was deep with emotion.

A sigh of relief from everyone was followed by wild whooping cries of approval from the Moon Riders.

Priam turned from his daughter to Atisha. "No patterned face for my child!"

"I agree to that," Atisha answered.

"And you must know this," he told her solemnly. "Though I do love this child of mine I give you warning, she is full of childish stories, fears, and imaginings. You must not believe all she says."

Atisha folded her arms, a stubborn and ironic smile on her face. "I have seen and sensed the things you speak of and I tell you this: it is just those qualities in the princess that tell me she is a true Moon-maiden at heart."

The king was puzzled by the frank reply but after a moment's reflection he bowed his head in acknowledgment.

"Now." Atisha turned away with a new sense of urgency. "Though I would not wish to behave with discourtesy to one who is now our friend, we must ride away fast toward the Sea of Marmara, as we've lost much of our journeying time."

"I can send Trojan ships to carry you across the Hellespont," Priam offered.

But Atisha shook her head. "I thank you," she bowed, "but we must travel north to the Place of High Cliffs, beside the Sea of Marmara, where the fisher-folk await us by the shore. They leave their nets to carry us across to Thrace each spring and in return we dance for their fishing and bring down blessings on their work."

Priam shook his head; this way of life was strange to him but courtesy to his new allies prevailed. He did not keep them there longer than it took to pack up and at last the Moon Riders were mounted again, galloping fast over the grassy plains while the sun sank in the west.

The light had almost gone when Atisha called a halt. They set up camp very quickly, the older girls moving fast and taking on extra jobs to make up for lost time.

Atisha called to Myrina, "Have you still got the food your mother packed?"

"Yes, it's here." Myrina lifted the bulging, strong leather bags down from Isatis's back.

"It's a blessing indeed," the Old Woman told her. "Will you carry it around? Ask Cassandra to help you."

"I will." Myrina nodded, uncertain about asking a Trojan princess to work with her, but Cassandra seemed willing enough and grateful to have something to do.

The dancers settled about the fire that they'd built, carefully putting out their own drinking beakers and setting up their tables. Myrina carried around the food-bags filled with Gul's flat, grainy bread. She took pleasure in the comments that came.

"So fresh!"

"Delicious!"

"Rare that we get bread as good as this!"

They ate heartily of the bread, smoked goat's meat, cheese and olives. Myrina set up her own table and began to eat Gul's bread, but though she was hungry, a sorrowful thought came to her. This meal was precious, the last that her mother would prepare for her for a very long time. A painful rush of longing for Gul and her familiar home-tent washed over her.

Terrible, shameful panicky thoughts rushed through her head. What would happen if she simply climbed up onto Isatis's back and returned to the Place of Flowing Waters? Would the Moon Riders pursue her? She'd never heard of such a thing happening. It would be sure to bring deep shame upon her family.

She gazed around at the unfamiliar hills. Which way had they come? She wasn't even sure of that. Suddenly her eyes filled up and hot, stinging tears started pouring down her cheeks.

The other girls who sat close by watched her stonily, not at all surprised; but Cassandra crept close and pushed her arm through Myrina's, offering simple silent comfort. This touch of kindness only made the tears rain down more fiercely.

Atisha looked over at her from where she sat. "Now is the time for weeping," she said. "This is good . . . this is right. You shall be happy again tomorrow."

CHAPTER TEN

Bow to the Moon

MYRINA COULD NOT stop crying. At last she got up, pushing Cassandra away, and ran in among the corraled horses. As ever, Isatis picked up her scent and came to her. Myrina flung her arms about the dark mare's neck. The touch and familiar sounds and smells gave comfort. Myrina cried into the silky mane while Isatis stood there patiently, whickering gently. At last her sobs eased a little and she raised her head, feeling much relieved.

Myrina blew her nose and dried her eyes. Her memory slipped back to the day that Isatis had been weaned and taken away from her mother, Midnight.

"You are to be her mother now," Aben had told the five-year-old Myrina.

He'd made a simple halter and showed her how to lead the young foal about.

"You stay at her side day and night," he said. "You see

her fed and watered, comb her coat and make sure that she's warm. You lead her to tender clumps of grass, and keep the flies away from her ears."

It had been hard work for such a small child, but Myrina had done as she was told and after one phase of the moon, Aben removed the halter. Myrina had been fearful that Isatis would simply gallop away and be very hard to catch again, but she needn't have worried. She could still feel the joy that came as she discovered that everywhere she went, Isatis followed unbidden. Whenever she rode in front of Gul on the steady brown mare, Isatis trotted at their side, and the following spring Aben lifted her onto Isatis's back for the first time. They'd been together ever since.

Myrina stroked the soft mane, digging her fingers into the shiny coat. She need never feel that she'd left all of her home and family behind, with Isatis at her side.

Calm now, she gave Isatis one last pat and turned to walk back to where Cassandra was still sitting, trying hard to regain a bit of dignity, despite her puffy eyes. Cassandra said nothing but handed her back the food that she had carefully kept for her. Myrina thanked her and started eating again.

When Myrina and Cassandra had finished their food, Penthesilea came to sit between them, putting a strong arm around each girl's shoulders. "Reseda used to look after me and I promised that I would do the same for you, little Snaky. We have much to teach that will bring comfort to you both, but now we must sleep, for it has been a long and difficult day."

"We honor the moon and then we sleep," Atisha announced.

The Old Woman took up a pipe and produced from it a slow throbbing melody while all the young women stood up, ready to dance. Myrina knew the movements so well that she did not even have to think about them, but Cassandra struggled, still determined to join in.

Myrina saw her difficulty and began a low whispered chant that gave instructions in time with the rise and fall of the pipe music.

> *"Bow to the moon,*
> *Dip to the earth,*
> *Turn to the mountain,*
> *Sway and sway."*

Cassandra quickly picked up the idea and found that she was moving in harmony with the others.

"Those two may do very well together," Atisha whispered to Penthesilea.

Penthesilea sent the two new Moon Riders off to sleep in her own tent. As they lay there side by side on soft cushions Myrina whispered to Cassandra, "Do you regret . . . ?"

"No," she answered firmly. "I lay myself down to sleep more happy than I can remember."

Myrina hiccuped. "I still have a tight pain inside my chest."

"Sleep now," Cassandra told her calmly. "In the morning there will be joy!"

"Will there?" Myrina yawned and closed her eyes.

"Yes," Cassandra said.

The next thing that Myrina remembered was hearing the sound of rustling in the darkness as Penthesilea shook her roughly. "Wake Cassandra!" she ordered.

Then quickly Myrina's muddled thoughts cleared and she remembered that she was with the Moon-maidens and that to rise and dress before dawn was part of their duty. They must be there, outside their tents, ready to salute the sun.

"Cassandra!" she whispered. "Get up!"

They both got themselves dressed with as little fuss as they could manage in the dark. Penthesilea laughed as they bumped into each other. "You'll learn," she told them.

Then at last they were out in the cool darkness. A touch of moonlight helped them to find a place, but

Atisha asked the newcomers to join her at the front. "You know the sun-welcoming dance?" she asked Myrina.

"Oh yes," she replied, raising her arms above her head, ready to send them swaying from side to side as soon as the first rays of light appeared.

Cassandra immediately copied her. "Yes," Atisha encouraged. "You are doing well."

Penthesilea took up a drum, and then, as the first touch of pink lit the eastern horizon, she began a steady beat and all the Moon Riders swayed their raised arms from side to side in time with the rhythm. The beat grew faster as more and more golden pink fingers streaked across the sky. A tiny bud of joy began to grow there inside Myrina's chest, chasing away the tight misery of last night. "I am here with the priestesses," she told herself. "I am here and I am one of them."

Then as the brightness grew the rhythm changed and suddenly the Moon Riders' arms rippled up and down like living snakes. At last, as the whole of the sky lightened and gleaming sharp sun-rays appeared, they began twirling around faster and faster, until the drum rang out with a trembling thunder, then stopped. Suddenly they were whooping and clapping and smiling at one another. Cassandra stood gazing toward the rising sun, her face bathed in pink light, a quiet smile of satisfaction on her face.

The Moon Riders fed and watered their horses first then sat down to eat themselves. "When we've packed our tents, we practice," Atisha told them. "Then we wash and dress ourselves for the evening rites, and ride on. You shall dance for the fisher-folk tonight, Myrina."

Myrina gasped. "I . . . dance tonight?"

The others, sitting close by, laughed. "Oh yes," Penthesilea insisted. "It is the tradition: the new priestess must dance at the evening's celebration."

"Do you mean me alone?"

"Yes!"

"But what shall I dance?"

"Whatever Atisha teaches you."

"What about Cassandra?"

Atisha cackled. "I think our hosts would like a song from Priam's daughter. They'd deem it a great honor."

For a moment Cassandra sounded uncertain. "The songs I have learned are all to honor Apollo."

"Sing whatever is there in your heart," Atisha told her, serious now.

Cassandra's unnerving eyes brightened. "I have songs in my heart that I've never sung out loud," she whispered.

"You sing them tonight, for us," Atisha told her firmly.

CHAPTER ELEVEN

Stone from a Fire Mountain

THE MOON RIDERS rode west all through the afternoon, moving fast, still making up for lost time. Myrina could think of nothing but the set of new movements that Atisha had shown her. She didn't care which direction they traveled in now, so long as she could remember what she'd been taught and not collapse in shameful tears again.

The Moon Riders were welcomed eagerly at the Place of High Cliffs, and provided with a feast of food and drink. Though both the dress and language of the tribe were strange to Myrina, there was no time to be bothered by such things. She worked through her new dance again and again.

"Let it flow." Penthesilea laughed. "Stop being so fearful and let it flow."

"How can I let it flow when I can't even think what comes next?"

The Moon Riders sat down to eat, but Myrina couldn't touch her food. Atisha looked in her direction and smiled. She put down her own food, then clapped her hands and picked up her drum. "Our performance shall begin at once," she cried. "I present our new Moon-dancer Myrina, in her first performance. Come forward, Myrina, and entertain our friends while they eat."

Myrina froze when she realized that Atisha was calling her forward. But Penthesilea was there behind, giving her a good shove, and suddenly she found herself in the midst of a crowd of strange faces, her mind gone quite blank.

Atisha set up a steady rhythm. Myrina missed the first movement but managed to jump in on the second.

"Yes!" Atisha cried.

Centaurea, a tall older girl with cornflower blue eyes, began a steady rhythmic clap of encouragement, soon picked up by the audience. Myrina grew in confidence and, though she missed another movement out, she smiled broadly at Atisha and carried on.

"Yes . . . yes!" The Old Woman nodded.

At last the dance built to a wild climax ending in warm applause and tongue-trilling cries of approval.

Myrina's heart thundered, but her face glowed.

"You will never have anything more difficult to do than that," Atisha told her. "Now you eat! Do you want to sing now and get it over with?" she asked Cassandra.

Cassandra shook her head. "I never eat," she said, and from her stick-thin arms Myrina could believe that.

Atisha shook her head, speaking reprovingly. "You are a Moon-maiden now. We ride all day and dance all night: to do that we must have good food and plenty of it. Your life has changed by your own choice; now you eat!"

Cassandra stared at the Old Woman, puzzled. The harsh words were softened a little as Cassandra received offers of food from the other young women, accompanied by lip-smacking noises.

"Have some of this," Centaurea offered. "Mackerel toasted in honey with sesame seeds: it's delicious." Cassandra stretched out her fingers for the tasty morsel and ate.

Later that evening Atisha called the princess to sing for them. The girl came hesitantly into the circle; her voice, a little shaky at first, soon grew in strength and at last the words seemed to come magically pouring forth from her throat. A song of the deep magic of the earth and the changing moon, of water and snow and bitter hail, and the joy of the returning spring.

Her voice was deep and pleasant. No wild whooping greeted her but a soft murmuring of approval, so that all were quiet and weary as the gentle moon-dance was performed.

* * *

The following morning the Moon Riders were up again before the sun, but then Atisha allowed them a little rest before they packed up their tents so that they'd have energy for the important fish-dances that were to be performed that evening. By noon many fishing boats were bobbing about beside the shore, ready to sail across. Each Moon-dancer led her steed aboard, two in each boat, for the restive horses might need the comfort of familiar voices.

When all the boats had safely reached the western side of the narrow sea, and women and beasts were helped ashore, then the dancers took their places for the watery rites.

"Blessings on our waters!" the fisher-tribe cried.

"Shoals of mackerel down from the Bosphorus!"

"Silver sardines, to light the night waters!"

As a steady drum beat began, half of the dancers took the role of swaying weeds, their hands drifting gently to right and left above their heads, while the others became fishes, weaving in and out, making wonderful finlike movements with their hands. When one round of the dance was completed, they swapped places, cheerfully doing the whole thing again to cheers and clapping.

Myrina slept soundly that night, with no sadness or thoughts of home.

The following morning the Moon Riders traveled on through Thrace.

There were no celebrations to perform for that night, so they made their camp by a cold clear stream, on a deserted grassy plain.

"Sleep well," Atisha said as Myrina and Cassandra staggered stiff-legged toward Penthesilea's tent. "I am very pleased with you both and in the morning I will share with you the greatest secret we possess."

"The mirrors," Myrina breathed. "At last."

That night they lay side by side, drowsily whispering. "We're to learn something wonderful," Myrina insisted. "The magic of our mirrors."

"Yes," Cassandra replied.

"Aren't you surprised at that?"

"No," she murmured sleepily.

As soon as the sun greeting was over and horses and dancers fed, Atisha called her two new recruits over to her side. "Bring your mirror, Myrina," she said. "I shall let you use mine, Cassandra, until we can have one made for you."

"I have my own mirror," Cassandra told her. "I couldn't leave that behind in Troy." She felt inside her tunic and brought out a bag, much smaller than the one that swung from Myrina's belt. She pulled open the strings and held up a crudely cut mirror of shining black glassy stone.

Myrina was a little disappointed, thinking that some

fantastically jeweled treasure was about to emerge, but Atisha gasped with delight. "Obsidian," she breathed. "Magic stone from a fire-mountain. Where did you get it?"

Cassandra stroked the mirror's polished surface. "I've had it for many years," she said. "Once when I was very young I ran away from the palace. I went out through the lower town and on and on until I came to the mound that they call the Tomb of Dancing Myrina."

"Yes?" Atisha listened with full attention.

"Well," Cassandra whispered. "There was an old woman there, washing clothes in a pool. She gave me the mirror and told me not to be afraid of what I saw in it."

"What did you see?" Myrina was as interested as Atisha now.

"I saw myself standing beside the pool but the water turned red as blood, and when I looked to ask her what it meant the woman had gone and guards were streaming out from the city calling my name."

Atisha nodded. "And you have kept it ever since?"

Cassandra stroked the glassy black surface. "It is my treasure," she said.

"And why do you treasure it so?" Atisha's eyes narrowed.

Cassandra hesitated. "Because . . . I see things in it, things that my parents call imaginings, but I know them to be truth."

"And what do you see now?" Atisha asked, while Myrina stood there quiet and awed.

Cassandra looked down at her night black mirror, then suddenly she smiled. "I see my friend Iphigenia, on the deck of a ship in the wide blue sea. She's watching dolphins jump from the water and she's happy. The creatures escort her safely home."

Atisha kissed Cassandra on the forehead. "Now I know truly why you needed to come with us: you have been chosen. Go back to Penthesilea and ask her to teach you the moon-dance. I can teach you nothing about mirrors; you have that magic already."

Myrina felt a little disconcerted as Atisha led her away from the camp and Cassandra wandered back to where Penthesilea was putting the dancers through their paces. Now that she was alone with her, Myrina felt a little afraid of the sharp-tongued Old Woman.

"Right." Atisha shaded her eyes from the sun. "Let's find a pleasant shady spot. Over there by the stream; that will do well."

Myrina obeyed, wishing that Cassandra were coming, too.

"Come sit beside me," Atisha ordered. "Sit so that you can lean against the tree. May I see your mirror?"

"It isn't like Cassandra's." Myrina spoke hesitantly, pulling the snaky mirror from its bag.

"No," Atisha agreed, gently touching Aben's delicate work. "But it is a very beautiful mirror, made with great love and care, and I think it is just the right mirror for you."

CHAPTER TWELVE

A Precious Secret

ATISHA MADE MYRINA lean back against the tree holding the mirror in front of her. "Now," she asked. "What do you see?"

Myrina frowned, still puzzled. "My own face."

"Good. Now let your eyelids droop a little, let your shoulders sink, slow your breathing down, as though you'd like to sleep."

Myrina suddenly felt very tired.

"Now tell me, what do you see behind your face?"

"I see the strong tree's bark, and green leaves dancing in the breeze, and a blue, blue sky," Myrina murmured.

"Forget yourself and gaze through the leaves into that sky."

Myrina felt as though she'd rather go to sleep but she tried to obey the Old Woman and soon she gasped.

"What do you see?" Atisha asked. "What do you see out there in the sky?"

"Clouds and swirling mist and shapes!"

"What shapes, child?"

But Myrina could only gasp again with delight as, through the swirling mist, familiar shapes emerged. There was Hati, holding a wreath of flowers, slipping them over Reseda's head. Then Gul was hugging her older daughter and Aben was there, too, slipping a fine silver bangle carved in the shape of deer's horns onto Reseda's arm.

"What do you see?" Atisha was smiling now.

"I see those I love the best," Myrina murmured contentedly; then suddenly she was alert with excitement. "Beno, my sister has chosen Beno for her husband; she's chosen well."

"And you have done very well. Come back now, back through the sky and the leaves and the tree bark," Atisha told her firmly.

At once the misty pictures merged together and faded. Myrina was staring at her own face again, reluctant to let the vision go.

"Now, just sit still for a moment," Atisha told her. "The first time that you mirror-gaze and truly see may leave you drained of energy. Now then, how do you feel?"

Myrina smiled and sighed. "Happy," she said. "Just happy. Reseda knew about my golden brown viper and now I know how."

Atisha nodded. "If you long for your family and friends now you know what to do."

"But," Myrina said, "will I be able to do such a thing myself, without you to guide me?"

Atisha laughed. "You did well, Snaky Girl; some find it much more difficult than that. The more you practice, the stronger your magic will grow."

"I didn't see Tomi," she realized.

"You will see whomever you want to see," Atisha told her. "There will be plenty of time for keeping an eye on your sweetheart."

Myrina jumped. The Old Woman seemed to know everything about her.

"Don't look so fearful." Atisha cackled crudely. "I didn't need my magic mirror to tell me that; the boy couldn't take his great calf eyes from you while you danced."

Myrina was pleased to hear that. "But what of Cassandra?" she asked. "Can she make this magic without being taught?"

Atisha turned solemn. "That ancient mirror of hers has strong mystical powers. In Troy, they would say she was chosen by the god Apollo, but I think there's a touch of Earth Mother, Maa, in the gift and maybe Dancing Myrina was her messenger."

This was deep magic that they talked of now, ancient magic that carried a great responsibility with it. Myrina could not help but feel a little resentful that the shade of the famous old warrior woman should visit Cassandra and not her who was her namesake.

Atisha nodded. "I am coming to understand that we are honored to have Cassandra here with us, and yet . . ." The Old Woman stopped, her lined face full of pain.

"Something troubles you about her?" Myrina whispered, hoping that she wasn't being disrespectful.

But Atisha smiled and patted her shoulder approvingly. "You are much like your grandmother," she said. "Yes, something does trouble me. Cassandra's gift will bring her sorrow. She doesn't just see, as I do, as you did—she feels. She feels the emotions of those she sees. That can be too much for one person to bear, far too much. What that one needs is a true friend."

Myrina frowned. She could see that such a gift could bring suffering, but she couldn't help but feel annoyed by the respect, almost reverence, that Atisha had so quickly given to Cassandra.

"What that one needs is a loyal and stalwart companion," Atisha repeated.

Myrina shuffled uncomfortably. She felt sure that the Old Woman was suggesting that she be this stalwart one. Didn't she have enough to do just keeping up with the other Moon Riders? Chryseis had seemed to be such a loyal companion but Cassandra had ruthlessly left her behind in Troy.

She was relieved when Atisha got up briskly and said, "Well, well . . . we shall see. We must return to the others. We'll cook and eat the fish that we've been given, then tomorrow we hunt. Are you good with the bow and arrow?"

"Yes," Myrina answered with confidence. "I can shoot from horseback in all directions, twisting north, south, east, and west, as Hati taught me."

"You are a born Moon Rider." Atisha smiled.

As the days lengthened and the bitter winter winds softened, the Moon Riders traveled on through Thrace. Everywhere they went they were welcomed and honored; their presence brought feasts and dancing.

Myrina had little time to mirror-gaze, or even think about her family. Every day brought a new journey, new people, a babble of strange languages, and unfamiliar food that must be received with courtesy. Cassandra struggled through it all with grim determination.

Atisha picked a steady mare called Arian for the Trojan princess, but even so, the first few weeks of riding alone brought her bruised thighs and an aching back. Myrina couldn't help but notice the persistence with which Cassandra clambered onto Arian's back each morning, gritting her teeth silently against the aches and pains. She readily joined the dancing each night, studiously copying Myrina's every twist and turn, willingly raising her fine voice in song whenever it was requested, even though she might be dropping from exhaustion.

As the two newcomers to the group they were often put together, and Myrina felt that she was being forced into the role of companion to Cassandra, whether she wished it or not. Atisha often spoke sharply to them both, but watched their struggles with approval.

Their journey took them first along the western shore of Thrace, through the lands of the old king Peiroos and the warlike Ciconi tribes. Myrina stared in wonder at the strange way the men wore their long hair, tied up in top-knots on the crowns of their heads. Before the Moon-maidens danced for them, the Ciconi men honored them by performing wild wrestling matches, making the young women cheer and swear that they were glad these people were their friends and not their enemies.

Two young women from the Ciconis were presented to Atisha and accepted as new Moon-maidens. Suddenly Myrina and Cassandra were not the only new recruits.

From there they traveled south to Abdera, and on to the lands of the Paionis, where the chieftain Pyraechmes ruled. Then they turned north to the lands of the great Thracian overlord Rhesus and the Edoni tribe, where two of the older Moon Riders would return to their families and two younger girls would be welcomed in their place.

In Thrace the Moon Riders were welcomed just as they were by the Anatolian tribes, but here they were known as Wolf-maidens in honor of Harpalyce, daughter of the Great Thracian Mountain Mother. The stories that Atisha told were different and Myrina listened with rapt attention to the adventurous stories of Harpalyce's childhood in the wilderness and mountains of Thrace.

At last their journey took them in an easterly direction, through the mountainous lands of the Moesians, and through the Month of Flies they rode back along the southern shore of the Black Sea.

Atisha brought her fine white stallion up beside Myrina and Cassandra. "Spring has come and gone," she told them. "We ride fast toward our favorite camping ground, where we'll stay and rest during the Month of Burning Heat. You have both worked hard and proved yourselves; now is the time for you to be happy and enjoy!"

"We will!" Myrina agreed, smiling and acknowledging the compliment, but Cassandra looked a little puzzled; enjoyment would not come easily to her.

CHAPTER THIRTEEN

Sting like a Scorpion

T HE MOON RIDERS crossed the narrow Bosphorus Sea then rode south again, along the shore of the Sea of Marmara, to Elikmaa, where they made their summer camp each year. Though Myrina had traveled far and wide with her family she'd never before been to this lovely spot beside a huge lake. They set up their tents beside the water; lush fertile hills with clumps of cypress trees stretched out behind them. Myrina breathed in the scent of iris flowers, mint, and sage.

A breeze from the water ruffled her hair. "A good cool place to be," she murmured.

"Yes," Cassandra agreed, seeming a little more at ease in this beautiful place. "And see the fig trees heavy with fruit and ripe golden peaches growing all about us; nobody will go hungry here. We are like the fish."

Myrina frowned, puzzled. "Like the fish?"

"Like the fish," Cassandra insisted. "We go north in the summer for coolness, then turn south for the winter to find warmth."

Suddenly Myrina understood and laughed. "You're mad," she told Cassandra cheerfully, making her hands float like fins, and her mouth gulp, to imitate a fish swimming upstream.

"Yes, that's what they always said in Troy," the princess answered, laughing back at her. "They called me mad!"

"You look beautiful when you laugh," Myrina told her truthfully.

"No one in Troy ever said *that*," Cassandra answered, happy for once.

Myrina smiled back at her. Being Cassandra's stalwart companion was not turning out to be so very difficult after all.

The tribes who camped near Elikmaa welcomed the Moon Riders with goat's milk cheese and delicious flat bread, rolled very thin and baked over fires glowing with charcoal. For once the only dance that was required of them was the gentle moon-dance that sent them all sleepy to their beds.

Though there was no more traveling for a while, there was still work to do, making sure that the horses were well fed, watered, and exercised. The Month of Burning

Heat went by all too soon and Atisha began to plan their next move south through the mountains. Bow practice was resumed, as soon as they'd saluted the morning sun.

The Moon Riders' tradition was always to shoot their arrows from horseback and in the old days, when they'd turned warrior, few enemies dared to face the formidable threat of charging Amazons.

The Moon Riders laughed at the name of Amazon as they strapped on their strong leather body armor that flattened and protected the right breast as they drew their bows. The Achaeans had given them the name of Amazon, meaning "breastless ones," and the story went about that the Moon-maidens were forced to burn or cut off their right breast.

"As if we'd ever do such a ridiculous and dangerous thing." Penthesilea shook her head, chuckling as she strung her curved bow.

"Ah, but it does no harm to let them think it!" Centaurea insisted. "If we'd cut off a breast without fear, what else might we do? A frightening reputation can do much to protect us."

"Do we really need all this practice?" Myrina asked. "All we ever do is hunt rabbit or deer."

"Foolspeak!" Lycippe snapped. She was a young woman with a sharp pointed face, well-suited to the pictures of jackals that adorned her cheeks.

"We must always be ready to fight!" Penthesilea waved her pointed spear in front of Myrina's nose. "Who knows when we may need to defend ourselves? The journey south takes us through mountains where bears and robbers hide. We must always be ready."

"All right, all right!" Myrina backed away red-faced, wishing she'd not spoken. They'd answered her just as Hati might.

Everyone knew that Penthesilea loved shooting with her curved bow; each morning she led the dancers in a mounted charge, astride her tireless mare, Fleetwind. They'd come and go in constant waves, never for one moment letting any direction go uncovered, aiming just as accurately behind them as in front. Back and forth they'd gallop at Penthesilea's command, until every horse and rider was bathed in sweat.

At last Atisha would call, "Enough!"

After they'd rubbed the horses down, Atisha would call for dancing sticks. Though the short, light sticks were gaily painted, the stick dance that they performed also bore a serious purpose. A sharp iron point fixed to one end would instantly turn the sturdy stick into a spear. The Moon Riders' sticks were free of pointed heads for the moment, but the way that Atisha made them train left no doubt in anyone's mind that these cheerful baubles might be turned to death-dealing weapons in an instant.

They advanced across the short-cropped grass, twirling their sticks steadily, then swung them fiercely above their heads. The clashing of wood on wood could be heard as the Moon Riders practiced with a partner—attack and defense, attack and defense. There were no holds barred and the dancers gathered many a bruised elbow and cracked ankle.

Myrina swung her stick at Cassandra but then lightened her efforts a little as she saw the princess shrink away.

"No! You're not helping her," Penthesilea cried. "Gentleness builds no strength. Sting like a scorpion, butt like a ram!"

Myrina hesitated for a moment, recognizing the truth of this, but while she was distracted, Cassandra advanced, catching her off balance with a sharp whack!

"Ha!" Penthesilea cried. "Well done! Strategy may win the day!"

Myrina staggered to her feet and advanced toward Cassandra with furious eyes.

"That's better," Penthesilea cried.

As the Month of Burning Heat came to an end, the Moon Riders' skills and strengths were honed. Cassandra grew dark-skinned and muscular, but at the same time a deep sense of contentment seemed to flow from her. Myrina grew stronger and more confident than ever. The two were rarely separated now. They both found themselves a little time for mirror-gazing and were content with what they saw.

Reseda seemed to be growing fatter and slower. "There may be a baby next spring," Myrina told Cassandra. "I think I shall be an aunt. Is all well in Troy?"

"I see that my friend Chryseis thrives, but I rarely look toward Troy," Cassandra told her. "It is Iphigenia in Mycenae that I fear for, but each time I see her in my dark glass she looks well and pampered. It's just that I feel she's not happy."

The Moon Riders packed up their camp ready for the southward trek, to find their winter quarters in the warmer clime of Lesbos, the Sacred Isle.

They set off riding south, but this time instead of returning to Troy, they skirted Mount Ida's eastern slopes and headed onward through the mountain pass. The narrow rocky route was hard going, and though the horses were sure-footed, everyone seemed to heave a great sigh of relief as they came cantering down the southern slopes. The sea lay before them and the fertile green lands that bordered the shore. Their pace slowed as they came into sight of the Isle of Lesbos.

"We'll be making camp here," Penthesilea told them.

Myrina was surprised. "But the sun is high in the sky," she said. "I thought we'd go on and look for boats. We're so close to the island."

Penthesilea shook her head. "We camp here for two nights," she told them. "Tomorrow is our gathering day. Surely you know about gathering day?"

Myrina vaguely remembered Gul and Hati talking of such a thing but she'd never taken much notice of what it meant. "Who is it that we gather with?"

Penthesilea laughed.

"It is the plants that we gather," Cassandra said solemnly. "Herbs and flowers for medicine and soothing potions."

"That's right," Penthesilea agreed.

"How did you know?" Myrina snapped, suddenly annoyed. She was the one who knew about the Moon Riders, not Cassandra.

Cassandra shook her head and shrugged her shoulders. "Look at the place," she said, waving her arm to encompass the whole circling bay.

Myrina saw what she meant. Lush grasses and wild flowers grew in wonderful abundance, where fingerlike spits of land stretched out into the sea, pointing the way toward distant Lesbos. Great clumps of rare wild lavender flourished there and golden fennel, with its green feathery leaves, grew all about the shore. There were delicate white asphodels, and the tallest hypericums that Myrina had ever seen. Then in the distance the curving land broke up into little islands. All around them washed a turquoise sea, streaked with darker blue and patches of purple where the water was suddenly deep.

Myrina slipped down from her horse's back. "Yes, I see what you mean," she said.

Just at that moment a great fish leaped up from the water and jumped twice. Then another followed as the Moon Riders pointed at them with delight.

"See," Penthesilea cried. "Even the fish welcome us here."

CHAPTER FOURTEEN

The Coming of Spring

T HE GATHERING DAY was frantic and exhausting:
the Moon Riders tramped through the grasslands, their arms full of wild herbs and flowers.
They picked hypericum for wounds and snake bite, bitter rue to strengthen the eyes, small purple flower
spikes from the chaste tree that would cool the sweats
of older women, and most important of all, the delicate
white opium poppy that brought merciful sleep to
those in pain.

Myrina found Cassandra standing amid huge clumps
of fennel, still as a statue.

"What is it?" she asked.

Cassandra shook her head. "Troy," she murmured.
"The Trojan plains that spread down to the sea are full of
fennel. The fishermen and boatmen gather fennel stalks
to light their lamps at night."

"You must miss Troy," Myrina said. "It is your home.

I've never lived in one spot, so it is my family I long for, not a place."

Cassandra shook her head. "I do miss Troy," she whispered. "I miss the great golden walls and towers, the fig trees, the tamarisks, and the sacred oak. The little huts of the lower town are built of mud bricks, but such wonderful bricks, for the baked mud is crammed with seashells."

"I have seen them," Myrina agreed.

"I miss all of that," Cassandra admitted. Then she looked down, rather ashamed. "I miss Chryseis, but I do not miss my family very much."

Myrina, arms full of sharp-scented lavender, bent toward her and kissed her cheek. "Why should you? I do not think they value you as they should."

Cassandra smiled. "Nobody ever kissed me like that in Troy," she said.

When the gathering was over, a small fleet of fishing boats came from Lesbos and carried the Moon Riders over the sea, with their steeds and their bundles of herbs. Once they'd landed they rode south toward Mytilene, named after the sister of the famous Dancing Myrina.

The people of this ancient city, founded long ago by the Moon Riders, had never forgotten how their town originated. They gladly provided a fine camping place, plentiful provisions and a warm welcome each winter.

* * *

The Month of Falling Leaves brought cooler weather but Atisha did not allow slackness. Horses must be exercised, dances improved, clothing dyed and mended, ready for the Spring Celebrations; herbs must be dried, pounded, and brewed ready for next year's supply of medicines.

In the Month of the Dying Sun, fires were built and slow sad dancing performed, in sympathy with the turning of the year. The Bitter Months followed, bringing snow and hail, but Atisha's merciless advice on keeping warm was to work harder, run faster, leap higher.

When at last the first signs of the sun's returning strength came, a great restlessness seemed to rustle through the Moon Riders' camp. Suddenly they were packing, ready to go off traveling again, for spring was coming. They'd soon gallop north again, for the Month of New Leaves, with spring romping along behind them.

Myrina could not wait to get to the Place of Flowing Waters. For just seven days she'd be there with her family again, at the great gathering. She knew from her mirror-gazing that Reseda hadn't given birth as yet. "I want very much to be there when my sister's baby is born," she confided to Cassandra. "But . . . I fear I've changed so much. I've grown so fast that my tunic needs replacing and my trousers letting down."

Cassandra smiled. "They will know their Snake Lady," she said.

"And Tomi. I must see Tomi, and make sure that he hasn't forgotten me. Each time I mirror-gaze, I see him hunting and riding and tending the horses. I've never seen him with a girl at his side, but I must remind him again that I'll marry him, if only he'll wait."

Cassandra looked at her, puzzled. "Does your father not choose a husband for you?"

Myrina laughed. "No, certainly not! The Mazagardi women choose for themselves, and a Moon Rider is never refused!"

"In Troy, a father always chooses!"

"But not for you! Surely you were promised to your sun god as a priestess."

Cassandra sighed. "I have broken that promise by going with the Moon Riders. I fear my father may change his mind if he thinks a marriage would be useful or bring more wealth."

"Hasn't the man got enough?" Myrina asked. Then she suddenly realized that perhaps she'd been very rude. "Forgive me," she muttered. "He is your father."

"There's naught to forgive." Cassandra was not offended. "You spoke the truth!"

The lookouts spied the Moon Riders coming and at once a great clamor of pipes and clapping began. Myrina felt great pride in this moment, arriving back among her people an experienced priestess, welcomed and honored by them all.

Pride turned to wild excitement when she saw Gul; dignity was forgotten as she leaped from the horse's back, and flung herself into her mother's arms. Aben hung back, a huge grin on his face, and Myrina caught a glimpse of Tomi standing behind looking hesitant.

"Father," Myrina yelled, hugging him.

"You've not forgotten your old pa then." Aben chuckled.

Then Myrina turned to Tomi, feeling surprisingly shy. They smiled then kissed, with just a little awkwardness.

"I've not forgotten my promise," Tomi whispered.

"I know," she said, then giggled at the puzzled look on his face, as shyness seemed to melt away. "Where's Reseda?" she asked, concerned not to see her sister there. "And Hati?"

"She labors to bring her child into the world," Gul told her. "Hati is with her, just in case, but Reseda swears that she's hanging on until her sister returns. You know that it brings good luck to have a Moon Rider present at a birth."

"I must go to her," she said. "I must go at once. I'll tell Atisha."

As she turned back toward the Old Woman she saw Atisha's bright monkey face bending over the princess with concern. This should be a joyous time for Cassandra, she thought, but where are her family to greet her? Where is her welcome home?

Then as she watched, a space appeared in the crowd, and people stood back for two armed guards, their tunics bearing the sun sign of Trojan Apollo.

"We come to escort the Princess Cassandra to Troy," they announced. A closed litter followed behind, borne by four strong slaves.

Cassandra hesitated but then bowed her head obediently, giving the reins of her horse to Atisha. She went toward the litter and for a moment Myrina felt that she couldn't bear to let her go back to Troy and such a loveless reception, but then the curtain in the litter was whisked back and the gentle face of the young priestess Chryseis looked out. Cassandra ran toward her smiling then, her arms outstretched. Myrina sighed with relief. Cassandra would not be friendless in Troy, after all.

"Right." She turned back to Gul. "Where are our tents? Where is Reseda?"

Reseda was breathless and elated when Myrina arrived. The birth was very close and there was no time for greetings. Myrina stooped at once to hold her sister's hand and there were only moments to wait before a baby girl slithered out of her mother's body into the world. Hati worked busily to tie the cord and cut it, then clean the small wriggling body with olive oil. At last the child was ready and handed over not to the mother, but to Myrina.

"The dance," Reseda whispered.

"Me?" Myrina asked.

"Of course." Hati laughed. "You are the only Moon Rider here. You must give the welcoming dance; there can be no one better!"

She took the little warm naked body into her arms and while Hati sang, Myrina gently twirled and turned, rocking her new little niece back and forth, while Gul and Reseda watched in silent respect.

"Catch the sun," Gul reminded her, lifting up the tent flap.

Myrina stepped carefully outside, still rocking and twirling, just as the sun went slipping away in the west. Then she turned the young child around and there was the moon looking down on them, picking up the last of the sun's rays so that it gleamed pink in the darkening sky, with one glinting evening star behind it.

Myrina took the baby back inside and handed her to her mother. "She has seen the sun and the moon and the evening star," she said.

All the women heaved a great sigh of happiness. "That is a great blessing," Hati said. "Very lucky and rare; this little one is blessed indeed."

"I shall call her Yildiz," Reseda said, taking her back with eager arms and snuggling her tiny daughter to her breast.

CHAPTER FIFTEEN

Back to Troy

OVER THE NEXT two days little Yildiz thrived on the care and attention that she received from her aunt, for Myrina couldn't put the baby down. "I'll be going away again so soon," she protested whenever someone tried to take Yildiz from her. "I've got to make the most of my niece before I go."

Reseda lay back enjoying the rest that she needed, watching her sister rock the baby. She was tired after the long labor and happy to let Myrina fuss over the child. "I never thought to see you so baby crazed." She smiled.

"Nor did I," Myrina agreed. "But then I never was asked to do the welcoming dance before; she feels special to me."

"When your time comes, you'll make a fine mother," Reseda told her.

Although Myrina and her family were wrapped up in the new member of the Mazagardi tribe, they could not help but be drawn into the excited gossip that filled the spring gathering. Sails had been spotted far out at sea, a fleet of fine ships moving up the coast toward the city of Troy. The second wave of news suggested that they'd been recognized as the fleet that Prince Paris sailed away in almost a year ago on his visit to Menelaus in Sparta.

"I know one who'll not be delighted at his return," Myrina murmured.

"Who? Your friend Cassandra?" Hati was quick to pick up on her meaning.

Myrina nodded. "She's filled with dread when her handsome brother is about, though she can't say why!"

Hati was thoughtful. "Poor princess," she murmured. "She's very sensitive, that one; such a gift will rarely bring happiness, though I'd say that those about her would do well to take notice of what she says."

"Ah! They never do," said Myrina. "In Troy they swear that she is jealous of Prince Paris and put everything she says down to that. They even call her mad . . . which she is not!"

Hati shook her head. "Poor princess," she repeated.

That night, the Lady Chryseis arrived from Troy in a fine curtained wagon drawn by two horses, with a message for the Old Woman Atisha and the Moon Rider Myrina.

"There's to be a great feast in Troy this evening to welcome Prince Paris back," she told them. "Cassandra begs you to come as guests."

Atisha agreed at once, though she insisted that she must ride her fine stallion, for she'd long ago forgotten how to ride in a wagon.

Chryseis turned to Myrina. "Oh no." She shook her head. "I cannot spare a day and night away from this fine new niece of mine and little Yildiz is best settled here with her mother."

Chryseis smiled rather sadly. "Cassandra told me not to press you, but . . . I know that your presence would be a comfort to her."

"Hmph!" Hati huffed agreement. "Not so fast with your refusals, my little Snake! From what you told me last night our tiny Yildiz might not be the only one who has need of you."

Myrina turned thoughtful at that. She looked across at Atisha, but the Old Woman shook her head, setting a gorgeous new peacock feather into her turban. "The decision is yours, Snake Lady."

Suddenly Myrina was smiling wickedly at Hati. "You want to go, Grandmother!" she accused.

Hati grinned broadly. "I should love to go," she admitted. "Curiosity was always one of my strengths."

"You may come as my companion." Atisha pushed her hand through her old friend's arm and they both rounded on Myrina.

"If you go," Atisha said, "you go for yourself."

"And maybe one other," Hati added.

Myrina looked about her. Reseda was up and strong enough now, her body tightening quickly back to its old muscular shape. Reseda and Yildiz didn't really need her and maybe the neglected princess did.

"I shall be pleased to come as Cassandra's guest," she told Chryseis.

The priestess of Apollo smiled with genuine pleasure at her decision. "Will you ride in the wagon with me?" she asked.

Myrina was about to refuse, for horseback was much more comfortable to her, but something in the hesitant invitation made her accept. "Yes please," she agreed.

Soon after the sun reached its zenith the wagon set off, with two Trojan guards with swords and short spears in front of it and the two old women riding behind, their bows strung and ready.

Chryseis pulled herself back inside the wagon. "We're certainly well escorted." She smiled.

Myrina agreed. "Those bringing up the rear are just as fierce as those in front," she said. "And crafty as jackals. I'd bet on them against your Trojan guards any day. Now tell me please, how was Cassandra received in Troy? Was she welcomed back?"

107

Chryseis's smile vanished and her head drooped to the side. "She was welcomed." Myrina could see that she was trying to be fair. "But of course there was no great feast in Cassandra's honor. Priam is suggesting now that as she has broken her promise as priestess to Apollo, she should be willing to marry instead."

"Oh no," Myrina cried. "Cassandra feared that."

"Priam is very keen to make some sort of alliance with the Achaean lords." Chryseis shook her head, clearly unhappy at the idea. "There is news of fearful raiding parties at Ephesus and Miletus. The pirate warrior Achilles swarms mercilessly up from his ships with his Myrmidon soldiers, snatching gold and women. They kill any man who gets in his way, leaving ruin behind, and it's just that same bloodthirsty man that Priam seeks to appease by offering him Cassandra."

Myrina shuddered at the thought, glad that she'd accepted Cassandra's invitation, but also glad that Atisha and Hati were riding close behind.

"At least Cassandra has you for her friend," Myrina generously told the young priestess.

Chryseis again looked sad. "But not for long," she said. She drew back the wagon curtains, pointing toward the deep blue sea of the Aegean. "Do you see that island in the distance? That is my home, the Isle of Tenedos. My father, Chryse, is the priest of Apollo in the temple there.

He agreed when I was younger to send me for seven years to serve Apollo as priestess at the temple in Troy, but my seven years are almost up. In the autumn I must return to my father and my home."

Myrina understood what this must mean. "So when Cassandra returns to Troy next spring, you will have gone."

Chryseis nodded. "See there," she pointed out. "That is Besika Bay."

Myrina looked and saw the curved bay filled with tall ships' masts. "Prince Paris's ships?"

"Yes." The priestess frowned. "No one can understand why he's moored there. Our ships usually arrive in the Bay of the City where everyone can watch from the city walls, to wave and cheer, then when important guests have disembarked the ships sail around to Besika for more permanent mooring."

"His ships are tall-masted and fine." Myrina could not help but admire them.

"Oh yes, and Paris is usually one for making a big entrance, so it's a bit of a mystery. He's hidden in Besika overnight, but sent messages to Priam announcing his arrival with an honored guest!"

"But he hasn't said who?"

Chryseis shook her head. "There's talk that he may have brought King Menelaus back from Sparta for another visit, for some of those masts bear the Spartan standard. Priam will be anxious if that is so."

Myrina caught her breath. "Not Achilles!" she whispered. "He's not brought Achilles to claim Cassandra's hand!"

"By Trojan Apollo, I pray not," Chryseis agreed with feeling.

At last Besika Bay was left far behind them as they crossed the low-lying marshy lands between the two rivers Scamander and Simois. The dirt track widened and the wagon ran more smoothly over a wide street of stone cobbles. Myrina enjoyed once again the impressive sight of the busy, high-walled city. Chryseis sat modestly back, hidden by the wagon's curtains as a good Trojan priestess should, while Myrina hung out of the window.

They rumbled into the citadel through the Southern Gate and up a steady sloping ramp, paved with golden limestone slabs. They left the wagon and horses at the stables and Chryseis showed them into the guesthouse once again. This time it was Atisha's turn to stare at the luxurious decoration and furnishings. Hati and Myrina smiled to see the Old Woman impressed for once.

CHAPTER SIXTEEN

A Beautiful Woman on a Shopping Trip

THE MAIN FEASTING hall gleamed with even more bronze and gold than Myrina remembered. It seemed Priam's wealth had grown noticeably in just one year. They were shown to a table on the women's side, and Myrina was pleased to see that she could twist around and there behind her on the royal women's table was Cassandra.

The princess got up and came straight over to them, hugging Myrina tightly. "Thank you for coming, my friend," she murmured. "I'm so glad to see you."

Myrina hugged her back, but saw with concern the quick tears that filled the princess's eyes. "I heard about Achilles," she whispered. "This guest that Paris brings, it's not him, is it?"

"No," Cassandra assured her. "Whoever it is, they've arrived in a closed litter, surrounded by slave girls and waiting women."

Myrina frowned. "Is it Clytemnestra back again?"

Cassandra shook her head. "If it is, she's not got Iphigenia with her. I saw her in my mirror-gazing last night, and now I recognize the palace at Mycenae."

Suddenly the deep notes of double pipes were sounding and Priam and Hecuba came in, followed by Hector and his young wife, Andromache.

They'd no sooner taken their seats than the pipes were sounding again and Paris was announced. He strode forward looking more splendid than ever, dressed in a robe of deep, dyed Syrian purple. He bowed to his parents but then turned back to introduce a veiled woman who followed him.

"Mother, Father," he cried. "Please welcome our honored guest Helen, Queen of Sparta."

Both Priam and Hecuba rose to their feet. They were a little puzzled by the arrival of King Menelaus's wife. Helen drew back her gauzy veil and at once a stunned silence fell.

Myrina had never before seen such a perfect face. Her eyes were deep turquoise, her skin smooth and white, golden curls framed all this beauty, drawn up high onto the back of her head and twisted into an elaborate headdress. The Spartan queen's gown was made of fine snowy white linen, trimmed with golden thread. The silence was so long and the surprised expression on the faces of Priam and his queen so funny that Helen suddenly laughed, a deep, pleasant, comfortable sound.

"Please excuse my unbidden arrival," she said. "But the fame of your Trojan fabrics has reached me in Sparta and I swore that like my sister Clytemnestra I must come on a shopping trip."

Everyone seemed to smile and relax at the friendly tone of her voice. She did not seem haughty or proud, even though she might look like a goddess. Priam shook himself out of his surprise and back to his usual courtesy. "You are as welcome to this city as spring sunshine," he said, and rushed to kiss her hand.

Priam led Helen to sit at his right hand; a great honor in this city where the women usually sat separately from the men.

Hector obligingly allowed the servants to shuffle his chair along so that Paris could take a seat on Helen's right hand. "For this courtesy you must introduce me, brother," he whispered good-naturedly to Paris.

After such an amazing start to the feast, it took a little while for the guests to settle down and the servants to rally themselves to start serving. Myrina turned and saw that Cassandra was staring down at the marble floor, looking troubled. Myrina almost rose to go to her but now that baskets piled high with soft white barley bread were being carried around by the slaves, she knew that it would be discourteous to get up. A touch of irritation returned. Why couldn't Cassandra just enjoy herself?

Large flat dishes of crayfish cooked in herbs, olive oil, and garlic appeared. The smell was delicious and Myrina couldn't resist helping herself, and enjoying such wonderful food. The strongest pangs of hunger satisfied, she looked over at Atisha and Hati, whose heads were bowed together, deep in conversation. The two old women stared up at the high table, to where the Queen of Sparta sat, then back to each other again, whispering furiously.

Myrina turned back to Cassandra and saw with dismay that she was eating nothing, pointedly ignored by Hecuba's waiting women, who sat either side of her. Myrina sighed; hadn't riding with the Moon-maidens at least taught Cassandra to eat properly?

The feast went on and wonderful steaming meat dishes arrived: beef, mutton, goat's meat, and pork, all oiled and spiced and roasted on sticks. Fruits dipped in honey, nuts, and aniseed followed, and Myrina swore that none of the feasts provided for the honored Moon Riders, excellent though they were, had ever quite come up to this. As the evening wore on, musicians appeared, and a message came around from Queen Hecuba, inviting Myrina to dance. Her stomach felt tight but she obligingly got up to dance, while Hati and Atisha nodded their approval.

Myrina didn't feel she'd performed well; the musicians

did their best to keep time with her, but they didn't have the Moon-maiden's touch. Despite that feeling, she was rewarded with enthusiastic applause. Cassandra did not even look at her, but sat with fists clenched, staring at the floor. When the cheers had died down, Myrina ran to the princess, holding out her hand in invitation.

"Come, show them what you have learned with the Moon Riders," she begged, longing for Cassandra to cheer up and show her family what a fine dancer she'd become.

Hecuba and Priam nodded indulgently at the suggestion, but Cassandra shook her head.

Then suddenly the princess rose to her feet and Myrina saw with apprehension that she was trembling from head to toe, her face turned white as snow. Cassandra pointed her finger at the beautiful Queen of Sparta. "How could I dance, on such a night as this?" She then swung around and pointed at Paris. "My brother brings us no honored guest; he brings destruction to Troy!"

A horrified silence fell. Guests sat there gaping, shocked beyond belief. This was the deepest discourtesy. Chryseis put her head down between her hands in shame.

"How dare you? How dare you?" Priam bellowed.

Myrina took Cassandra's arm. "Hush, my friend," she whispered, trying to calm her. "You do none of us any good."

But Cassandra was awash with tears that came flooding down her cheeks, though her arms had gone stiff as sticks. She turned her gaze once more to Paris, her mismatched eyes deeper in color than ever. Then her voice sank suddenly low, though in the quiet every word was heard. "This is no shopping trip. King Menelaus's wife is your lover and you bring her here to Troy! You bring us death."

Both Priam and Hecuba were on their feet, Hecuba in tears and Priam purple-faced with rage. "You are no daughter of mine," he shouted, then he was lost in a violent fit of choking.

Cassandra stumbled to the side as though she'd faint, but Hati was there, taking her arm, Atisha on the other side, supporting her around the waist.

The king recovered his breath for a moment. "Get her out of my sight!" he growled.

"I shall go!" Cassandra gasped. "Away with the Moon Riders again!"

"Go—and don't return," Priam told her. "If these are the manners that you've learned you'd best stay with the wild barbarian dancers."

"No!" Hecuba cried.

Suddenly Atisha was speaking, her deep soothing storyteller's voice carrying well across the great hall. "Forgive this discourtesy," she begged, bowing to Helen.

"The princess suffers much from sudden melancholy. We will be honored to have her travel with us again. I beg that you will not think too unkindly of this disruption."

Her calm sensible manner seemed to restore a little of the good feeling that had prevailed at the beginning of the feast. Hati and Atisha both bowed deeply to the high table, then turned and walked swiftly away, Cassandra borne along between them.

Myrina hesitated for a moment, stunned and sickened at what had happened. Chryseis rose from her place at table, and came to her. They both bowed to Priam and followed Cassandra out.

CHAPTER SEVENTEEN

The Troublesome Daughter

T HE TWO OLD warrior women did not stop once they left the hall. They marched Cassandra out of the palace, down the steps and the slope that led toward the stable block. Cassandra went white-faced and obedient, moving between them like a sleepwalker. Myrina and Chryseis broke into a run to try to catch up with them. When they reached the stables, Atisha rode out on her stallion, Cassandra mounted in front of her, supported in the Old Woman's strong arms. "We go at once," she told them. "The king may change his mind and want his daughter back."

"Then should we not wait?" Myrina cried. "He might forgive her."

Hati followed them out of the stables, mounted on her own mare, shaking her head. "There is no safe harbor here for Cassandra, not after tonight! Not for a while, at least!"

Chryseis seemed to accept this as wise. She stretched up to take Cassandra's hand. "Good-bye, dear friend," she whispered. "I don't know when we'll see each other again, but you will always be here in my heart!"

Cassandra nodded though she couldn't speak. Myrina was reminded of the bond that still lay between Iphigenia and the princess. "Few friends," she murmured. "Few friends, but true friends."

Atisha galloped through the Southern Gate while Hati bent to pull Myrina up behind her, then they trotted down the stone-paved ramp and into the lower city. As they moved out onto the plain, leaving the small winding streets behind them, Hati brought her mare up to a gallop. Myrina clutched her grandmother tight about the waist, feeling a little better. She whispered into her ear, "No fine bedchamber for us after all, Grandmother!"

Hati laughed. "Nay, sleeping safe is better than sleeping in luxury."

"Priam surely wouldn't have harmed us?" Myrina said.

"Not Priam," Hati replied.

"Who then?"

"His son Paris! Did you not see the look that passed between Paris and the Spartan queen? Did you not see the way his hand flew to his dagger?"

"No," Myrina answered, trying hard to understand what this might mean. "Was there truth in what

Cassandra said?" she murmured. "Prince Paris and the Spartan queen are lovers!"

Hati slowed the pace a little, bowing her head in respect as they passed the ancient burial mound of Dancing Myrina. "Oh yes!" she said. "Cassandra did not pick a very suitable moment, or the best company to announce such a thing, but Atisha knew she spoke the truth. She always does!"

Myrina fell silent as they galloped fast across the plain, back toward Mount Ida and the Place of Flowing Waters. It must have been that the beautiful queen had willingly come away with Paris, for she herself had cheerfully announced that she'd come on a shopping trip. Did her husband know, or did he too think this a shopping trip, like Clytemnestra's?

"What do you think King Menelaus will do?" she asked her grandmother.

Hati shuddered. "I dread to think," she whispered. "I suppose he'll go to his brother Agamemnon for help. All I know is that between them they now have just the excuse that they've been looking for, to come here and wage war on Troy!"

Myrina knew what such a war would mean. The whole of Anatolia would be dragged into it and the tribes and those who traded in Troy would lose their livelihoods and maybe their lives.

Hati rode on grim-faced.

"But Grandmother, you said that Troy would never be an easy place to get into," Myrina reminded her.

"No," Hati agreed. "That's still true. It could take a long time to wear the Trojans down and a great deal of death and misery first." She sighed and her lined face seemed more skull-like and fragile to Myrina. "I'm too old for this now, too old and weary to turn warrior again."

"Maybe Menelaus will think himself best rid of Helen. If she wants to go away with Paris, let her. He has his kingdom to rule."

They were coming in sight of the great spring camp now and the mare slowed her paces. Hati swung down from the horse's back and looked up at her granddaughter, her face drawn with anxiety. "It's not as simple as that. Menelaus will have to come seeking his wife. You see, Helen inherited the kingdom from her father, so that Menelaus only rules Sparta as her husband. If Helen chooses Prince Paris as husband, who then is the true King of Sparta?"

Myrina began to understand the seriousness of Cassandra's outburst, when Atisha came pushing back through the crowd toward them. She looked worried.

"Where is Cassandra?" Myrina asked her.

"Safe with Penthesilea; go to her!"

Myrina went into Penthesilea's tent. The older girl

supported the princess, making her sip a sharp-smelling herbal brew. Cassandra tightly clutched her precious obsidian mirror.

"Can you see something in there?" Myrina asked, sitting down beside them.

Cassandra shook her head. "Gone," she murmured.

"But you did see something?"

Cassandra nodded and shuddered.

Penthesilea got up. "I must see Atisha," she told them. "Will you look after Cassandra?"

"Of course." Myrina nodded.

They sat together in silence for a moment. Myrina hadn't even thought of rushing back to Reseda and baby Yildiz. "What was it that you saw?" she whispered at last.

Cassandra answered her in a flat quiet voice. "Blood," she said. "Blood everywhere and falling walls, crumbling towers, fire and screaming—terrible screaming!"

Now Myrina shuddered. "Where was it?"

"Troy," Cassandra mouthed, her voice still flat, her face blank. "It started in Troy, then it spread."

"Spread where?"

"Here," she said. "The plain, Mount Ida, everywhere. I know it to be the truth, but they will never believe me."

"Atisha believes you," Myrina told her firmly. "She believes you and so do I. Rest now and I will stay here and keep you safe."

To Myrina's surprise Cassandra obediently lay down on the cushions, closing her eyes; she fell asleep almost at once, like an exhausted child. Myrina took the dagger from her belt sheath and held it ready, clasped in both hands. She never had trusted Prince Paris, not one bit.

When Atisha and Penthesilea returned with Hati they found Cassandra still sleeping and Myrina alert and on her guard.

"Well done," Atisha told her. "A better guard dog I couldn't find. We have agreed that Cassandra must go ahead with Penthesilea and wait for us in Thrace."

"I shall go with them," Myrina said with determination, then politely added, "if you think fit, of course."

Atisha smiled and nodded. "Three is a good number, more might attract attention, but you will have to ride fast."

"Isatis will carry me like the wind."

"Little Yildiz?" Hati reminded her.

"She is safe with her mother." Myrina didn't hesitate. "And especially with her great-grandmother to look to her safety. Cassandra has greater need, I think!"

Hati kissed her. "You are turning into a fine young warrior, my young Snaky," she said.

CHAPTER EIGHTEEN

Escape to Thrace

L THOUGH IT WAS a sacrifice to miss the spring dances, Myrina couldn't help but feel excited at the task ahead. Penthesilea would be expected to do such a thing, but Myrina was pleased at the way Atisha seemed to put trust in her as well.

The three young women went off the following morning, walking their horses calmly away, while the other Moon Riders rose to greet the sun. Once they had left the great gathering behind they mounted and cantered steadily around the foothills of Mount Ida. Then at last they set off at a gallop, skirting the plain of Troy. They stayed up on the high ground, passing the tall towers of the city in the distance, riding fast toward the narrow sea crossing of the Hellespont.

Cassandra did not even glance at her home city but rode white-faced and quiet, staring straight ahead with Myrina and Penthesilea on either side of her. They all had their bows strung, leather breast-straps in place, and daggers in their belts covered by long cloaks. Their horses were fastened into felt-padded chest guards that might deflect an arrow or spear, covered and disguised by the usual riding blanket.

Though Cassandra never turned, Myrina looked toward the high windy city of Troy and the deep blue sea beyond. She saw a gang of riders leave at the Southern Gate, heading southeast toward Mount Ida, their helmets and weapons glinting in the sun. She said nothing, but she couldn't help but wonder if they'd just got away in time.

As they came to the sea they turned north, away from the very narrowest point, riding up the coast toward a small village of huts and boats. Penthesilea swung down from Fleetwind and walked straight to the biggest hut. The headman of the fisher-people sat outside with his wife, mending nets in the spring sunshine.

"We need a boat," Penthesilea said, thrusting at him a silver medallion bearing the image of the crescent moon on one side and the plump figure of Earth Mother, Maa, on the other.

"In the service of Maa!" He spoke in the Luvvian language to his wife. She nodded and they both stood up, immediately putting down their nets.

Orders were shouted and six young men rose at once,

leaping onto the largest of the boats that were tied up. They started to haul the ropes and unfurl the sail, but then suddenly all the fisher-people were shouting at one another; Myrina's heart beat fast as her hand crept to clasp the handle of her dagger. But the headman was talking again in Luvvian, explaining the argument. "The wind is turning to the west, not ready yet. You eat first. Roast mackerel—anchovies—fresh bread."

Myrina wanted to smile, letting go of her knife, but Penthesilea looked anxious. "Our journey is important," she told them. "We cannot wait."

"Can't wait to eat?" The fisherwoman was surprised.

"No," Penthesilea insisted.

Then suddenly it was all agreed. Strong wooden oars were brought from the nearest hut and a wooden ramp set up against the boat so that they could lead their horses aboard. When at last everything was made ready, the fisherwoman pushed a basket into Myrina's arms; it contained fresh bread, a gray stoneware flask of olive oil and three smoked mackerel.

"You take—eat," she told her. "This one—too thin." She prodded the slender wrist of the Princess of Troy.

Myrina wanted to laugh and cry all at once. She took the basket and thanked her; they were not going to get away without food.

The young men took the oars and started to row out into the sea. It was a heavy load with three restive horses and hard for them to row against the strong current flowing southward into the Aegean. The men were sweating and grateful when at last a westerly breeze filled the sails and they could draw up the oars. Then with the wind, the water turned choppy, ruffling the surface.

"Look to the horses," Penthesilea ordered, and though the three mares stamped their hooves, the soothing of their riders kept them from panicking.

Penthesilea and Myrina kept glancing back in the direction of Troy; only Cassandra seemed careless of whether they were pursued or not. The headman saw the agitation of his passengers but asked no questions. When at last the Thracian side of the Hellespont was reached, the three Moon Riders climbed out and mounted their mares as quickly as they could, hurriedly thanking the fisher-people.

"Blessings of Earth Mother, Maa," the head fisherman told them. "Nobody will follow you; not in our boat, anyway." He cackled.

They galloped north along the Thracian shoreline, stopping only once in the midday heat, when they were grateful for the food that they'd been given. They rode fast until the sun began to sink in the west, then

Penthesilea slowed her pace. "I think we're safe now," she told them.

"Yes—we are safe," Cassandra confirmed it. She drew breath like a swimmer who had feared drowning, coming to the surface at last. "I am hungry," she announced.

Suddenly they were all laughing at one another, cheerful with relief.

They slowed their horses, looking back across the Sea of Marmara as it gradually grew wider and wider on their right-hand side. Ships loaded with copper, iron, and bronze could be seen passing steadily back and forth, after paying Priam's dues.

Myrina frowned in puzzlement. "The current flows south to the Aegean," she said, "and yet the great shoals of fishes swim north toward the Black Sea."

Cassandra and Penthesilea both smiled. "There's another strong current, deep below the surface," Cassandra told her, full of knowledge. "My father is always discussing it with his sea captains. A deeper current goes northward, making sea journeys difficult."

Cassandra seemed to have thoroughly recovered her spirits now that she was safe on the Thracian shore and Myrina felt that their fast ride had been worth it, just to see her happy again.

Penthesilea led them along the western shore, following their usual journey. They were welcomed as ever, and though no questions were asked, Myrina sensed a touch of curiosity as to why three young Moon-maidens were riding ahead of the Old Woman. They reached Abdera and made camp, deciding to stay there to await the arrival of Atisha. They enjoyed their few days of rest, but were relieved to hear that the lookouts had spied Atisha and the other Moon Riders in the distance.

When they arrived they were full of worrying news. "Menelaus and his friend Odysseus, King of Ithaca, sailed into the Bay of the City, demanding that his wife be returned," Atisha told them.

"So Priam knows now that Cassandra spoke truth?" said Myrina.

"Oh yes." Atisha nodded. "Paris and Helen refused to be parted and Menelaus has gone away swearing vengeance, though Odysseus stayed a little longer trying to act as mediator."

Cassandra herself admitted that she knew this to be true. "I saw my father in my mirror," she told them. "He is full of sorrow, but what can he do? Paris is filled with such a passion for Helen he will let nothing stand in his way. He has lost control of his feelings and suffers truly from a kind of madness of desire. At last, I do feel some sympathy for him."

"But—your father could order both Paris and Helen to leave Troy," Myrina suggested. "That might at least keep Troy safe."

Cassandra shook her head. "My father will never again send away his dearest boy. For good or ill he will not be parted from Paris."

CHAPTER NINETEEN

Who Has Done This?

AS THE SPRING PASSED the Moon Riders followed the usual course of their journey, heading at last to their summer lakeside camp. Wherever they went there was rumor and fearful gossip. Old people remembered how they'd suffered when Hercules and Theseus came raiding their towns and villages.

"Is it Hercules come again?" they asked.

"Is it only Troy they think to seize? Or do the Achaeans want slaves, gold, and iron?"

The year turned and the Moon Riders packed up their tents and baggage, setting off for Lesbos with some anxiety. The journey through the mountains was always difficult, but it was shorter than taking the easy-going route through the plains. When they descended the southern slopes, they found small towns and villages turned to smoking ruins. Dead men lay unburied by the roadside and the few survivors wandered about dazed and desperate, somehow clinging to life.

"Who has done this?" Atisha asked, her lined face grim.

Wherever they went the answer was the same. "Achilles!" They would spit on the ground as they spoke the name. "Achilles and his band of Myrmidon warriors. The man runs riot in our lands and Agamemnon and his brother Menelaus encourage him. Those who trade with Troy are being forced to pay for Paris's love of Helen."

A frightened young girl spoke nervously to Myrina; they'd found her struggling to bury her father and small brother. "I hid," she said. "Ran to the woods as Father told me. They even killed my baby brother and they've stolen my mother away!"

"And this is the man they wished me to marry." Cassandra shuddered.

"Well, whatever happens, you are not going to marry him now!" Myrina growled.

The Moon Riders did what they could to help the bewildered people; sharing the small stores of grain and oil that they'd brought with them from Elikmaa. When they arrived in view of the Isle of Lesbos, they found more desolation there, though it seemed that a bitter battle had been fought. Telephus, the king of that land, had succeeded in putting Achilles and his men to flight, but they'd lost many of their own warriors and the land was burnt and crops destroyed. Lesbos itself had been plundered.

Penthesilea looked about her at the ruin of the beautiful peninsula and scattered islands, agitated and angry. She furiously suggested that they leave the late summer gathering of herbs and search for boats to pursue the Achaean robbers. The other priestesses were angry but uncertain of what to do.

"Turn warrior?" they murmured. "Should we turn warrior?"

"It is not the time," Cassandra said.

"It's not up to you to decide," Penthesilea told her sharply.

But Atisha shook her head. "Listen to the princess," she insisted. "Besides, the herbs and medicine plants are still flourishing; Achilles' men had little interest in them. I too want these wicked raiders to feel the fury of the Moon Riders' arrows but the truth is that they've sailed away where we cannot easily follow. Wherever Achilles makes his winter camp, at least we know that he'll not be raiding again till the spring."

"I'm as ready to fight as you," Centaurea agreed. "But we may be in great need of medicine and ointments in the coming year."

Penthesilea listened with frustration, but then at last

her smile returned. "Of course you are right, Old Woman!"

Atisha touched her arm. "I was no fool when I chose you as my successor. Your courage will never be in doubt, but we must gather now as we've never done before."

They worked with doubled energy, letting anger drive them on. Myrina was bending her back, scooping up armfuls of scented lavender, when the uncomfortable feeling came upon her that she was being watched. She pretended to carry on with her work for a moment then suddenly swung around, an arrow notched in her bow.

At once her face relaxed: it was the frightened girl who they'd helped to bury her father and brothers.

"What are you doing here?" Myrina demanded.

"I followed you," the girl said, shocked at being caught, but stood her ground, while from out of the bushes three more ragged young women emerged.

"But your home was at the foot of the mountains. It's a full day's walk."

The girl shook her head. "Where is our home now?" she demanded. "Our families are gone. We want to learn how to fight, then we'll never hide in the woods again. We want to be Amazons!"

Myrina put down her bow. "What are your names?"

"I am Coronilla. This is Bremusa—Alcibie—and Polymusa."

"Come with me," Myrina told them. "We will see what the Old Woman says."

Atisha listened to their story and after a few moments of thought she agreed that they should join them. "I put them in your charge," she told Myrina.

Myrina was a little shaken by that, but Atisha cackled. "If you bring new recruits, then you can train them," she told her. "Best set them gathering herbs."

"But we want to fight!" Coronilla cried.

"You can fight once you've learned to heal the wounds that you cause with your fighting!" Atisha told them stubbornly.

That silenced them and they seemed to see some sense in what she said. "We will gather," they agreed.

The new recruits worked very hard, while Myrina ordered them back and forth. They staggered uncomplaining through the grasslands with bundles big as themselves on their backs and began to call themselves Myrina's gang.

When at last the Moon Riders crossed to Lesbos, they arrived with more herbs and berries than ever before. The boatmen who carried them over the water warned that Mytilene had suffered near destruction, but still they were not prepared for the sight of the fine city in ruins, and again, so many people dead or stolen away.

Atisha wondered if they should travel on and find a

new place to camp over winter, for the struggling survivors had enough to do trying to feed themselves, but the people begged them stay.

"The Moon Riders are our luck," they told her. "You bring the spirit of Maa back to us."

So they did stay over winter and their hard work and care, along with the singing and dancing, put better heart into the reduced population. They managed to rebuild enough of the houses to shelter those who needed it. Atisha insisted that bow practice and stick dancing must be performed every day without fail, and Penthesilea led them with warriorlike enthusiasm. Myrina could feel her muscles growing stronger and tighter than ever before and she rejoiced in the determined progress of her new recruits.

When spring came the Moon Riders were restless to be on the road again despite their fears of war. Myrina wondered how Cassandra would be received by her family, but the princess seemed unconcerned.

When the Moon Riders arrived they were greeted, not just by the Mazagardi and the tribes, but by a finely dressed group of Trojan nobles, headed by Priam himself, Hecuba at his elbow. They welcomed Cassandra with honor and also with apology.

The princess went contentedly back to Troy with her

family, exchanging her mare for a gilded litter. Myrina noticed that neither Paris nor Helen was part of the welcoming group, and sadly Chryseis had returned to the temple of Apollo on the island of Tenedos.

The rest of the Moon Riders arrived at the Place of Flowing Waters to find that trade was a little slack. Some of the herders had sold their best horses to Mycenaean dealers, who were making the best of a bad situation and selling good strong horses to Achaean warriors for high prices.

Myrina was delighted to see the growth in strength of her little niece. Yildiz was full of lively babble, staggering about enthusiastically, wanting to touch and taste everything in sight. Tomi was still unmarried but Myrina sensed a new restlessness in him. Late one evening as they sat together by the fire, she dared to ask him about it.

"What is it, Tomi?" she whispered. "Do you love another? Is that what troubles you?"

He shook his head fiercely. "How can you think that?" he asked, his voice full of pain. "I miss you more with every moon that passes and I try to be patient, but it is very hard. I want to be with you all the time but you go bravely riding away while I sit by our campfire like a tame goat doing nothing."

"That's not true," she insisted. "You go away trading

our horses. The tribe depends on your success and my father values your trading skills; he tells me so."

But still Tomi sighed. "I want to ride south and let these Achaean raiders feel the sting of our bows," he growled. "I want to be a warrior."

Myrina touched his arm, feeling the tight muscles beneath his skin. "Be patient, love," she whispered. "Atisha swears there will be time enough to fight them, but the time is not yet here."

CHAPTER TWENTY

An Evil Dream

THE SPRING CELEBRATIONS passed all too quickly and when the day for leaving came, Cassandra reappeared, escorted by both of her parents. "My daughter wishes to travel with you again," Priam told Atisha. "If you are willing, so am I! These are troubled times and she may be as safe with you as she is here with us."

Both Priam and Hecuba looked older and grayer. This favored son who'd returned from exile wasn't making life easy, however much they doted on him.

Atisha agreed to let Cassandra ride with them again. "Your daughter will know if you need her," she told them.

"How did Paris treat you?" Myrina asked as they rode away from Troy.

Cassandra shrugged her shoulders. "He and I will never be good friends," she said, "but one thing I do begin to understand. Helen has a magical charm about her; she swore to me that they were sorry for the deception. Paris is desperate to stay with her and I begin to see why. Father will do anything to keep Paris at his side. Hector just shakes his head and prepares for war."

"So you managed to be civil to each other?"

Cassandra nodded. "At least my brother has learned something about war from his support of the great Hittite empire to the east of Troy. Paris fought for the Hittites against Egypt and discovered from them how to make weapons of iron and how best to defend a city. He has set them building new towers to strengthen the walls of Troy."

Myrina saw practical sense in that. "And those walls are strong already."

The Moon Riders were welcomed in Abdera with renewed warmth, but they soon became aware of the many loads of bronze and iron, carried both by cart and sea, heading for the Achaean mainland. The Ciconi tribe and the Sapei were angry that Troy was threatened with attack and swore that they would rush to Priam's aid, should a battle fleet be sighted. But it was clear from the heavy trafficking through the mountainous routes and the sea that some of the southern tribes were profiting from the war-gathering of their Achaean neighbors.

During the night that they were due to travel to the north Myrina was woken by low whimpering sounds and muffled cries. "No, no—please no."

She felt about in the darkness. Cassandra was having one of her bad dreams. "Waken, Princess," she called, gently shaking her arm. "Waken. You are safe here in Thrace with the Moon Riders."

"Dream. Terrible dream." Cassandra roused herself, but Myrina could feel her still trembling.

"Tell me," she said.

"Too bad to tell," Cassandra murmured. "Too bad."

"Tell me," Myrina insisted. "If you tell then its power will wane."

At last the princess managed to whisper the words that brought such dread to her. "Iphigenia," she said. "Iphigenia looking up and a knife—a great glittering, gilded knife—coming down toward her throat."

Myrina shuddered at the picture these words brought to her mind, wishing she hadn't been so insistent that Cassandra speak out. Perhaps some fears were best unspoken. She sat there for a moment deep in thought, quietly stroking Cassandra's arm, though the trembling wouldn't cease.

"Stay here!" Myrina whispered. "I won't be a moment."

She crawled out through the tent flaps, returning quickly with a pine torch that she'd lit from the turf-banked fire they always left smouldering at night.

"Now," she ordered. "I will hold the light; you look in your mirror. You will see that Iphigenia is safe and this just an evil dream."

Cassandra slowly reached for her belt with shaking hands and drew the dark obsidian mirror from its sheath. For a moment she hesitated, as though afraid of what she might see, but then she took a deep breath and looked.

"What can you see?" Myrina asked.

"I see her in bed," Cassandra began.

"Is she safe?"

Cassandra shrugged. "She sleeps and all about her chamber hang fine new clothes, rich jewels." She suddenly gasped. "They are wedding clothes."

"But—Iphigenia; she's just a little girl."

"She's thirteen." Cassandra spoke sharply. "Quite old enough for an Achaean king like Agamemnon, if he wants to make some powerful alliance." She turned back to look in the mirror again and the expression on her face changed from anxiety to horror.

"What have you seen now?" Myrina demanded.

"Ants. Jeweled ants all over her clothes, around the hems, at the sleeves, and even around the neck—they are ants!"

"What can that mean?" Myrina was puzzled.

"Don't you see? It's Achilles! His Myrmidon warriors—their symbol is the ant."

"No," Myrina cried, understanding at last. "That brute! We have seen what he can do. You can't mean that they are going to marry her to him!"

Cassandra was calmer now, her eyes closed in concentration, her face very white in the yellow torchlight. "They are, and yet I feel somehow that they are not." Suddenly she shuddered and the trembling returned; she could hardly speak through gritted teeth. "There is something even . . . worse!"

"Worse than marriage to Achilles?"

Myrina remembered that both Atisha and Hati had sworn that it was best to take notice of Cassandra's troublesome gift. "Come." She put her arm around her friend. "You and I shall wake Atisha and tell her what you've seen."

Atisha made no complaint when they came whispering at her tent flaps.

"We're sorry to wake you, Old Woman," Myrina started.

"I wasn't sleeping," Atisha told them. "Sleep comes rarely to me these days. The aged have little need of it."

She listened carefully to all that they told her. "And is she important to you—this little princess of Mycenae?"

Cassandra nodded. "She's younger than me and looked to me as though I were an older sister. She's lived

143

in luxury and innocence, cocooned in the great palace at Mycenae, but I promised her that I would always be her friend."

Atisha pulled a grim face. "A child such as that to be married off to Achilles!"

"We must do something!" Myrina insisted.

Cassandra shook her head. "The mirror tells me one thing, but deep here in my belly I feel that there is something even worse."

Atisha took her hand. "If you feel that, my child, then I believe it. There is something worse!"

"But what do we do now?" Myrina brought them back to practicalities. "Could we beg or borrow a ship and persuade some of our fishermen friends to take us south toward Mycenae?"

Atisha shook her head, frowning in deepest thought. "The weather is treacherous and the sailing month has not yet arrived. It is far to go and I fear that it would end in capture."

They sat together in silence for a few moments then Atisha spoke again. "It would be possible to ride south through Thrace."

"Yes!" Myrina agreed. "Many Thracians would join a war party. There's much anger that Troy is threatened."

Atisha smiled at Myrina's enthusiasm but she shook

her head. "I'm not suggesting that we make war on Agamemnon."

Myrina subsided, discouraged.

"Don't look so disappointed, young Snaky. You are thinking well. A small determined task force may have a much better chance of success." She wagged a gnarled finger at the girls. "The best riders, the best archers; Centaurea, who knows the land to the south of Thrace; Penthesilea, whose courage cannot be beaten. A small group, who may pass secretly through the Achaean lands and quietly watch over this little princess so that no suspicion may be roused."

Myrina let her breath out slowly. "Yes," she agreed. "This plan makes sense. It is just that I'd thought that— perhaps I might . . ."

Atisha laughed. "You shall go, my little Snaky, you and Cassandra both. You have an important part to play; this poor princess must have someone that she can trust and she will trust you both."

"Yes!" Myrina was triumphant. "We must both go!"

Cassandra looked at them, her eyes full of doubt. Such an undertaking seemed wild beyond belief to her, but the terrible memory of her dream flooded back and she began to shiver again.

"Have faith in yourself, Princess," Atisha told her. "We have faith in you!"

"Yes," Cassandra agreed at last. "If anyone must go, I must go. This is what true friendship means; it is just that I am fearful. I cannot be brave like Penthesilea."

"You have courage of a different kind." Atisha patted her cheek.

CHAPTER TWENTY-ONE

To Steal a Bride

P ENTHESILEA AND CENTAUREA agreed immediately to the suggested plan. "Will you come?" Penthesilea asked the Old Woman.

"No." Atisha shook her head. "I am too old for such a race. I give you no orders; you spy out the land and make your own decisions. All I say to you is this: listen to Cassandra. If she is troubled, take good notice of her."

"I will." Penthesilea was clearly delighted to be put in charge.

Cassandra thanked her graciously for her willingness. "And you do not even know Iphigenia," she said.

"Never mind Iphigenia; this is my chance to punish that foul pirate Achilles." Penthesilea smiled fiercely. "If we can steal away his poor little bride that will be a fine reward for me. When do we go?"

"Go tonight," Atisha told them. "It will be safest to ride at night, and the moon waxes more and more powerful for the next half of the month."

"Then let us set about it!" Penthesilea was impatient to be off.

They tried to rest during the following day and took their leave at sunset. All the Moon Riders gathered to dance and sing as they went; a song of ancient magic, begging Mother Maa to bring them safely back to their friends.

As the tiny group rode fast away, Myrina struggled with some misgivings. Was this all madness? And might she be responsible for it all? Should she have told Cassandra to turn over and go to sleep, forgetting her dream? Her young recruits had looked lost when she said good-bye, but Atisha had promised to watch over them.

Once the horses had got into their stride and clouds cleared so that the moon gave silvery light, her spirits rose. What an adventure she would have to tell Gul and Hati about! She turned to Cassandra and saw that the princess urged her horse on with grim determination; this would be a much more difficult journey for the Trojan princess than for herself.

They rode all through the night and as dawn came they slowed up by a river, looking for a shallow ford.

"This is the River Strymon," Centaurea told them. "Once across the other side, we will be in the land of the Macedonians."

They found a safe ford, and having crossed it, stopped to eat the bread and mare's milk cheese that they'd been given. Centaurea thought they should travel on through daylight as the Macedonians were friendly to the Moon Riders.

"We will have to go slowly later on, once we reach Thessaly and come close to the Achaean lands."

Atisha had insisted that they all wear breast straps and leather protective body armor. Their bows were strung and ready, fastened to their full quivers, daggers at their belts. They rode on across the gentle slopes of a grassy plain, traveling openly all through the morning, but when the sun rose high in the sky, they stopped at the edge of a wooded stream. "We'll rest," Penthesilea ordered, and Myrina, drowsy at last with the need to sleep, was relieved.

Penthesilea told them to sleep while she stood guard.

"Does she never weaken?" Myrina muttered.

As the sun went down, Myrina woke and found that Centaurea was now on guard. "We must eat again and be on our way," the older girl told her. "Can you wake Penthesilea and the princess?"

They traveled on through the night, crossed the River Axus and on toward the mountainous southern parts of Macedonia. The journey turned into a blur of riding, sleeping at the height of the noonday sun, hidden among trees and undergrowth, snatching bits of food. On the fourth day they'd eaten all that they'd brought and were growing hungry, so they stopped to ask if they could buy food from a group of shepherds roasting meat in front of a hillside hut.

The men stared suspiciously at the four sunburnt women riding through the lonely hills with weapons at their belts and strapped to their backs. Then Penthesilea brought out from her pouch the small silver medallion that Atisha had entrusted to her once again, with the crescent moon on one side and the goddess on the other.

"Ah." They suddenly seemed to understand and bowed respectfully. "Magic women, Amazons," they said. "Amazon women eat much meat!"

None of the women disagreed with that, for the smell of roast mutton and herbs was delicious. The shepherds were soon hacking great slices of mutton from the sheep that they were roasting, only begging the blessings of the Mother on their flocks in return. The women went on with full bellies; their bags stuffed full of cooling meat, barley bread, and rough red wine.

On the seventh day they skirted a huge mountain, its head lost in the clouds. "Mount Olympus," Centaurea told them.

"Ah." Myrina looked up with respect. "Olympus—home

of the Achaean gods. I can see why they might think such a thing."

Centaurea agreed. "They say that Zeus the God King lives up there, but we Thracians swear it's the home of Mountain Mother." Then for the first time in their journey she looked hesitant. "Tomorrow we begin to pass through Thessaly. It's the farthest that I've ever been and I don't know which direction we should take."

Penthesilea was silent for once and Myrina had a brief moment of doubt, but that quickly passed for Cassandra turned her head toward the southeast, almost as though she'd caught a scent on the wind. "That is the way," she pointed. "Iphigenia travels in a litter beside her mother Clytemnestra, and a young babe lies between them. They are followed by baggage trains and wagons heavy with goods and gold."

Penthesilea frowned. "It is hard to trust to dreams and visions," she said. "I'd rather look for the remains of a fire or horses' dung, but if you say that is the way, Princess, then that is the way we'll go."

They traveled on through Thessaly, taking good care now to hide their weapons beneath their cloaks, cantering through the morning, without any look of urgency. If any asked, they said that they were horse traders. Each night they rode as fast as they could in the growing moonlight. As they passed through the south of Thessaly and into the land of Phocis, it became clear that they were not alone in the direction that they took. Real horse dealers, wagons of iron and bronze weaponry, cartloads of wine and smoked fish took the same road. The name of one place was on everyone's lips. "Aulis. The warriors gather at Aulis."

"They'll buy weapons and horses."

"Wine and olives!"

"Cloaks and leather goods!"

Though they found it unnerving at first, Penthesilea soon realized that traveling within the growing crowd gave them protection. "Who could pick out four women spies among this lot?" she whispered. "Is it to Aulis that we must go, do you think?"

Cassandra nodded. "Yes. My mirror tells me that Iphigenia is with her father now, but though she greets him gladly, he looks away from her with fear and—and shame."

"And so he should." Myrina was adamant. "Marrying a child like Iphigenia to a brute of a warrior."

Centaurea frowned a little. "Of course I agree with you, Snaky Girl, but in his world such a marriage would be all he could hope for. By marrying Iphigenia to Achilles, Agamemnon will secure the loyalty of his most renowned warlord and provide his daughter with wealth and honor at the same time. You'd expect him to be glad and not ashamed."

Penthesilea quickly saw what she meant. "Yes," she agreed, narrowing her eyes. "If Cassandra is right and he feels shame then there must be some other reason for that shame. Marrying her off to Achilles should bring him joy."

They all turned to Cassandra, the unspoken question in their faces. She shook her head, looking miserable. "I cannot see the horror that lies beneath it all."

"Don't distress yourself, Princess," Centaurea soothed. "Your mirror and your visions have brought us safely to where the father and the daughter camp. I'm sure that you will know it all when the time is right."

Myrina had given small notice to Centaurea in her two years with the Moon Riders, thinking her strong and daring but thoughtless. Now she saw another side to her, a side that was perceptive and calming, proving very helpful in this nerve-racking adventure. Atisha had chosen well.

Cassandra suddenly asked with urgency, "How many nights to the full of the moon?"

Centaurea looked surprised, but she counted under her breath and held up three fingers.

Cassandra nodded. "The full of the moon. That will be the moment of greatest danger: that's when we must act."

CHAPTER TWENTY-TWO

Aulis

THE FOLLOWING MORNING they arrived at the town of Aulis, where they found the great Achaean fleet of ships anchored three and four rows deep all along the bay. The sight of it took their breath away as they stopped for a moment on the hillside above the town. The tall masts rose in countless numbers, spreading as far as the eye could see.

They fell silent, understanding how deep a shock this must be for Cassandra. Every one of these warships was bent on threatening her home city of Troy. Myrina leaned from the saddle and took her hand.

Cassandra stared. "I knew there would be many," she said. "But I didn't know it could look like this. It seems all the world has gathered against Troy."

"Not *all* the world," Penthesilea insisted. "Come, we must find Iphigenia."

It wasn't difficult. The princess was staying with her

mother in the fine palace that belonged to the Lord of Aulis. Penthesilea went off boldly to speak to a woman who sold olives outside the palace gates but returned to them, her face ashen white.

"What is it?" Centaurea asked.

They were all concerned at the way she looked. Nothing frightened Penthesilea, but for once she was clearly shaken. "We must find somewhere to talk in secret," she told them. "I cannot speak the words out loud here in this bustling place."

So in silence they hurried back the way they'd come and out of the city. They found a quiet spot beside a stream and only then did Penthesilea manage to tell them what she'd learned.

"Sit down close together," she insisted. "Take the princess by the hand and pour her some of the shepherds' wine."

They followed her instructions fearfully. Myrina had a terrible sense of foreboding growing deep inside her stomach.

Penthesilea began, choosing her words carefully. "Iphigenia is here in the palace," she told them. "I pretended to the olive woman that we wished to sell one of our best horses to pull the wedding cart. Well, she looked at me as though I must be mad or stupid. 'You don't still believe that, do you?' she said. 'I thought everyone in

Aulis knew by now. The old priest of Chalcis has had a message from Artemis: he swears the wind will not change direction and allow the ships to sail unless a sacrifice is made.'"

Myrina and Centaurea were still puzzled. It wasn't unusual to sacrifice a lamb or a deer or a goat when a fleet was setting off, but Cassandra began to shudder.

"Look to the princess," Penthesilea cried. "Give her a sip of wine."

"No." Cassandra pushed the cup away. "I do not need wine. I have known this horror deep in my heart ever since that dream. I have known this foulness but I couldn't look it in the face."

"What horror?" Myrina took her friend's hand and then she remembered the terrible words that Cassandra had used to describe her dream. "I saw a knife held above Iphigenia's throat."

The growing sense of sickness inside Myrina's stomach threatened to make her vomit. She clapped her hand over her mouth. "This is it!" she cried. "This is why the king looks away from his daughter with shame. They are going to sacrifice Iphigenia!"

Penthesilea nodded, her face gray and grim. They all sat there for a moment clinging together as they began to understand. The wedding plan had only been a ruse to get the princess to Aulis.

Then Penthesilea spoke again with determination. "But we are here to stop this foul thing and we will. How, I don't know, but we have come here to carry Iphigenia away and now we cannot allow ourselves to fail."

"We must think." Centaurea was trying to be calm and practical. "We must find out where and when this sacrifice takes place. We must find out every last scrap of information. Who will be there? Does the princess know? Does her mother know?"

Cassandra shook her head. "I think Iphigenia lives in innocence. I cannot believe her mother knows, for she does love her child though she treats her like a doll."

"We must set out and spend the afternoon listening," Centaurea insisted. "Though we need one another at this moment, we will find out much more if we split up and wander about separately. We'll meet here again, at sundown."

"Will you be all right alone?" Myrina was concerned about Cassandra.

But the princess nodded, swallowing hard. "I feel better now," she said. "The wickedness is shared; it's not mine to bear alone. I can be strong for Iphigenia and I will be."

Penthesilea bent and rubbed Cassandra's shoulders. "Well done," she cried. "We are Moon Riders, we are Amazons; we will find a way through this!"

"I know when the sacrifice is planned," Cassandra told them. "It is on the evening of the full moon; tomorrow at sundown."

They should have known. Cassandra had continually told them that the full moon was the moment of greatest danger.

They met again that evening by the little stream to share the knowledge that they'd gained. It hadn't been too difficult, for the whole of Aulis was buzzing with the news and, though some were sorry for the young princess, many had little love for Agamemnon and his family.

"This priest Chalcis is a wicked man." Centaurea spat on the ground. "It seems that the fleet has been restless here for months and unable to sail for Troy against the cold wind that blows down from the north. He has told the generals that the wind will change only if this sacrifice is made."

"But the wind always blows from the north at this time of year," Myrina said. "It blows down from the Black Sea, right through the Hellespont until the full of the moon and the Month of Flowers, then it dies away and a warm steady wind begins to blow from the south."

"We know that, and the priest knows that," Centaurea said. "And I swear Agamemnon must know that the winds will change soon, whatever Artemis wishes."

"Achilles must know that, too," Penthesilea insisted. "He's done enough sailing; I hear he lives in splendor at the palace, along with the rest."

"Is he a party to the plan?" Myrina asked.

Penthesilea shook her head. "He is in a great rage, having just discovered it. Though I hate the man bitterly, it seems this sacrifice is even too horrible for him to stomach."

"Then why in the name of the Mother and Artemis are they doing it?" Myrina was almost despairing.

"It's their generals," Centaurea insisted. "And that priest. Many are men who've never been away from their homes before. They understand little of winds and sailing and they are desperate to get to Troy and fight if they must so that they may return home again as quickly as they can. They are full of ignorance and fear."

"Yes," Penthesilea agreed. "There is real danger of rebellion if this evil priest is disobeyed. The great mass of warriors are with him and demand the sacrifice."

Cassandra suddenly lurched forward, her lips twisted as though in pain. Myrina grabbed her and held her tight. "What is it?"

"She knows," Cassandra whispered. "Iphigenia knows what they plan; her mind has gone dark with fear."

They looked at one another for a moment, frozen as ice, trying to understand what the young princess must be feeling. It was too much—too bitter, too terrible to bear.

Then Penthesilea shook herself back into being practical again. "We need to find out where this is to take place."

"I know that," Cassandra told them. "An altar is being prepared in front of the temple in the grove of Artemis, on the hill above the palace."

"Well done." Penthesilea would have no sorrow, only action. "Now we have all the information that we need and I know what we will do."

They spent a restless night, but on the following afternoon they stood together in a tiny circle, heads bent in prayer to Maa; beside them tethered and steadily cropping the grass was a small and perfect white deer. "If all moon goddesses are one," Penthesilea whispered, "may the Lady Artemis and our own Moon Mother join together and help us this night!"

Then slowly, very slowly they raised their arms to the sky, dancing to the right and then to the left, tiny shimmering movements flowing from their hands and feet. They performed the most magical dance known to them, an ancient dance of power. Somewhere far away to the north an Old Woman sat beside her camp watching them in her mirror, while the whole great company of Moon Riders performed the same sacred dance, sending to Aulis all the magical strength they possessed.

CHAPTER TWENTY-THREE

The Full of the Moon

A S SOON AS the sun began to slip toward the
horizon, the four women ceased their dancing.
Penthesilea took hold of the young deer firmly.
"Forgive me, little one," she murmured. Then she
brought the hard muscular heel of her hand down sharply
on the back of its neck, dealing instant death.

The others helped her to strap the carcass, still warm,
onto her belly. They covered it carefully with her cloak,
so that Penthesilea bore the unmistakable shape of a
pregnant woman near to her time.

They set off, leading their horses toward the public
entrance to the place of sacrifice. Many people walked
beside them, young and old, thronging the streets and
heading up toward the hill to see the sacrifice performed.
Some of their faces were blank, but some were lined with
sorrow; a few of them wept.

They passed by the palace and found a small group of

bystanders gathered about the walls, pointing and distracted. They heard loud bangs and thumps coming from one of the high windows, and then the sound of splintering wood. The guards who stood by the gates ran back inside, leaving their posts unattended.

"It's Clytemnestra," the whisper spread from person to person.

Myrina stopped by the gates, hesitating. "No." Penthesilea shook her head. "We must ignore it. Iphigenia must be our only concern if we are to succeed."

Myrina nodded; Penthesilea was right. They turned away and moved on toward the temple of Artemis.

Centaurea stopped at the gates. She carefully gathered all the horses together, then wishing the other three well she turned away, leading the mares to a patch of fresh grass at the bottom of the sacred grove.

Penthesilea led the way, followed by Myrina and Cassandra, who clung together, hand in hand. With steady determination, Penthesilea pushed to the front, the other two following in her wake.

Whispers flew around the crowd. "Does the princess come willingly?"

"Clytemnestra is locked up in her room, guards at her door. You can hear her screams of rage from outside the palace."

"Where's Agamemnon?"

"He will not come, but sends his brother in his place, while he calls for a pitcher of the strongest wine."

"His wife swears that she will bring the foulest revenge. Her curses are enough to frighten the strongest warrior."

A young woman with a baby in her arms shuddered. "I'm glad it's not my child who must die."

Penthesilea could not contain herself. "Many a mother's child shall die," she told the woman fiercely, "before these kings are done with their war on Troy."

There was silence all about them for a moment and Myrina caught her breath. Those about them looked with suspicion on the two strange women with decorated cheeks. But then the woman who'd been speaking looked with pity on Penthesilea's swollen stomach. "What you say is true," she answered.

"Aye . . . true." Agreement came from all around.

At last they stood before the stone altar and Cassandra saw with a gasp that the glittering gold knife of her dream lay upon it. Flames rose from a gilded fire-basin. Behind the altar stood the sacred grove with the statue of the goddess, forbidden to all but the high priest and priestess.

"It is death to anyone who goes in there," Myrina whispered.

"It is death to anyone who does what we plan," Penthesilea answered. Then she added with bitter humor, "If they are caught!"

Myrina almost smiled, though her stomach churned fiercely.

The crowd began to chant, swaying from side to side.

"Where is he?" Penthesilea hissed. "Where is this bloody man that calls himself a priest?"

Three notes were heard on a flute followed by the light tinkling of cymbals, then from down the steps of the temple a procession slowly came into view. "There he is." Myrina nodded. "Ah—how can they?"

Ten young girls led the procession. They were dressed in long tunics dyed in a rainbow of colors, the fine material swirling as they danced. Two clicked cymbals while the others began strewing flowers onto the ground. If the purpose of it all had not been so terrible, it would have been beautiful.

Then at last they saw Iphigenia, a small figure dressed in a long white tunic that fell to the ground; about her neck was a single silver crescent moon. Her face was bloodless and blank; almost, Myrina thought, as though she were already dead. She walked forward as though in a dream, stumbling a little, but then somehow moving on.

Staying calm for that moment was the hardest thing that Myrina had ever done; Penthesilea, too, had great difficulty holding back. For two pins she'd have leaped up, dagger at the ready, and killed the priest where he stood. Cassandra went very still and white, never taking her eyes from Iphigenia's face.

"You must make her see you," Penthesilea whispered.

It seemed that Iphigenia saw nobody: not the dancing girls or the crowd. The priest arrived at the altar and picked up the knife, turning to urge his victim forward. At that moment Cassandra let her veil slip from her face. It slid down her back and onto the floor; her blue and green eyes burning into the face of Iphigenia, slowly she touched her hand to her brow, in the priestess's salute.

At last Iphigenia seemed to look at her friend, though no sign of recognition crossed her face.

"I think she has seen you," Penthesilea whispered. Her hands moved inside her cloak to loosen the dead deer. "Whether she has understood I cannot tell. We must act, whether she understands or not. Are you ready, Myrina?"

"Yes."

Myrina clutched in her hand the open bag of incense that Atisha had given them. Usually Atisha would use but one grain to give a strong scented smoke, but this time, as the priest Chalcis carelessly threw a small handful of incense grains into the fire-bowl, Myrina leaned forward and tipped the whole of Atisha's bag into the flames. There was just one short moment of surprise when the few people who'd seen the gesture stared at her, puzzled and suspicious, but then immediately thick white clouds of powerful smoke billowed out of the dish.

The women wasted no time, leaping forward at once. Cassandra and Myrina snatched Iphigenia, one on each side, while Penthesilea flung down upon the altar the body of the slaughtered deer. Then they dashed straight ahead, into the forbidden grove, running past the statue and fast down the hill through the sacred olive trees, to where Centaurea was waiting at the bottom with the horses.

Behind them smoke billowed thick as a cloud, making eyes run and throats gasp and cough. The Moon Riders didn't stop to see it.

Penthesilea was the first to leap onto her horse. "Give her to me," she cried.

They had half-dragged, half-carried Iphigenia, like a limp doll between them. Now they hauled her up into Penthesilea's arms and without waiting for them to mount their steeds and follow, Fleetwind was off, heading north, out of the city and out of that land.

Myrina and Cassandra could hear rising cries of anger and frustration behind them as the tightly packed crowd pushed and shoved in panic.

"Don't stop!" Centaurea shouted.

Cassandra sprang onto Arian's back.

Myrina swung herself up onto Isatis. Within moments

they were cantering after Penthesilea, urging their horses to a gallop as they reached the outskirts of Aulis. "If ever you ran like the wind, the time is now, my dear Isatis," Myrina whispered. And the blue-black mare did not let her down.

Back at their small camp by the stream, Penthesilea stopped for a moment so that the others could catch up with her. Cassandra was distraught when she saw the glazed look and still limp body of Iphigenia.

"She's drugged," Penthesilea told them. "Don't fear for her. She cannot seem to hear or speak, but she lives and breathes. Force a drop of water between her lips, then we must ride again."

Centaurea brought fresh water and they managed to get a few drops down Iphigenia's throat, but then they remounted and rode north without stopping all through the night.

CHAPTER TWENTY-FOUR

A New Recruit

S DAWN CAME, they began skirting the lower slopes of Mount Parnassus. Penthesilea insisted that they must stop and eat and drink at a clear spring.

"Come here, Cassandra," she called. "Here's a sight will cheer your heart." She swung down from her horse, Iphigenia still in her arms, but they could see at once that a faint rose blush had touched the young girl's cheeks.

Myrina took the rug from her horse's back and spread it on some soft grass. "Lay her down here," she said.

They bent over her, full of concern, and Iphigenia moved her lips as though they were numb and stiff. "Moon-lady," she murmured. "Moon-lady!"

Penthesilea chuckled. "She seems to think that I am Artemis and I have spirited her away."

Then suddenly Iphigenia looked up at Cassandra, her eyes full of recognition. She lurched forward, stiffly holding out her arms. Cassandra scooped her up and they stood there hugging each other tightly, while the other three watched, huge smiles on their faces and tears in their eyes.

"Dear little friend!" Cassandra murmured, gently rocking Iphigenia.

"I knew that you were there with me," Iphigenia whispered.

"Did you see me there in front of the temple?"

Iphigenia spoke solemnly. "You were there with me, long before that," she said. "I was never really alone, just as you promised."

"Now we must eat." Penthesilea insisted that they be practical. "We've bread, olives, and cheese from Aulis market stalls. We must all eat whether we feel like it or not, then quickly ride on and not stop for anything else."

Iphigenia clung to Cassandra and wouldn't leave her side but she obediently ate what they gave her and smiled at Myrina. "You are the Snaky Horse-girl." Her voice was croaky. She was still shivering from shock, but they were encouraged that she recognized Myrina, too.

"Did somebody give you something to drink?" Centaurea asked.

Iphigenia looked vague for a moment, then she spoke. "Mother," she said. "My mother gave me strong wine to drink."

Centaurea nodded. "Poor woman," she whispered.

"What else could she do?"

When they got up to remount, Cassandra led Iphigenia to ride on Fleetwind again. "Penthesilea is the best horsewoman of us all," she told her. "We'll all be able to move faster if you ride with her."

Penthesilea hauled the girl up in front of her. "Moonlady," Iphigenia murmured.

"Ha!" Penthesilea laughed.

They traveled on for four days, stopping only for the briefest rests. At times the horses carried them half-asleep on their backs. The beasts seemed to sense the importance of constantly moving on, and at last they began to travel more slowly again, with Centaurea happy to be back in her homeland of Thrace.

"We must make camp and rest for a few days," Penthesilea told them as they neared the familiar town of Abdera. "Our horses have carried us like magical steeds, but we must not push them further. Besides we've no food left and I think we are safe here."

They all agreed, glad to be among the friendly tribes again. They were welcomed and feasted, but decided that it was wise to keep Iphigenia's identity secret for the time being.

"This is my niece, Genia," Penthesilea announced. "We take her north to join the Moon Riders; she is our new recruit."

"I *would* like to join the Moon Riders," Iphigenia told them.

Penthesilea held her as she spoke, whispering gently, "You know that you cannot go back?"

Iphigenia nodded.

"I know something of what that feels like, for I left my family when I was your age to travel with the Moon Riders and I have never been able to go back to them."

Iphigenia understood. "I'd rather be here with you and Cassandra and the Snake Lady," she told them firmly. "It is just that—I wish my mother knew I am safe."

The weather was warm while they camped at Abdera. Iphigenia slept peacefully each night, snuggled up to Cassandra. Myrina was relieved to see that both the troubled princesses seemed to have found peace at last.

A few days of rest and good food made them all feel stronger, and on the third day some Thracian horse traders passed through the town telling everyone of the miracle that had taken place at Aulis.

The marketplace at Abdera was alive with gossip. "They say that Artemis herself appeared and snatched the little princess up into her arms! She flew away with her, high into the sky."

"I should think so, too," was the general response.

"Damned shame—the very idea of it—sacrificing a young girl like that!"

"The goddess left a white deer in the princess's place and the priest sacrificed that instead—now the wind has changed."

"Doesn't the wind always change at this time of year?"

The Moon Riders listened to it all with satisfaction. "We've gotten away with it." Myrina laughed.

"Yes. But we mustn't let our guard drop," Penthesilea insisted.

The following morning brought sadness again when Cassandra told them that she must leave them and return to Troy.

"Have you had another dream? Have you seen something in your mirror?" Myrina asked.

"No." Cassandra was very firm and clear about it. "This is no dream or vision; it is simply that I think of my family and I think of the city that I love. All those ships, that bronze weaponry, all those warriors, rank on rank of them; they carry their war to my city and I must be there."

"There's nothing that you can do to help." Penthesilea didn't like the idea at all and Myrina even less.

"Why should you go home to a family who've never believed a word you said, or ever given you much of their love?"

But Cassandra wouldn't give way. "I must be there with them," she said.

"Can I come with you to your city?" Iphigenia begged. The thought of being parted so soon from her dear friend was terrible to her.

Cassandra took her hand. "You wouldn't be safe there and I would worry about you all the time. You must travel on to the Moon Riders' camp. Atisha, their chief, will take good care of you. I shall be happy knowing that you are safe with them. Please try to understand. You and I will never be parted in our hearts." Cassandra touched Iphigenia's face.

"Yes," Iphigenia agreed. "As before. I will not be alone."

Tears sprang to Myrina's eyes as Iphigenia took the pearly crescent moon from about her neck and slipped it over Cassandra's head. It seemed this pampered child had grown up and lived a whole lifetime of experience in just one phase of the moon.

Then Cassandra was fumbling at her belt with shaking fingers and suddenly Myrina knew what she would do. The Princess of Troy held out her precious obsidian mirror wrapped in its leather pouch.

Iphigenia took the gift, a little puzzled as to what it was.

"This is more than the dark shining stone that you will find inside," Cassandra told her. "Its magic will give you power if you learn to use it well."

Iphigenia took out the gleaming, black mirror and smiled. "It is beautiful," she whispered. "What will I do with it?"

"I will teach you how to use it," said Myrina.

When they saw that Cassandra was determined to return to Troy, they set their minds to making plans. They would travel on through Thrace together, cross the Hellespont and see the princess safe inside the city walls. Then they would head north toward Elikmaa, where they'd wait for Atisha and the other Moon Riders.

CHAPTER TWENTY-FIVE

The Towers of Troy

W HEN THE SMALL band of women reached the land they called the Thracian Chersonese, they found warriors camping by the riverside, their spears and weapons visible as they approached. Penthesilea slowed them all up, wondering whether to take a more westerly route. Though she'd willingly challenge any warrior, the safety of her two royal charges was uppermost in her mind.

She need not have worried for Myrina stared ahead at the tents, joy rising in her.

"Mazagardi!" she cried. "Mazagardi tents and horses!"

"Your tribe?" Penthesilea laughed with relief.

"But what are they doing here?" Myrina puzzled. "They should be by the Black Sea at this time of year."

As they moved forward, a single warrior rode out to meet them. Myrina urged Isatis ahead. "Tomi, it's Tomi!" she cried.

The others followed her, smiling, as the two perfectly trained mounts slowed down, side by side, so that Myrina and Tomi could lean across to kiss each other, still on horseback.

"Why are you here?" Myrina gasped.

"Looking for you," he told her, his face flushed pink with pleasure. "Atisha sent a message to Hati, telling us what you'd set out to do. I begged Aben to let me take an armed gang to see you safe back to the homelands."

"So—you have got your warrior band at last!"

"Yes, I have, thanks to you! And now we will see you safe back to Elikmaa: all the country is alive with the story that the princess is rescued, though they do not say the Moon Riders had anything to do with it."

Myrina smiled at him a little sadly then. "If you wish to escort us, you must come first to Troy."

Penthesilea raised her eyebrows at the idea that she might need an escort but said nothing. They all rode on together down the narrow spit of land toward the Hellespont. Myrina and Tomi were happy to be together, but as the wind changed direction, blowing warm and steady up from the south, for once it made them shiver.

They and their horses crossed the narrow sea in style when one of Priam's ship-captains recognized Cassandra.

"Your father will welcome you, Princess," the man

assured her. "Prince Paris has been adding new towers to Troy, like those on the strong Hittite forts that he's seen. Nobody could breach the walls now, but still your father calls in provisions from near and far. Some say that they expect Menelaus and his brother any day, others laugh at all these preparations and say they'll never come."

"Oh, they will come," Cassandra told him.

They made camp at Abydus on the Trojan shore and spent their last night together watching the fishermen haul in nets full of glinting silver mackerel. When they arrived in sight of Troy, they could see at once that strong new towers had been built to strengthen the sturdy walls.

Myrina grew full of sadness. "Atisha bade me guard you," she told Cassandra. "She told me that you needed a stalwart friend to keep you safe and now here I am, letting you return to a home that is preparing for attack."

Cassandra drew Arian up close to Isatis. "It is through your friendship that I'm strong enough to go home and face the hardships to come. I have a new charge for you." She inclined her head toward Iphigenia, who rode with Penthesilea, now quite at home astride a horse. "Here's another princess who needs your friendship," Cassandra told her. "Will you see her safe into Atisha's care?"

"Of course I will," Myrina promised.

They approached the city from the high plateau, arriving

at the Eastern Gate that Hati had admired so much. Now a strong new curtain wall had been built that curved in front, protecting the wooden doors.

Penthesilea was impressed. "Clever—very clever," she pointed out to Tomi. "Nobody could get a battering ram inside there. These Achaeans will not find Troy easy to sack."

Cassandra rode ahead of her friends. When she got to the gate, a guard from the tower above recognized her and called out in welcome. The stall keepers and horse boys heard his cry and turned to see her approach, then warm cries of welcome surrounded her.

"The priestess returns," they called. "Now we shall have the blessing of Maa as well as Trojan Apollo. We will be safe."

Cassandra dismounted and led Arian back to where the others followed. "This is my last gift to you," she said, holding out the reins to Iphigenia. "I do not need Arian, now that I am back in Troy. She will carry you safely. Can you ride her?"

Iphigenia didn't wait for any change of mind, but slid down from Fleetwind and strode confidently to Arian's side. She went to gently stroke the pale cream nose while Arian whickered friendly approval.

"Well done," Cassandra whispered. "She gives consent. You are her mistress now. Climb onto her back."

Cassandra held her clasped hands low to help Iphigenia mount. With a jump, Iphigenia was up, looking as though she'd been riding all her life. "I will take good care of her," she promised.

"Go now," Cassandra ordered. "Ride fast away! There is no more time to say good-bye."

They took her at her word, reluctantly turning their horses' heads toward the north, as Cassandra disappeared behind the protective wall, and in through the hidden Eastern Gate, to her home in the city of Troy.

Penthesilea led them on over the high ground, but stopped after a while to look back. "What is it?" Myrina asked.

Penthesilea frowned, shading her eyes from the bright sun. "I'm not sure—I thought I saw . . ." Her voice trailed off.

Myrina and Tomi turned to look. From that high place, they could see the Hellespont to the right of them and the southern spit of the Thracian Chersonese in the distance. Straight in front of them stood the high towers of Troy with the deep blue Aegean Sea beyond and the islands of Imbros and Tenedos in the distance.

Then Tomi gasped. Penthesilea had not been mistaken in her concern, for from behind the Isle of Tenedos dark spots appeared, growing bigger and blacker as every moment passed. At last the shape of masts and sails could be seen.

"They are here," Myrina said. "I knew they would come and yet, I hoped . . ."

As they watched, more and more sails appeared until at last the whole of the horizon was dotted with them; an unbroken line stretching as far as the eye could see. The towers of Troy seemed suddenly small.

Iphigenia and Centaurea turned to see what they were looking at. They watched in silence for a moment, then Iphigenia spoke. "I do not want to look at that," she said.

"There's no need for you to look," Centaurea told her. "Come with me and we will lead the way to Elikmaa."

As Centaurea and Iphigenia rode on, Penthesilea seemed to snap back into life again. "We must be on our way," she said.

"What can we do?" Myrina felt a great desire to ride back again to Troy. "I hate to leave Cassandra and her city to face those warships."

"There is much that we can do," Penthesilea insisted. "We get this child to safety, then we set about getting them help."

Tomi seemed to hesitate. "If you wish to return to Troy, I shall go with you," he promised.

Myrina hesitated, thinking hard. "The Thracian tribes would help," she said.

"Oh yes," Penthesilea agreed. "The Thracians and the Mysians. The Lycians and Carians—but they must be roused."

"You are right," Myrina said at last, turning her horse away from Troy. "There is much to do! Come, Isatis!"

They turned and rode north.

Part Two

THE SNAKE LADY

CHAPTER TWENTY-SIX

The Raid

N INE YEARS PASSED after the dark shapes of the Achaean sails were seen heading toward Troy. Many warriors from the Anatolian tribes rode to defend the city, but endless battles followed and the plain of Troy was soaked with the blood of both attackers and defenders. Despite the bitter warfare, the sturdy walls remained unbreached.

Atisha took Iphigenia and Centaurea and retired to the Moon Riders' homelands on the banks of the River Thermodon, saying that she was too old for this new battle and leaving her trusted Penthesilea to lead the young women. The Moon Riders struggled to continue their travels, bringing the rites and dances of Maa to the tribes of Anatolia. They had to fight many skirmishes on their way, for Achaean raiding gangs constantly roamed the hills and islands, seeking to replenish their food stocks and supplies.

It was now early spring in the tenth year since the war began, and the Bitter Months were at last behind them. Myrina looked forward to the great meeting of the tribes at the Place of Flowing Waters. The Moon Riders cantered north from their winter quarters on the island of Lesbos.

The Spring Celebrations would bring a brief time of joy, even though the countryside around Mount Ida was bleak and comfortless since the coming of the Achaeans. The nomadic tribes found desolation everywhere. The fertile plains and valleys that had welcomed them before were burnt and ravaged, so that it was difficult for the Moon Riders to stop and feel secure during the Birthing Months. The horses, goats, and sheep in their herds were always under threat of pillage, and as they traveled through countryside once safe and familiar, they had to keep a constant lookout.

Myrina stared into her mirror, but the Moon Riders had ridden hard all day and she was tired, so that for once her powers of true seeing were slow to come. She propped herself up beneath the gentle shade of a tamarisk tree, Isatis quietly cropping grass beside her. The mirror showed her nothing but herself, a dark-haired young woman with high cheekbones and a challenging expression.

"Where are you, Mother?" She sighed. "I just need to

know that you are safe."

Then she tried again, breathing in deeply and lowering her shoulders gently. She tried to look into the mirror and see beyond her face, the ferny green branches of the tamarisk, and the distant mountainside behind her. Though sharp sunlight lit the water in front of her, dark clouds, gray laden with rain, bowled down from the mountaintops. She relaxed a little more and let her gaze wander into the rolling mist reflected in the polished silver, then at last the vision began to emerge. She caught a quick glimpse of Tomi, riding alone through a mountain pass. Myrina heaved a sigh of relief; he looked well and full of purpose but so alone. Since they had parted at the last spring gathering, she'd been concerned for him. He'd ridden to Thrace to act as a messenger, linking the tribes. A vague mist descended. As it quickly cleared, she saw the peaceful camping place of her own nomadic tribe, the Mazagardi, with the blue waters of the Lake of Storks beside the tents. They would be packing up tomorrow and heading south to the Place of Flowing Waters, where Myrina would soon meet up with them.

Her mother, Gul, was kneading bread dough, with her granddaughters on either side of her. This would be Yildiz' eleventh Spring Celebration; the girl had grown tall and she pounded her ball of dough skillfully, while three-year-old Phoebe poked inquisitive fingers into

Gul's creamy mound until she was given her own small piece to pat.

Myrina smiled, remembering that she had done just the same at that age, but then she frowned, seeing Gul look up sharply from her work. Reseda came running toward them to snatch up Phoebe. Then, distantly, as though through water, she thought she could hear the faint sound of screams and sobbing, and even the light metallic clash of swords. She watched, transfixed with growing horror, the mirror shaking in her hands. Her mother and sister were shouting at each other, but their words weren't clear; then Gul grabbed the fish-gutting knife from her belt and thrust Yildiz inside the home-tent, while Reseda vanished with Phoebe in her arms.

Myrina's hand stole involuntarily to the knife at her own belt as she saw her family and friends rushing to snatch up bows and quivers. Before they had a chance to strap on armor or draw bow to defend themselves, warriors were upon them, wielding swords and spears, blazing torches in their hands, the hated black symbol of ants upon their banners. The peaceful scene had swiftly turned to terrifying chaos and Gul's mouth gaped with fear. Myrina struggled to hold the vision as she saw her mother trying to fight off some huge unseen foe. Suddenly one loud and terrible scream shattered the picture and Myrina lurched forward with a jolt.

Isatis flattened her ears and rolled her eyes as Penthesilea leaped across the fresh grass to wrap her strong arms about Myrina. "What is it?" she demanded.

"That scream! That terrible scream!" Myrina clapped her hands to her ears.

Penthesilea whispered urgently in her ear, "It was you, Myrina. That scream came from you! What is it that you've seen? What was your vision?"

It was hard to find the words. "The bloody-handed Ant Men—the ones we saw in Aulis!"

"Where were they?" Penthesilea bellowed.

"My mother . . . they have killed my mother!"

Penthesilea swore and held her tightly.

"They were killing them . . . all my tribe."

"We will ride at once," said Penthesilea, pulling her to her feet.

The Moon Riders did not spare their horses as they galloped through the night, around the foothills of Mount Ida, past the gathering place, over grasslands and hills toward the Lake of Kus. Penthesilea rode at their head on Fleetwind. Moonlight touched the cheeks and arms of the young priestesses as they traveled, revealing glimpses of their astonishing body pictures. Curling snakes, racing panthers, leaping deer gleamed in the gentle silver light, giving them a touching beauty that was at odds with the furious clenched jaws, gritted teeth, and rippling, rope-hard muscles of both horses and riders.

Dawn was breaking as they came to the Lake of Kus, but they saw the devastation before they reached the shore. Where once there'd been huts, now patches of smoking rubble lay, with corpses piled everywhere. All that remained of the strong Mazagardi tents was shreds of stinking, blackened felt hanging from scorched sticks. A few stray animals with raw flanks wandered distressed among the rubble; the corrals were smashed open and the bulk of the fine Mazagardi herd of horses gone. Most of the sheep and goats, which provided milk and meat through the Bitter Months, had vanished, too.

"So that's the way it is," Penthesilea hissed through gritted teeth. "All this murder, so that Achilles' warriors may have fresh teams for their war chariots and meat to roast on their campfires."

Myrina had ridden Isatis wildly, whipping her on as never before. Now she sat white-faced and silent on her mare's back; only her eyes moved frantically, sweeping to left and right, searching every dead face as Isatis picked her way delicately through the wreckage of the Maza-gardi camp. Beno was there among the slain.

At last Myrina saw what she dreaded most: her mother's body on the ground, knife still gripped in her hand, her father, Aben, lying close by. She climbed down from Isatis's back, her knees giving way as her feet touched the ground. She crouched in silence beside her mother, stretching out a trembling hand to stroke the fading pattern of roses that had been pricked into her cheeks. Gul meant "rose," a true symbol for such a gentle, loving woman as Myrina's mother had been. Myrina sat down between the bodies of her parents, her face still blank, her eyes and throat aching and dry. She reached out to hold her father's cold, stiff hand on one side and her mother's on the other.

She turned to her father. "You told us this would happen," she said, her voice level and emotionless. "You warned us! Priam's greed . . . any excuse would bring the Achaeans swarming over our traveling routes. Not just Trojans—the whole of Anatolia must suffer. . . . Blood across our lands . . . You were right, Father, you were right!"

Myrina did not know how long she sat there, talking on and on until she grew hoarse and the words made no sense. The other Moon Riders searched for survivors, their voices low and growling with anger.

"The poisonous Ant Men!"

"Let me get at them!"

"They'll get my arrow in their back!"

"Death is too good for them!"

"Poison-spewing creatures! Why this?"

"Foul poison everywhere!"

At last, under Penthesilea's grim direction, they began to drag together the remains of the tents and corrals to build a pyre, laying out the charred and blood-soaked bodies close by.

Friends stopped from time to time to touch Myrina's shoulder in sympathy, but she shook them off and remained sitting between her parents' bodies. At last she became aware that someone was standing still and silent in front of her; someone waiting both patiently and fearfully for the moment when she looked up.

Myrina was afraid to lift her head, afraid of what she might see. Then a young girl's voice cut through the confusion, grabbing her attention. "Snake Lady?"

When Myrina did at last look up, it was into the deeply lined face of her grandmother, Hati. The old woman's cheeks were smudged with ash, her mouth a bitter line of sorrow; in her arms a small bruised child, Phoebe, lay still as death. Yildiz stood beside her, clutching tightly to Hati's worn smock, her face red and blistering, part of her hair burnt so that it stuck out in short rough tufts.

"Aunt Rina? Snake Lady?" Yildiz murmured again.

Myrina struggled to her feet, where she rocked for a moment as though she might fall, but then she steadied herself beneath Hati's flinty gaze. "Phoebe? Is she . . . ?"

Hati shook her head. "She sleeps," she said, her voice faint and breathless.

"Reseda?"

Hati spoke sharply. "Gone. They have all gone. I found Phoebe beneath her mother's body, then pulled Yildiz out of the burning tent."

Myrina tried to make her mouth say something, but no sound came out.

"Come." Hati lifted her hand from where it rested on Yildiz' shoulder and held it out.

Myrina went to them like a child, wrapping one arm around Yildiz' small shoulders and the other around her grandmother's stick-thin body and the sleeping Phoebe. "So we are all that's left?" she murmured.

"Yes," said Hati. "We are all that's left."

CHAPTER TWENTY-SEVEN

Dancing for the Dead

P ENTHESILEA CAME UP and stood beside them
quietly. When Myrina at last pulled away from
her grandmother, she saw that the Mazagardi
corpses had been carried to a freshly built funeral pyre—
all except for those of her parents. "Now we must take
them, too," Penthesilea said firmly. "We have found
Reseda. Shall we take your parents to lie beside her?"

"Yes." Myrina nodded. "The children . . . they must say
good-bye to their mother."

Myrina saw at once that Coronilla and Bremusa were
carrying Reseda's body carefully between them, while
Alcibie and Polymusa stood ready to help pick up Gul
and Aben, their eyes dark with angry sympathy. Myrina
remembered that they had lost their own parents in just
such a raid as this.

"Now I know," Myrina said to them. "I know the pain
you felt."

"Yes." Coronilla spoke for them all. "You know the pain now and it is terrible. But it was you who made us live through it and survive. Since that day we have called ourselves Myrina's gang and now we will help you."

"Yes," said Bremusa quietly.

"It is our turn to help," Alcibie repeated.

They bent to the terrible task of gently cleaning the bodies, smoothing the singed clothing and carrying them respectfully to the funeral pyre. Black smoke rose again above the desolate landscape. The Moon Riders made a circle around the flames, dancing and singing the Songs of Leaving that would carry the spirits of those who had died safely into the arms of Earth Mother Maa. None could send Mazagardi souls swiftly to rest better than the young priestesses.

Myrina stood beside her grandmother, still dry-eyed, watching the smoke drifting high into the sky. Phoebe had woken, and though they knew she must be hungry now, she did not cry for food but watched the fire quietly, her eyes wide and solemn. Yildiz stood between her great-grandmother and her aunt, clutching tightly onto them both but making no complaint about her sore and blistered skin.

"We too should dance and sing for them," Myrina murmured.

But Grandmother Hati shook her head. "Never

again," she whispered, her voice low and bitter. "Not I. You go and join them."

Myrina looked at her grandmother, surprised. She could not remember a time when Hati had refused to dance, for their dancing was more, much more, than just enjoyment; it was a sacred duty that expressed their deepest emotions. Not to dance in honor of those who had died was shame indeed.

"But, Grandmother, you have lived all your life to dance for Earth Mother Maa," she said. "We must dance now to honor our closest ones."

"Not worthy." Hati's mouth curled with self-disgust. "I'm not worthy, not anymore. I wasn't there when they needed me; I was away up on the hillside. And when I saw it happening—I . . ." Her voice shook, then came back firmly with a terrible honesty. "I hid. I could have raced to join the fight, but I hid. I never thought that I, Hati, could ever do that. To hide from a fight is the deepest shame and sorrow to me."

There was a moment of silence. Myrina sighed. She understood this extra pain. Never through all her long life had Hati's courage been doubted by any. All the Mazagardi children knew the story of how, as a young woman, she had ridden down through Thrace to Athens and fought the Athenian guards.

"Grandmother," Myrina said at last, quiet but determined, "perhaps there is another way to look at this. Maybe Maa was holding you back, for you have never dodged a fight, not in all your life. If you hadn't saved yourself up on the hillside, you wouldn't have been here to take up Phoebe from her mother's arms and you wouldn't have been here to pull Yildiz from the burning tent. When you saved yourself, you saved these two precious children."

Hati frowned for a moment, but then she reached over to Myrina with gratitude and grabbed tight hold of her hand. "Your words are like raindrops on parched land," she whispered.

"And there will be more raindrops," Myrina insisted, her voice gaining strength and conviction. "Until at last we flood the land and wash away all the filth that has been spread over it."

Hati looked up at Myrina with surprise and grudging respect. "You are right, my Snake Lady. We must not forget that we are Mazagardi and we must dance to honor our dead, whatever shame we bear. There will be time enough to rid these lands of invaders. Come, Yildiz, you and Phoebe will be part of our ceremony."

So all four of them went to join the circle of dancers, as the night sky darkened and the moon came out.

When the fires died down, the Moon Riders brought out what food they had and shared it about. Nobody felt much like it, but Penthesilea gave the order that everyone must eat, for a funeral feast also brought honor to the dead. "And we will need our strength for the days to come," she said.

There were murmurs of agreement and everyone obeyed. Coronilla quickly made some flat, coarse bread from the rough flour they carried with them and produced a small but sustaining meal, with goat's cheese and olives. All the Mazagardi stocks had been stolen along with the horses and kine. As they forced the food down their throats, angry conversations grew among the women, like the fierce buzzing of hornets whose nest has been disturbed.

But Penthesilea again gave the order: "Silence now! We dance for the moon and then we sleep. Tomorrow we hold a council—and believe me, it will be a council of war."

The slow, gentle moon-dance at last brought with it the release of tears. Myrina and her grandmother wept openly as they turned and swayed, touching hands, singing the familiar, soothing songs of the night. Then Myrina took what was left of her family into her tent, and they lay down together, so weary that even the terrible bitterness of the day could not keep them from their sleep.

In the morning there was another job to be done before they could begin their council of war. Earth had to be heaped over the charred bones and ashes where the pyre had burned. It was a solemn job that required the help of everyone—Yildiz and even little Phoebe. At last the large hump of earth was patted smoothly over the burnt remains of the dead, so that it seemed to them that Maa had taken back her children, sealing the wound with life-giving soil, soon to be covered again in grass and flowers.

Myrina pointed out to Hati the straggling survivors who had appeared throughout the morning. "Grandmother, you are not the only one who hid," she told her. The local fishermen and their families, who knew the country well, came down from the hillside caves where they'd taken refuge. Such flights had become a way of life for them in recent times.

At noon, dust was seen rising in the west, and as they all watched fearfully the sound of horses' hooves could be heard. The Moon Riders ran to mount their horses and snatch up their bows, but they soon saw that the approaching warriors wore their hair tied up in topknots. It was the elderly warrior Peiroos riding at the head of a gang of Thracian tribesmen.

"Welcome," Penthesilea cried, striding out to meet them.

"Naught to fear," Myrina told Yildiz. "They are old friends of ours."

Peiroos had been following in the wake of Achilles'

raiding party, hoping that he could cut them off and chase them back to the southern shore. When he and his tribesmen saw the mound of earth and all the devastation, they shook their heads, understanding that they'd come too late. They dismounted and offered the Moon Riders what help and supplies they had. Just as their tents were raised, another lookout spied a smaller cloud of dust rising in the north and the Moon Riders were cheered a little, for they recognized the banners of Atisha, approaching with her caravan.

Neither Myrina nor Hati was surprised. "She has been mirror-gazing and seen it all," Hati murmured.

Penthesilea rushed forward to welcome Atisha and help her out of the litter that she now used for travel, since her old stallion had died. The Moon Riders were a little shocked to see how thin and fragile she had grown and how slowly she moved. But still, despite that, she looked sharply about her, recognizing each face and giving them all their names.

A special hug was given to Hati. "What times we live in," she whispered.

Hati pulled back a little. "You have seen it all?"

"I have seen that you saved your grandchildren," Atisha told her sharply, coming forward to kiss her cheek again. "What times! I thought Theseus was bad enough, but . . ."

They both nodded and words failed them. Then Hati took the two children away to Myrina's tent. "They do not need to hear all that must be spoken of," she whispered.

"We are glad to see you, Old Woman," Penthesilea said to Atisha warmly. "You are just in time for a council of war. Come speak to Peiroos, who has ridden here from Troy."

Atisha nodded. "I have seen such doings in my mirror visions as I hoped never to see. I have no strength of body left, but I still have my wits and advice to offer. Call this war council and let us plan what must be done."

So everyone sat down. The first to speak was Penthesilea, who vented her fury and urged that they ride at once to Troy in the wake of the Ant Men to take back the Mazagardi horses and slaughter the warriors in revenge. The bitter anger that held Myrina's heart in a tight grip of misery made her wish to follow Penthesilea's plan at once, but then another voice, full of warning, spoke up.

The Thracian lord Peiroos applauded Penthesilea's courage, but he feared that an ill-prepared attack would go amiss. "Troy's troubles are greater than ever," he told them. "King Priam's son Hector, the one we called the Tamer of Horses, has been killed by the Ant Men's leader, Achilles. We all thought Hector invincible, but with his death that high-walled city has lost its heart. The people have withdrawn inside the citadel like a snail into its shell and Agamemnon and his Achaean leaders strut and crow outside on the plain. The walls of the citadel are still strong, but the Trojans' stocks of food are as low as their spirits. The Achaeans raid the countryside and take whatever food they find, so that those towns that would willingly send supplies to Troy have nothing left to give. I myself have lost more than half my warriors, and many of the survivors are wounded men, who grit their teeth every day against pain, but still fight on. An ill-prepared attack on the Achaeans, with our small numbers, would mean that we'd be swatted like flies—and who would then be left to stand by the Trojans and defend the tribal traveling lands?"

"So do we sit here on our backsides and let Achilles' Ant Men destroy us?" Penthesilea demanded.

CHAPTER TWENTY-EIGHT

Bitter and Wise

ENTHESILEA'S ANGER MADE the whole company flinch and there was a moment of silence. But Peiroos got up again, shaking his head. "I still counsel patience—we must have patience. We have received word from King Memnon of Ethiopia that he is coming himself, leading an army of his fiercest fighters. He reviles the thought of Agamemnon's rule spreading throughout the whole of Anatolia as much as any. No, my fierce Daughter of the War God, we will not sit here on our backsides; we will train and gather support while we wait for the Ethiopians and hone our weapons. Then, with King Memnon's aid, we will have an army, sharp for battle, that can truly ride to the aid of Troy and throw the Achaeans back into the sea."

Penthesilea answered him through gritted teeth. "I like it not, warrior man. Patience is hard to find, but . . . I do see the sense in your words."

Atisha stood up and gave her approval of Peiroos's plan. She seemed relieved that Penthesilea, though burning for a fight, had agreed to wait. The Moon Riders had always respected the fierce Thracian tribesmen. They would be able to work together well.

"Let all the tribes go to the Place of Flowing Waters to carry out our Spring Celebrations just as we always do," Atisha suggested. "The Achaeans know of our rites; they will suspect nothing. But this year our songs and dances will disguise a war gathering. All the traveling tribes have suffered bitterly over these past years and I swear the survivors are ready to make their last and final stand. This time we cannot let the Achaeans swamp us with numbers."

Myrina could not help feeling a welling sense of disappointment. Her stomach churned with fury as she saw in her mind the swift punishment that she longed to hand out to Achilles' Ant Men. She wanted to leap up at once and ride after them, shooting all the warriors full of arrows until they looked like falling porcupines. A desperate desire for action grew in her, while those around her seemed to do nothing but talk and talk. It was difficult to sit still, listening to it all; she shuffled her feet constantly, her heart bursting with hatred.

Peiroos and Penthesilea argued on about tactics, but Myrina's gang was aware of their Snake Lady's inward struggle. They never left her side, always ready to stroke her back or hold her hands. Bremusa, always the practical one, brought food and drink and stood over Myrina, insisting that it was consumed.

The war council was at last coming to an end as the sun began to sink. There seemed to be grim agreement all round, but before they could start to disperse, Atisha once more struggled to her feet, demanding that they listen to her. Her voice had lost its old strength, but her powerful storyteller's sense of timing held her audience in silence.

"This plan has all my blessing," she approved as her gaze swept about the gathering, "but there is one more thing that we should do. The Trojans should not be left in this deep despair, ignorant of our intentions. They should know that there are many who care for their plight, and they must be told that their allies gather together in the shelter of Mount Ida."

"Ah yes! The Old One speaks true." A wave of murmuring agreement rose from all sides.

"But how?" Penthesilea demanded.

"A small number may get into Troy unnoticed by the Achaeans. We need someone who knows the land well and whose courage lies in subtlety rather than in strength; somebody whom the Trojans will trust."

Myrina suddenly looked up at Atisha, but Penthesilea

cried out with wild excitement, pulling the knife from her belt and brandishing it above her head. "I shall go. I shall go ahead and defend the Trojans until you come."

Atisha smiled but shook her head. "We need you to stay with the tribes, my fierce warrior woman, to lead them and marshal our allies. You must work like a tigress at that job . . . and then your time will come. No, if she is willing, Myrina is the one who must go to Troy. She knows the city and the land around it better than any of us and, even more important, the princess Cassandra is her special friend. Myrina and her gang should go, and if they can gather a bit of food on their way, so much the better."

Myrina's heart raced. "Yes, I will go," she cried at once with gratitude. This would do much to satisfy her need for action. Ten years had passed since she'd seen Cassandra. Her mirror-visions told her that the princess was alive and somehow struggling on, but she longed to see her properly, to hug her and speak to her and know how she truly fared.

Coronilla, Polymusa, Alcibie, and Bremusa clenched their fists in salute, grinning at one another. It was clear that Myrina's gang were willing.

Penthesilea's mouth closed in bitter disappointment but, as was always the case with her, she could not hold a grudge for long. She quickly looked up again and nodded her agreement, clapping Myrina on the back. "Of course Myrina is the one," she acknowledged with quick generosity. "Sneak inside those walls like the snake you are and take good care of yourself, little one."

The council broke up and the Thracians shared the small amount of food that they carried with them. It was only when Myrina returned to her tent to tell Hati what she must do that her heart sank.

She found Yildiz sitting cross-legged on a cushion, her small fists tightly clenched. The young girl's face was drained of color and she seemed to see nothing of what was going on around her. Myrina squatted beside her niece and gently stroked her rough, scorched hair. "How are you, Little Star?" she whispered.

Yildiz did not even seem to hear her.

Myrina turned to Hati. "I can't go. They want me to go ahead to Troy, and scavenge for food on the way, but how can I go? What of these two little ones? I am their aunt; I should adopt them as my own. How can I take Yildiz with me into the dangerous city of Troy?"

Hati shook her head. "You can't," she said, "that's clear—but do you wish to go on this mission, Snake Lady?"

"Oh yes." Myrina nodded firmly, baring her strong teeth. "I want to have a chance to get my hands on those . . . But I want to see Cassandra, too—"

"Then you shall go, and you will not worry about these little ones," Hati cut in. "I have been thinking that with so many Mazagardi gone, it might be best if I travel north with Atisha to the Moon Riders' sanctuary beside the River Thermodon, where they keep Iphigenia hidden away. If you go to Troy, then I shall take the children with me to the safety of that place."

Myrina looked up with concern. "Then we will be parted, Grandmother, even though you are all the family I have left."

"Not forever, I hope," Hati told her. "I will wait for you there by the wooded riverbanks, with Atisha and the princess. I hear that Centaurea is there with her and that Iphigenia grows strong and well, studying the healing arts and Earth Mother's magic."

"Yes," Myrina agreed, "I know that is true. I look for her in my mirror-visions and see that the place where she lives is beautiful and full of peace."

"Well, that is where I shall take these children, and I will keep them safely there until you come to join us. I am not such a crazy old fool as to think that I can still be a warrior."

Myrina smiled sadly and kissed Hati. "For that I am grateful, Grandmother. I do see that they will be safer with you on the banks of the Thermodon than here with me. It's a harsh struggle indeed that's taking place in this dying land of ours."

Hati nodded. "You grow both bitter and wise, Snake Lady."

The following morning Myrina's little gang of four got themselves ready to set off westward with her, along the southern shore of the Sea of Marmara. They covered their bows and full quivers with long cloaks, tying scarves about their heads, so that they looked more like horse-driving Mazagardi than Moon Riders in full battle-dress.

Atisha called Myrina to her side and gave her some practical advice, along with some of the valued herbs and medicines that she made and carried about with her. "You are like to have more need of these than I, Young Snaky."

Then she sighed and her fading blue eyes gazed into the distance, where Penthesilea was energetically putting the Moon Riders through stick-twirling dances before the sun reached its full heat.

"What is it, Old Woman?" Myrina asked.

Atisha smiled. "You could always see into people's hearts, Myrina. That's why I know that you are the right one for this tricky job. You will snake your way inside the walls of the citadel and you'll bring much comfort to the Trojans, but . . . my heart is heavy, for I know that Penthesilea is likely to rush headlong into battle with these Achaean raiders. I have given my advice, but I doubt that she'll have the patience to wait for Memnon and his Ethiopian warriors. All we can do is slow her down as best we can. I'm fearful of the outcome and I want you to do something that you may find very difficult when the time comes."

"What?" Myrina was puzzled.

"When our allies arrive at Troy . . . you, Myrina, must not go out to fight alongside them."

Myrina frowned at that. From an early age she had been trained, like all the Mazagardi women, to defend her home-tent and her tribe whenever necessary. In recent years she'd taken part in many skirmishes as a Moon Rider, fighting against Achaean raiding bands. She was skilled with her bow and arrows and not afraid to fight. "You'd have me turn coward?" she asked, shocked.

"There are many different kinds of courage," Atisha snapped back. "Look at it this way: if aught should happen to Penthesilea, who will lead the Moon Riders then? I will not be there with you. It must be someone with a quick brain and resourcefulness, and that is you, my Snake Lady."

"But . . ." Myrina started to protest, but then remembered her own words of comfort to her grandmother and nodded thoughtfully. "I said something like that to Hati myself—that it might be good to hold back, so that you are there to clear up the mess and . . . and save what can be saved."

"Exactly. You see"—Atisha's wrinkled monkey face lit up—"you understand so quickly. I hope desperately that Penthesilea will win victory for the Trojans, but I am not like Cassandra, I have no pictures of the future in my mind and we must plan for whatever the fates may bring. If the time comes for you to act, do not fear to follow your instincts, or to break the rules. The ancient traditions of the Moon Riders have served us well for many generations, but now, though it breaks my heart to say it, I think that time is coming to an end. We must look for new ways to live. . . . We must simply find a way to survive."

Yildiz

MYRINA WAS AWED by the seriousness of Atisha's words, but soon the Old Woman became practical again and took her over to speak to Peiroos, who had promised them three light carts so that they could gather produce along the way and arrive with some stocks of food for the hungry Trojans.

"Have you seen aught of a young Mazagardi warrior named Tomi?" Myrina asked Peiroos. "He went to Thrace to act as a messenger, riding fast from tribe to tribe." Myrina had looked again in her mirror for Tomi and saw him riding through a landscape that was unknown to her; sometimes he was alone, sometimes he led his horse through rough terrain accompanied by dark-skinned men in turbans.

The old warrior smiled and gently touched her cheek. "There's a touch of blush on that fierce body picture," he said. "I know well the young man you speak of and he is worthy of a Moon Rider's concern. Your Tomi rides far to the east, looking to meet up with King Memnon and guide his army back to the walls of Troy."

"Ah." Myrina blushed again and thanked the old man. At least she understood now why she saw him traveling through strange lands. The coming of the Achaeans had changed the marriage plans that Myrina and Tomi had made. The Moon Riders had been desperately needed to act as messengers, translators, and warriors, keeping the nomadic tribes in touch with one another. The Moon-maidens had become a strong symbol of unity, bringing together most of the Trojan allies in their reverence for the Great Earth Mother, Maa. Myrina, like many a Moon Rider, had stayed with the priestesses much longer than her seven years, setting aside her marriage plans to swell the ranks of warrior women to more than one hundred. Few recruits were taken on, and, sadly, many intended marriages had been spoiled by the deaths of young warriors, both men and women.

Peiroos had seen much hardship in his long life, and he felt great sadness now in his waning years. The fight in defense of the tribal traveling lands had turned so many young lives bitter. "I hope that you will find your warrior man," he told Myrina gently. "If all goes well with the Ethiopians, your Tomi will arrive with them, but when, I cannot say."

The time for leave-taking came and Myrina had to hold back the tears as she kissed Phoebe's soft, warm forehead. Hati was agitated because she couldn't find Yildiz and felt she should say good-bye properly to her aunt. "I couldn't see her anywhere when I woke up," she said. "I fear she's wandered off and got lost, for I swear her mind has gone all misty."

Myrina was unwilling to leave with this uncertainty, but then a small figure came out from behind the tents, leading one of the few remaining Mazagardi horses, with raw blistered flanks; her right hand she held behind her back.

Yildiz led the horse right up to Myrina and said in a small but determined voice, "Snake Lady, I come with you."

Myrina took the young girl's face in her hands, deeply touched. "No, I must leave you with Hati, Little Star, for Atisha has given me important work to do. I must help the Trojans get rid of these Achaeans who destroy our lands. It is far too dangerous for one as young as you. No one can join the Moon Riders until they've seen thirteen summers."

But Yildiz stood her ground, her words quite clear and measured. "Older Mazagardi girls are dead. There are none left to join the Riders—only me."

Myrina looked up at Hati with concern, but the old

woman shrugged her shoulders. Though Yildiz had seen only eleven springs, the truth of her words could not be denied.

Penthesilea came to see what the holdup was. "Let her come with me to the Place of Flowing Waters—I will make a Moon Rider of her, though she is so young."

But Yildiz shook her head. "I ride with the Snake Lady. She is my aunt and I make her my mother now. I kill Ant Men—it's my right. I'm not afraid to die."

Penthesilea drew in her breath sharply, hissing through her teeth in admiration.

Myrina looked at the horse that Yildiz led. It was a sturdy bay mare, small enough for a young girl to ride. She touched her blistered muzzle and sniffed closely. "Who treated these burns with lavender oil?"

"I did," Yildiz told her, turning to stroke the muscular neck. "She is Silene and I've been riding her all through the Bitter Months; she knows me well and I know her."

Myrina walked around the mare, prodding gently at her raw, but treated flanks. "Hmm! Silene is a good strong steed," she had to agree.

"She will never leave me," Yildiz insisted.

"I think she has proved that already. Why do you hold your hand behind your back? Is it injured?"

Yildiz slowly brought her hand around to the front to show Myrina a freshly made body picture on her forearm, wrist, and thumb. The skin was swollen and sore, but the crude shapes of a crescent moon, a star, and the sun could be seen, the star's lower point coming down onto her thumb. "I have made my own body picture," Yildiz said.

"You did this to yourself?"

Yildiz nodded. "I took Hati's picture juice. I must have a body picture if I come with you. You have your snake, which makes you the snake lady. I must have my star, but . . . my bow and quiver were all burnt up in the home-tent."

Myrina took the swollen hand in hers, finding it hard to speak, but she forced out the words, "On the day that you were born, Yildiz, I held you in my arms and I welcomed you with the sacred dance. The sun, the moon, and the evening star looked down on you and me. Now, I will be your mother and you will ride with me and be my daughter."

"Ha!" Penthesilea was delighted.

Hati nodded solemnly and kissed them both, then she lifted over her head the quiver full of arrows that she always wore strapped across her chest and slipped from her shoulder the bow that she carried ready strung in these dangerous times. "Take my bow and quiver, Little Star," she said. "You may take my place as a warrior woman, and all who cross your path had better watch out!"

Penthesilea bent to kiss her. "I salute you, warrior

woman. If any Achaean harms a hair of your head, he will have Penthesilea to deal with. Go with the blessings of Maa!"

As they traveled west Myrina's gang passed through small fishing villages. The people, who lived in hovels and had been continually robbed by Achaean raiding bands, were cheered to see a small group of Moon Riders. The spring dances so long neglected were performed that year, bringing back hope to their lives, and though they were struggling to feed themselves, they managed to find some grain and salted fish to spare for those inside the walls of Troy.

There was so much to think about during the day that Myrina had little time to spend with Yildiz, but every evening she made space for them to talk together. Her doubts about taking the child along were soon put to flight. Yildiz, though still very solemn and thoughtful, was willing to talk, and as they sat together remembering happier times Myrina came to understand that Yildiz had grown up very fast indeed. Sometimes she comforted her adopted daughter, but just as often Yildiz gave practical and simple advice to her Snake Mother. Now and again a bitter, quiet mood overcame the young girl and she would not speak for a while; when at last she did, she growled out her anger. Myrina allowed her to do so, thinking that such terrible feelings were better let out than held in. Yildiz needed action just as much as her new mother, and she was willing to ride all day. The hard riding and energetic pleading for supplies brought some kind of comfort to them both. Myrina also saw that the presence of a young girl gave them a less threatening, less warlike aspect, so that the hard-pressed shore dwellers were reassured.

They traveled on down the coast and at last reached a small peninsula where the land stuck out into the sea like a pointing finger, catching the warmth of the sun. This area was green and pleasant, the hillsides rich with perfumed roses and oleanders, small pink sage flowers adding sharpness to the warm, scented air. Humps of islands in the Sea of Marmara could be seen in the distance, the green tips of their hills making them shine like a necklace of emeralds set in a turquoise sea. It seemed the Achaean raiding parties had not ventured so far north. This verdant coast and islands looked beautiful and peaceful in the bright sunlight; it was hard to believe that, just over a day's journey to the south, a fine and ancient city was besieged and all the surrounding countryside laid waste.

Myrina's gang breathed deeply, with much-needed pleasure, looking longingly across the sea toward the islands.

"They look so lovely in the distance." Coronilla spoke with feeling. "I want to step away from this war and float across the sea to them, to a land of peace and plenty."

Myrina smiled. "That is the Isle of Marble out there. I once went there to dance at King Daris's wedding." Daris had insisted on marrying Ira, a young bride from the common folk, whom his uncles had scorned but whom he himself adored.

The Isle of Marble, though small, was rich, for the cities of Anatolia traded with the islanders, giving gold and jewels in return for the fine marble that came from the quarries there. Though trade had waned while the fighting raged, still the island must thrive, for it was also rich in sheep and cattle and grain. It was even said that the old adventurer Jason had stopped there for supplies of grain and wine. He had passed through the Sea of Marmara, seeking to trade with Colchis, bringing back a fine breeding ram from their flocks of golden-fleeced sheep.

Myrina turned suddenly thoughtful. It would slow them down for a day or two, but King Daris had welcomed the Moon Riders in the past and he might well have better supplies to offer than the poor fisher folk along the shore. Marble Islanders honored a goddess of the earth called Dindymere, but they readily acknowledged that she was simply Mother Maa by a different name.

"Ask those fishermen," Myrina told Coronilla. "And if you can make them understand our language and find any willing to carry us across, you shall have your wish for an island visit."

CHAPTER THIRTY

The Isle of Marble

C ORONILLA FOUND THE Marmara dwellers' language difficult, but she smiled broadly and went off to speak to the fishermen, determined to make herself understood. "They'll be willing," she said. "I'll make them. You'll see!"

Myrina watched her, chuckling, as with a great deal of arm-waving and laughter, Coronilla managed to get their assent. They were indeed prepared to offer their boats in the service of the Earth Mother, for what better way to bring down her blessings on their watery harvest?

Myrina followed Coronilla, striding over the rocks to rescue her and offer her own language skills to make the arrangements now that Coronilla had succeeded in her mission. But as Myrina spoke to them, explaining their purpose in detail, they looked uncertain and shook their heads.

"Bad time to ask anything of King Daris," they said.

"Very bad time!"

"Queen lady Ira is sick and like to die."

"King and queen have wanted child year after year, but none came; now at last son is born to them, six days ago, but Ira has terrible fever after childbirth and all say she will die. King Daris is distraught and will not look at child. He is very angry with everyone."

Myrina frowned. She remembered the young queen whose wedding they'd danced at; Ira had been little more than a girl and the king a boy. Myrina stood on the hot sands, gazing uncertainly toward the Isle of Marble, surrounded by the pungent smell of hot seaweed. Reluctant to leave this pleasant spot, even though there were other pressing needs, she turned and looked back longingly at the green hillside sprinkled with fragrant, pink-flowered sage.

Then suddenly she smiled. "A remedy for childbed fever!" she murmured. "Ah, yes, Atisha would have known at once: the means of saving Ira is all around us. Get ready the boats—and, Coronilla, can you find good stabling for the horses? I shall be back very soon."

While the fishermen and Moon Riders prepared to board the boats, Myrina wheeled Isatis around and cantered back to the hillside that sloped to the sea. It was covered with roses and sage plants. She dismounted and quickly stooped to pick handful on handful of fresh sage, then stopped for a moment's thought and used her knife to dig up some of the plants, taking care not to injure the roots. She took off her cloak and made a bundle of the sharp-scented herbs, carrying them carefully to the waiting Isatis.

She arrived back to find the boats ready. "I swear I shall soon have Queen Ira back on her feet," she told the fishermen.

They shrugged their shoulders and wished her luck; Moon Riders were known as good medicine women and perhaps if anyone could help the queen, it was this young warrior priestess who led her small gang with such confidence.

Leaving the horses in stabling, they crossed the stretch of water in the evening and arrived as the light was fading. Myrina told her gang to make camp beside a small spring that bubbled out of the hillside below the palace steps. She took the rooted sage plants from her bundle and handed them to Polymusa and Coronilla. "Plant these carefully around the spring and water them well," she told them.

"Blessings of Mother Maa!" they whispered, giving Myrina the priestess's salute.

She marched toward the heavily armed guards at the main gates of the palace, Yildiz following her like a dog.

Myrina turned to her, a question on her lips, but Yildiz forestalled her. "You are my Snake Mother—I go where you go," she said.

Myrina bowed her head and smiled. There was no time to argue about it; she would very likely need some help and she couldn't be sure that the palace servants would be of much use.

"Tell King Daris that Myrina the Moon Rider has come, bringing her healing magic," she told the captain of the guards.

He had drawn his sword at their approach, but he replaced it at once and bowed respectfully. "Too late." He shook his head.

"Is there life still?" she demanded.

The man shrugged his shoulders.

"If there's life there's hope," she insisted. "What will the king say if he knows you have turned away his last hope?"

The other guards put away their swords, too. "Let her try," they said.

The captain sighed and nodded. "There is nothing to lose by it," he agreed. He opened the gate and led her inside and up the magnificent marble staircase to the queen's bedchamber, Yildiz still following determinedly behind.

The captain knocked on the door and Daris himself opened it, his hair and clothes awry. "I said not to disturb us!" he growled.

Myrina pushed in front of the guard, taking the king by the shoulders as though she were his mother or aunt. "I am Myrina the Moon Rider," she told him. "I danced at your wedding feast. Now I bring you our magic woman's medicine. I can help!"

He stared at her for a moment, too surprised to be angry; then at last he nodded and pulled her into the chamber.

Ira, the young queen, lay on an elaborate gilded bed hung about with gossamer drapes in rich colors. She muttered through dry lips, her eyes rolling, her face puffy and red and her skin mottled. As she turned this way and that she threw off her soft, woolly sheepskin covers. Waiting women fussed and fretted all about her, offering wine, strange smelling powders and rich jewels to touch.

Myrina went straight to the young woman's side and put her hand on Ira's burning forehead; then she turned back to the boylike king and grabbed his arm. "I have the medicine that's needed here in my magic woman's bundle," she told him. "But I must have peace and quiet if I am to make my healing work and I must be left alone with my assistant here."

Daris stared at Myrina and Yildiz again, still having little idea who they were, but somehow Myrina's strength of purpose cut through his confusion and he imperiously waved the waiting women out.

"You, too," Myrina told him.

But he objected to that and sat down quietly at the end of his wife's bed, shaking his head like a determined but disobedient child. "I stay!"

"Oh well . . ." Myrina had no more time to waste. "You must help us then."

He looked up, surprised at that, but then nodded.

"Two pots of water!" she demanded. "Some boiling water and some as cold as you can make it, then I must have cotton cloths torn into strips! Quickly! Do you understand? Water: hot and cold! And some rose water!"

King Daris strode to the doorway and shouted orders. Meanwhile Myrina felt Ira's brow again, then delicately touched her cheeks and breasts. "Can you brew a strong sage potion?" she asked Yildiz, opening her bundle of sage and tearing up some of the leaves.

The girl nodded. A waiting woman appeared nervously at the chamber doorway; she carried a small brazier with glowing charcoal, all set in a tripod. Yildiz took over at once and set about steeping the herbs in a pot. Another waiting woman appeared with a small beaker of cold water and a jeweled jar of rose water.

"What is this?" Myrina demanded, pointing to the beaker.

"Cold water!" the woman whimpered.

"No, no, no!" Myrina shook her head with impatience. "I need buckets of cold water, buckets of it."

At that the young king rushed out of the room, returning almost at once with a huge ornamental golden ewer filled with cold water.

"That's more like it," Myrina encouraged.

The waiting women fled once more, but hovered in the doorway. They were shocked to see Myrina remove the fleecy bedcovers, then look swiftly about the room and reach up to rip down the queen's fine bed-hangings. She poured the whole jar of rose water into the ewer, then stooped to soak the torn drapes in it. The whole room was at once filled with a fresh, gentle scent that reminded them all of childhood days in a garden.

Myrina squeezed out the cold, dripping drapes and began wrapping them about Ira's fevered limbs. Then she took the knife from her belt, making the women gasp with fear. King Daris hushed them. He'd never seen a woman work so fast and efficiently and by now he was willing to put his faith in this strange intruder. Myrina used her knife to fish out a soggy wad of boiling sage from Yildiz' brew.

"This is fine medicine," she announced.

She carried it to the ewer and cooled it, then squeezed it out and bound the damp compress of herbs gently about Ira's swollen breasts with another torn drape.

Almost at once the young queen was soothed, and she responded by ceasing her continuous tossing and turning.

Understanding better now, Daris took a jeweled knife from his own belt and began to split and tear up the linen coverlet, then, rolling up his fine embroidered sleeves, he soaked the strips in the golden ewer, passing them over to Myrina as soon as they were ready.

"Yes, yes," she encouraged. "Well done!"

At last the young woman's body was covered with cooling cloths and damp herbs. Myrina looked up to call Yildiz, but saw that the girl was already approaching the bed with a golden goblet of warm, aromatic sage tea and a gilded spoon.

"Honey!" Myrina commanded, sending the waiting women scattering again, to return quickly with a simple stone pot of honey. "Now you're getting the idea," she approved.

Myrina carefully fed Queen Ira with small spoonfuls of honeyed sage tea. Now the bedchamber was pungent with the sharp, clean smell of the herb as well as roses. At last she stood back. "Well . . . now we must just wait and be patient," she told the king.

He still refused to leave and throughout the night he dozed, exhausted, on a couch while Myrina and Yildiz worked together to feed the queen more sage and honey tea, regularly changing the cooling cloths.

As morning light came in through the palace windows, Daris awoke and saw that both his mysterious helpers had fallen asleep on cushions beside the bed. Ira lay quite still, but the bandages had been removed, and she was covered with a light, dry linen sheet. He stood shakily and went to bend over her. Her skin was pale and clear again and her face had lost all the red swellings, though her lips were still dry and flaky. He saw that she breathed easily, and as he bent over her she opened her eyes and smiled with recognition. He snatched up her hand in his, lowering his lips to kiss it, then began to cry with relief, howling freely like a baby. "Ira . . . my Ira . . . safe. She is safe!"

Both Myrina and Yildiz woke with a jolt at the sound of his sobbing. But when they saw that Ira's fever had gone, and that it was joy that made him cry so loudly, they hugged each other.

"We make a good team, you and I," Myrina praised, and for the first time since the massacre Yildiz really smiled and looked happy.

CHAPTER THIRTY-ONE

To Feed an Army

D ARIS'S CRYING BROUGHT back the waiting
women; they ventured nervously into the
royal chamber, but when they saw how well
Ira looked, their faces broke out into quiet smiles and
sighs of relief.

Myrina gave a few more orders, suggesting that honey-
stewed apples and some fresh eggs would make a good
meal and nourish the newly recovering queen. A trou-
bling thought had come into her mind at brief moments
during the night, but she'd been too busy to stop her
work and ask about it. Now, once again, it came to her.
She looked around the bedchamber in a puzzled way,
frowning and still seeing no sign of a cot or cradle. She
spoke gently, fearing that perhaps it had not survived:
"Where is the baby?"

The waiting women said nothing and hung their
heads.

Daris shrugged. "Gone to a wet nurse," he told her, surprised that she should ask.

Myrina shook her head and folded her arms across her chest in determination. "That will not help this new mother," she insisted. "Bring the child here at once. The child needs its mother's milk, and the feeding will help keep the fever away and make the queen get better."

"But all the palace children are fed by nurses; it is too lowly a job for the queen."

Myrina sighed, wondering how to explain, but Ira, who was now sitting up propped on pillows, came to her aid. "I do not consider it too lowly a job for me," she whispered, her voice still faint.

The young king scratched his head and bent low to kiss his wife's hand again. Then he called to the women, "Well, what are you waiting for? You'd better fetch the child at once."

Ira put the tiny boy to her breast, and though she was still weak and sore, she smiled happily as he began to suck strongly. King Daris watched them both with a foolish smile of deep contentment on his face as they snuggled together beneath the ravaged bed-hangings.

At last he turned to Myrina. "I will do all you say," he told her. "Everything. Stay here and be our royal healing woman. I will give you gold and jewels, a fine carved litter and slaves to carry you about."

"No, no." Myrina shook her head. She yawned again, for she was now truly exhausted and her mind a little confused. Then the real purpose of her visit came back to her with a wave of clarity and she remembered that there was little time to spare. "No," she said firmly. "I cannot stay, but . . . if you think I have given you good service this night, then you have it in your power to repay me well, for you have something that I want very much."

Daris looked a little anxious as he wondered what this might be, but Myrina went on. "I want carts of grain, as much as you can spare, and olives and raisins, casks of salt fish and wine and . . . and honey, pots of it."

Daris stared at her, amazed. "You sound as though you wish to feed an army!"

"That's not so very far from the truth," Myrina agreed. "I wish to feed the struggling city of Troy."

He stared at her again, wondering if he were having a crazy dream, but then he glanced back at Ira and the baby. "Ha!" He laughed. "You are a madwoman, a crazy Moon Rider! But if that is really what you want, it shall be done—at once."

"Thank you!" Now it was Myrina's turn to smile with relief.

"Well, well!" Daris was suddenly thoughtful and practical. "You will need armed guards to protect your carts from the Achaeans. You shall have armed guards as well."

But Myrina was uncertain about that. "No, no," she said. "If you have strong warriors whom you can spare, send them to the Place of Flowing Waters, where the tribes and Trojan allies are gathering. Just a small number will suffice to help us into Troy. I have my own plans."

"Whatever you want shall be done," he said. "Now you and your assistant must rest and when you wake, I swear I shall have all that you have asked for ready to leave."

They were led to a sleeping chamber and served with rich food, but they were both too tired to appreciate it, or the splendor of their surroundings, and soon fell into a heavy sleep.

Daris did as he had promised, and when Myrina and Yildiz woke up and returned to the waiting gang of Moon Riders, they found them giving orders to hordes of servants, who were loading a magnificent collection of supplies and carts onto a line of cargo boats. There were huge stone pots filled with grain, barrels of well-salted fish—sardines, mackerel, and whiting—casks of olives preserved in olive oil, two cartloads of raisins, stone jars of dried apples, honey, and wine. Mules were led aboard each boat, with drivers and guards to protect them. Daris came down to oversee the loading and to say good-bye.

Myrina saw that Coronilla had planted sage all around the spring, just as she had asked her to. "Keep these plants well watered and cared for," she told Daris. "Then use the leaves as I did whenever any should suffer from fevers."

He bowed low and kissed her hand. "It shall be called the Spring of the Moon Rider in your honor," he said. "If ever I can help you again in any way, you have only to ask."

Myrina went aboard her boat with a sense of bursting joy; she had somehow managed to gather together supplies beyond any hope or expectation. All her gang was excited and eager to get on and carry the goods to Troy. The wind was blowing in their favor as they sailed away from the Isle of Marble and they arrived on the southern shore of the Sea of Marmara just as light was fading. They reclaimed their horses from the stables and wearily made camp for the night.

Next morning they were up at dawn, anxious to be on their way, leading the great wagon train south across the hilly scrubland toward Troy. It was only as evening came that Myrina's spirits began to fall. She had told the young king confidently that she could manage without many guards and that she had her own plan for their arrival at Troy. Now, as she gave orders for setting up camp, misgivings began to creep in. She had been so cheered and excited by her healing success that nothing seemed beyond her, but as they traveled on through the wasteland, getting closer and closer to the besieged city, she had to admit to herself that she had no real plan and no idea how they would get their goods safely within the city walls.

They trundled on southward all the next day, the Moon Riders chatting happily with King Daris's men. The well-armed guards seemed to feel that it was all a great adventure; they were interested to see for themselves the struggling city of Troy, whose fight for survival had recently been the focus of all the news. Meanwhile Myrina racked her brain as to how they would get into Troy without the Achaeans stealing all the excellent provisions that they had collected together.

Yildiz seemed to pick up on her growing anxiety and spoke her thoughts out loud. "Can we get into Troy without the Achaeans seeing all this food?" she asked.

"I shall think of something!" Myrina answered sharply.

Coronilla overheard them and laughed. "Atisha told us to sneak into the citadel like a snake. Not much chance of that, with all this lot behind us! Perhaps you are too successful, Snake Woman."

Myrina's unease grew. It was all very well for Atisha to tell her to be resourceful, but now her mind had gone blank. Maybe she had overdone the food-gathering and had just brought another problem with it.

"We could get in by the hidden gate," Coronilla went on cheerfully, "so long as Agamemnon hasn't posted guards about it."

Myrina bit her lip. "Let's hope for that," she told Coronilla sharply, refusing to join in the laughter. There was no way that the Achaeans were going to get this precious food—on that she was adamant.

"What if there are guards?" Yildiz insisted.

Myrina shrugged. "We work it out when we get there."

At last the landscape became familiar and Myrina called a halt. "We make camp here," she cried. "Once we cross the brow of the next hill we will be within sight of Troy and that means within sight of Achaean lookouts."

As her gang set up their tents and built cooking fires, working together with King Daris's men, Myrina tethered Isatis and marched ahead up the steep hillside by herself, determined to have a look at what lay ahead.

I should have listened to Atisha, she argued with herself. Small amounts would have been best—but then, small amounts would not feed so very many starving people.

She reached the summit of the hill and stood there, looking down. Though a wagon train might be spotted from that distance, one young woman could not be seen.

The golden limestone walls of Troy stood beneath her; then, beyond them, the main spread of Achaean tents and huts made a dark gray smudgy shape all along the far shoreline to the south of Troy. The northwestern citadel walls were built above a precipitous drop, which provided good natural protection on that side; nobody could scale that steep height. The once busy lower town outside the walls of Troy seemed to have become a no-man's-land, almost deserted and half destroyed. The eastern side, with its cleverly built hidden entrance, was closest to where she stood; it was protected by a curtain wall and it would almost have been possible to get the carts down there, had it not been for a camp of Achaean guards settled just above the Southern Gate with their flags and standards. Her hopes were dashed; it seemed that Agamemnon had set a watch on who came into and went from Troy.

CHAPTER THIRTY-TWO

Mazagardi Horses

MYRINA SAT DOWN and took her silver snake-carved mirror from the pouch that hung from her belt. She let her shoulders relax a little and thought of her friend Cassandra, not far away at all, but hidden within the strongly built citadel that lay before her. At last the tension that she saw in her face began to ease and she looked deeply into her own eyes, seeing there, in the golden brown depths of her iris, a small figure that grew and grew until at last there was the slim shape of the Trojan princess, with her strange eyes, one green, one blue, turning to her with a smile.

"Almost as though she knows that I watch her," Myrina whispered.

Cassandra slowly raised her hand to touch her temple in the priestess's salute.

"She does know." Myrina smiled and raised her own hand in response. Cassandra had not forgotten their friendship, and though getting inside the city might be difficult, a warm welcome was waiting there.

A small sound behind made Myrina turn away, so that the mirror-vision vanished. Yildiz had followed her, creeping from bush to bush like a shadow. Myrina clicked her tongue with impatience and put her mirror away. "You can come out from behind that cistus, my little flower," she called.

But then, seeing that the girl looked crestfallen as she emerged, she made a space where they could both sit and not be seen. "Come and see if your young eyes can spy out more than mine," she ordered.

Yildiz moved forward eagerly and her eyes swept across the landscape below them. "No gates on this side," she said as she stared in awe at the citadel walls. "We can't get in at all, can we?"

"Ah." Myrina smiled. "These Trojans have built cleverly," she said. "The Eastern Gate is concealed. See there! Look carefully!" She pointed to where two small towers flanked the hidden entrance. "That is where we must take the wagons in. The doors are big enough for horses and carts, and those above can shut them quickly and defend the narrow space below. It's all protected by the curtain wall."

Yildiz nodded, impressed, her eyes wide. "Very clever," she said. "But how can we get our carts down to the gate without their coming up here from that camp to kill us?"

Myrina shook her head and sighed; she had no answer to that question. A panicky feeling of desperation was growing inside her. How could they come so far, then fail at the gates?

They sat there in silence for a while, gazing down over the rocky hillside and the plain beyond Troy. Myrina's thoughts swung about, but still she couldn't think how they could possibly sneak quietly into the city. Suddenly Yildiz stiffened and a little cry came from her lips.

"What is it?"

Yildiz grabbed Myrina's hand, her small strong fingers trembling and pressing angrily into her Snake Mother's palm. "Horses," she whispered. "Mazagardi horses. Our horses."

Myrina followed the direction that her sharp young eyes had taken and saw what she meant. Beyond the Southern Gate, where once golden crops of barley had grown, a great corral of horses stood. That was another reason why there was an Achaean camp nearby: Agamemnon's men watched over the whole herd of stolen Mazagardi steeds.

Suddenly the small seed of an idea began to grow in Myrina's mind. "Mazagardi horses," she whispered. "Mazagardi-trained! You have made me think, Little Star!"

"What? What do you think?" Yildiz begged.

Myrina got up, her cheeks flushed with excitement, then she started to laugh with a sudden fierce joy; at last she knew what must be done.

"Those blundering Achaeans will have no idea what to do with Mazagardi horses," she said. "How can Achaean warriors control our steeds?"

Aben had always given generous instruction to those who bought their horses honorably, but those who stole could do little with their prizes.

"I could create chaos with that herd down there," Myrina cried. "And maybe I could win our horses back as well."

Yildiz also leaped to her feet, quickly understanding what Myrina had in mind. "You and I, Snake Mother! With a 'Yip! Yip! Yip!' We can take the Mazagardi mares from under their noses."

Myrina stopped smiling at once and shook her head. "Not you, Little Star. Helping to cure a sick queen is one thing, but to ride down there, as you say, beneath the noses of those who killed your family—that is too much for one as young as you. I wouldn't be a good mother if I allowed that. You must let me do this alone."

But Yildiz set her mouth in a determined line. "You need me, Snake Mother," she said. "One must lead and the other follow behind, using the secret horse magic that we both know. Your Moon Rider friends are fine horse-women and they know the everyday horse cries, but they aren't trained Mazagardi as I am; they don't know the secret of herd-leading. You cannot do it alone and if I get the chance to kill one of those Ant Men, I will not care that they kill me."

Myrina was alarmed at the thought and still shook her head, but she couldn't deny that Yildiz was right. Of all her gang, only she and Yildiz knew the mystical horse cries that made it possible for just two riders skilled in Mazagardi ways to control a whole herd. None of the others had this secret knowledge, but the cries would come to Yildiz as easily as breathing, and on Silene's back the horse moves would be as natural to her as the steps of a familiar dance.

Myrina heaved a great sigh, thinking hard. "I would care very much if they killed you," she said, "but . . . that would not be likely to happen if you took the lead. The guards are bound to be startled at first and if you went ahead that would be safer: I must be the one who follows behind."

Yildiz smiled, realizing that she was winning her argument. "Then we will do it together, Snake Mother. I will allow you to take the more dangerous role and ride at the back of the herd."

Reluctantly Myrina agreed.

* * *

They returned to the camp in high spirits. Myrina had her plan—and confidence that it would work, dangerous though it might be.

That night they sat around their campfire, talking it all through. "I will go ahead with Yildiz and we will make such madness and chaos around the Achaean horse guards that they will have no time to look up here and see a wagon train descending from the hills."

King Daris's guards offered to ride down with Myrina when they heard the plan.

"I should go with you," Coronilla insisted. "I will go instead of Yildiz."

"No," Bremusa butted in. "It should be me. I am the tallest, strongest woman among us."

But Myrina shook her head. "No, none of you will come. I do not want to risk Yildiz, but height and strength are not what's needed. You don't know the secret horse-leading ways that we Mazagardi learn as little children. You would bring more trouble with you. Believe me, only Mazagardi can do this, and though I am loath to take Yildiz with me, she has pointed out very clearly to me that I need her. Coronilla . . . Bremusa . . . you and the gang must lead the caravan of carts down to the hidden gate and get them safely inside. That is your job and it is important that I can depend on you."

"But just the two of you!" Alcibie protested still.

Myrina laughed and touched her cheek. "Not just two of us—we have our Mazagardi horses to help us, Isatis and Silene: they will have their own important part to play. You must bring the wagons to the top of the hill and be ready to roll as soon as you see a disturbance start. Then, quick as you can, straight down to the hidden gate in the citadel wall."

"You can depend on us," Bremusa agreed. "But will the Trojans let us in?"

Myrina paused, thoughtful for a moment, but then she smiled, remembering her mirror-vision. "Yes. When they see our loads of grain and olives, I do not think they will hesitate long, but there is one inside the walls who will know well what we plan—that is my friend Cassandra."

"But how will she know?" Bremusa insisted. "Did she not give that precious obsidian mirror of hers to Iphigenia?"

Myrina nodded. "Yes, she did, but Atisha always swore that Cassandra had no need of mirrors, and when we rode south so long ago to rescue Iphigenia, that proved to be true."

They all shuddered, remembering again how Agamemnon had been willing to sacrifice his own daughter in the hopes of bringing a good sailing wind for his fleet.

"That man is camped just down there." Alcibie shivered. "That man who would have had his own child killed."

Bremusa came in quickly: "All the more reason to trick his guards and get this food into Troy. We will feed new strength into the Trojans and trust that your princess still has her powers and will help us."

CHAPTER THIRTY-THREE

What Mazagardi Steeds Can Do

T HAT NIGHT MYRINA slept soundly, though all through the next day she was restless. She saw Isatis well fed, watered and groomed. Her stomach churned and she was eager to make her move, now that the idea had come to her, but she knew that there would be a much better chance of making it work if she waited till dusk. She rested her cheek against Isatis's shoulders and gained strength and patience from the familiar warm scent of healthy horseflesh. Yildiz too spent the day grooming Silene, whispering her excitement and anger into the flicking ears.

By late noon they had drawn the wagons close to the brow of the hill. Moon Riders, guards, and drivers alike were strained as tense as bowstrings.

Myrina watched and waited until at last the moment came when the sun began to disappear into the dark land-mass of Thrace, across the narrow strip of water that was the passageway to the Black Sea. Then she made a silent signal and she and Yildiz started out, down the hillside toward Troy.

They set off at a steady pace, their cloaks wrapped closely to hide curved bows and full quivers, braided hair flapping freely behind them. They rode close to the hidden Eastern Gate, where a small group of Ant Men camped, but made no attempt to head toward it. As they passed they looked up at the gate towers and saw two guards and a slender figure with long dark hair, braided just like their own, her hand raised to her brow in salute.

Myrina briefly returned the gesture, then rode on to the south, toward the plain.

"Is that her?" Yildiz whispered.

"Oh yes." Myrina rode on, smiling. "Cassandra has not lost her gift."

They passed a huge patch of burnt earth that smelled foul and smoked a little. As Myrina looked closely, wrinkling her nose, she saw that the earth was strewn with the charred bones of both men and beasts. Many a funeral pyre had been built on this spot, until the very earth was hollowed and charred with the burnings. They looked away from the dreadful sight and approached the huge horse corral at the same moderate pace. A few of the Achaean guards looked over toward them with curiosity, but none of them seemed alarmed at the sight of a young woman and a girl riding around the ramparts of the ruined lower town. It was an unusual enough sight for them to stare, but they saw no threat.

One or two of the guards grinned at each other and made crude signs as the pair came closer. If they could find the energy, this might be an opportunity to have a little vulgar fun at the women's expense. The Mazagardi horses peacefully cropped the marsh-watered grass of the plain. Achaean war chariots lined the northern edge, but they looked rusty and unused.

"Fools!" Myrina hissed. "You won't get our steeds between the yokes of your chariots! Our beasts will accept none but those skilled in true horse knowledge." She wanted to laugh at the thought of them trying to set thoroughbreds to pull a chariot, but then the threatened laughter fled as Gul's bloody wounds came into her mind, making her veins seethe with bitter fury. "We will show them," she muttered through gritted teeth. "We will show them what Mazagardi can do."

She turned to nod at Yildiz; the last rays of the sun were fading and it would soon be dark.

Myrina began circling the wooden fence of the corral, while Yildiz slowed Silene up and went on at a leisurely pace, close to where the guards were camped, as though she were admiring the corraled horses. A few of the men shouted crude remarks at her, but they still lolled lazily in front of their tents, eating and drinking.

Myrina rode on at the same steady, ambling pace, but as she circled the fence she began a low whistling, which made many of the horses prick their ears and stop cropping grass; they raised their heads, listening and alert. As she moved on, her whistle changed to the quiet gathering call that came from deep in her throat: "Yoh, yoh, yoh!" At once all the other horses lifted their heads, standing still and attentive. They did not turn or move, just tossed their manes back and forth, a little restive.

The guards looked up from their food to watch uncertainly. "Mad bitches!" one cried. "Are they interfering with the beasts?"

"By Poseidon, I swear there's something amiss!"

"Is yonder witch charming the beasts?"

Myrina knew that she was running out of time, but by now she was at the far end of the corral from Yildiz. The time had come; she raised her fist and took a deep breath, yelling, "Eeey yip! Yip! Yip!"

The horses responded immediately by starting to trot round the field in an orderly manner, all in the same direction. They gathered speed and broke into a canter, quickly forming themselves into the shape of a great turning wheel.

The guards leaped to their feet, swords drawn, the food they'd been eating falling to the ground. "Get them," they cried. "Get the bitches! By Poseidon—to your bows!"

But Yildiz was ready for them. She sent her arrow whizzing through the air to bury its head deep in the neck of the nearest guard. "That's for my mother," she cried. Then she wheeled Silene about and rode away fast toward the higher land to the east, yelling, "Yip, yip, yip-yip, yaar!"

Before the men could get their arrows notched the thudding sound of galloping horses made them glance over their shoulders in terror. The herd moved as one toward the edge of the corral where Yildiz and Silene had been, heads lowered, nostrils flaring wide. Dust rose all about them as they charged toward the fence. Seeing that they were in the pathway, the men dropped their bows and ran.

The first horses leaped the wooden corral with ease, but as the great mass approached, the fences fell under their trampling hooves, snapping like sticks before the wave of tossing manes and rearing heads. The whole herd moved off to the east in a thundering cloud of dust, following in Silene's wake.

Myrina galloped behind on Isatis, echoing the "Yip, yip, yar!," her bow notched and ready.

This was the dangerous bit, for she must try to head off any straggling youngsters who might not yet be fully trained in the Mazagardi ways, and at the same time the guards were recovering from their shock, as she knew they would. The men who'd been camped outside the hidden gate ran down through the lower town to give aid to the horse-guards. One ran at her with a spear, but with the quick twist of the waist that the Moon Riders were famous for she swung right around and let fly an arrow that struck his chest. The man staggered to the side, his spear flying uselessly to the ground. Another spear-thrower came up beside him, but Myrina twisted again, letting another arrow fly, while sure-footed Isatis carried her away into the dust and the darkness, following in the path of the Mazagardi stampede.

In the distance three war chariots appeared from the long trailing spread of the main Achaean camp, but Myrina rode on, smiling fiercely; there was no way that those rumbling chariots could catch up with Mazagardi thoroughbreds galloping at full speed.

Meanwhile in the citadel Cassandra had given the order for the hidden gates to be opened. While under cover of darkness, the caravan of carts piled high with food and wine rumbled safely down the steep hillside and in beside the curtain wall. Soon the sound of cheering filled the streets as people came out of their houses and rushed up onto the walls, waving and singing and dancing about in welcome.

Yildiz rode on through the night, a small brave figure at the head of the great herd; it was only when they were well away from the plain that she slowed down a little, crying, "Low, low-low!"

The horses slackened their pace obediently, but Myrina urged Isatis on to catch up with Yildiz and lead the herd in the direction of Mount Ida, following the guidance of the stars. Myrina's face was filthy and caked with dust, but she dared not stop to find water. They rode on all through the moonlit night, Myrina closing her eyelids from time to time, gratefully trusting Isatis to carry her safely onward. There was no danger of falling asleep, for though she was tired, her heart was racing with delight at the small victory they'd achieved.

They slowed their pace again as the first light of dawn lifted the darkness and they saw in the distance ahead of them the dark shapes of riders on horseback. They cheered as they heard the ululating joy-cry of the Moon Riders. Penthesilea had ridden out with her gang from the Place of Flowing Waters to give them a wild welcome of waving spears. She pulled Fleetwind up beside Isatis and leaned across to hug Myrina, laughing at the filth that covered her comrade and now smudged her own face. "I saw you in my mirror, Snake Lady," she bellowed. "I watched until the darkness made my eyes ache. Well done! Well done! Now our allies will have matchless steeds and plenty to spare!"

Despite the long ride through the night, Yildiz, too, was filled with wild energy and excitement. "I killed a man," she cried, waving her bow at Penthesilea, her eyes gleaming. "And now I shall go back for more."

"Stay here with us and train for the big fight," Penthesilea suggested. "The Trojans have their food now and they will hear of our plans from Coronilla and Bremusa. You two could stay here with us and prepare for battle, then you will have your chance to send your darts into the hearts of many Ant Men."

Myrina was tempted for a moment but then she shook her head. "I saw Cassandra from the distance, and I knew that seeing her in my mirror is not enough; I need to be at her side."

"What about our fierce Little Star?" Penthesilea asked.

Myrina turned to Yildiz. "You must make your own choice—you have earned the right to do that."

"I follow my Snake Mother wherever she goes!"

Myrina smiled at Penthesilea, remembering Atisha's advice. "There are many different ways of joining battle," she said. "We have found our way, me and my Little Star, and I think I will always feel safer with Yildiz at my side."

Penthesilea shrugged her shoulders and laughed.

"Every army needs its secret agents," she said. "It's true enough that two crafty spies may achieve more than a whole gang of armed raiders." A shadow of deep sadness crossed her face. "It is just that such a way is not for me. Take care of our brave young fire star—I swear she will spit flames at those Ant Men."

CHAPTER THIRTY-FOUR

The Streets of Troy

T HEY STAYED TOGETHER that night, feasting around the campfire and performing dances to honor the horses, imitating their delicate stepping movements and their powerful warlike gallop to end the night. The slow, sleepy moon-dance sent them to their sleeping cushions, and in the morning Penthesilea and her gang set off for the Place of Flowing Waters, leading the Mazagardi herd, while Myrina and Yildiz turned their horses back to Troy, braids bound up in scarves like traveling tribeswomen, their bows and arrows hidden once again.

They kept to the high ground, well away from the Achaean camping sites, even though it was a much longer way around. Myrina was cautious, knowing that they'd be killed at once should they be recognized as the women who'd led the horses away. Twice they saw Achaean raiding gangs in the distance, and dismounted to hide among scrub and rocks until the men were well past.

Again they waited till dusk before they attempted to go down toward the hidden Eastern Gate, but they were cheered to see that an armed party of Thracian allies, with their distinctive topknots, were now camped outside the walls in the lower town. Good smells of cooking food and the sound of a blacksmith's hammer were bringing the half-ruined shacks back to life. The hidden doors behind the curtain wall stood open once again and it seemed that the food and the sight of the Mazagardi horses' breakout had truly put new strength and determination into the Trojan cause.

Cassandra was up there on the tower with the lookouts. She came running down to greet them as soon as she saw them leading their horses through the smoky pathways of the Thracian camp.

Myrina and Cassandra hugged each other tightly, while Yildiz hung back a little awkwardly. When at last they pulled away from each other, Cassandra turned to the young girl. "Welcome, Little Star," she said, holding out both her hands to her. "You were a very little star when I last clapped eyes on you; now you shine as bright as the moon."

Yildiz smiled, but could not help but stare at the princess. Though she was used to the body pictures of the Moon Riders that some found strange enough, she hadn't remembered from her early childhood that Cassandra had one green eye and one deep blue, just like the Aegean Sea that edged the plain of Troy.

"You are too thin," Myrina butted in, putting her hands out to circle Cassandra's tiny waist. "You must start eating the food we brought. Remember what Atisha taught us: 'Strength comes from a good appetite.'"

Cassandra laughed. "We've all done nothing but eat since your caravan of carts arrived," she told her. "But before that we were close to starvation." Her voice shook a little and the smile fled. "You will see others just as thin as me. Troy is a very different place from the city you remember. We managed quite well so long as we had allies camped outside and we could keep the top gates open for supplies, but after Hector died . . . Well, all our hopes died, too."

"It must have been hard," Myrina sympathized.

Cassandra nodded. "Particularly for my mother . . . you will see. Of late the Achaeans have set up a guard to stop food getting through to us. I think they meant to starve us out, but never mind that now—you have come to our rescue and my father wishes to see you. I cannot tell you how grateful we are. Come up to the palace and we'll find somewhere for your horses; we have so few left—the stables are crammed with other beasts."

Cassandra led the way and they followed her through

the streets, staring about them as they went. To Yildiz all was new and interesting, but to Myrina, who remembered the elegant, wide walkways of the citadel, there was much that was shocking. Little huts and shacks had been built everywhere, crammed inside the old palatial dwellings. They sheltered ragged children and desperate-looking women, who bowed to them as they passed, crying out in the Luvvian language their gratitude for the food and drink.

They followed Cassandra through winding alleyways and as they walked Myrina had time to look at her friend more closely. Cassandra was now dressed like a beggar, the hems of her once fine, layered skirt frayed and ragged. She remembered the beautiful saffron priestess's gown that her friend had worn when they first met.

As they strode on, women and children fell to kissing their feet, which troubled both Myrina and Yildiz. As Cassandra had warned, many who sheltered inside the walls had arms and legs like sticks, and their bloated bellies told of hunger sickness.

"How are you giving out the food?" Myrina asked, suddenly understanding that it would not be an easy task.

"Don't worry." Cassandra smiled. "Bremusa and Alcibie are taking charge of that and rationing it strictly so that all are fed, but none can gorge. They even rationed my father, and he accepted that they were right!"

Myrina was amazed. She could not imagine the proud old King of Troy taking orders from a young Moon Rider, although Bremusa had always been a determined person to argue with. But when she met him, she understood.

King Priam had grown thin; his shoulders were hunched and he stooped. His face was deeply lined with sorrow and his hands shook as he shuffled forward to welcome them. Tears streamed down his cheeks and he bent to kneel before Myrina, but she begged him not to. It touched her deeply to see this once proud and stubborn man so humble. Queen Hecuba also looked very different: her gown was worn and a stale smell seemed to hang about her. Her once bejeweled throat was grubby and bare. She smiled briefly at Myrina as though she recognised her vaguely, but her eyes quickly moved on, constantly searching each face as though her interest lay elsewhere.

"It's Hector's death that has brought them to this," Cassandra whispered. "While Hector lived and fought for us they had hope, but since his terrible death and dishonorable treatment my mother cannot seem to make sense of anything and she refuses to wash or put on fresh clothes."

Myrina stretched out her hand to comfort her friend. She had heard of troubles turning people's minds like this. "It's not that she has naught to wear?" she asked.

Cassandra shook her head. "She refuses." She smiled ruefully. "And I cannot seem to find time to dress as I should."

In a mist of perfume Helen arrived, followed by Prince Paris. "I remember you, my sweet Moon Rider," she cried, kissing Myrina on both cheeks. Myrina saw that Helen had the sense to dress plainly in these difficult times, but she still smelled of roses and her hair was washed and carefully arranged in gleaming golden ringlets that bore just a touch of silver-gray.

Though Myrina wanted to feel angry with this dangerous woman who had brought such trouble to Anatolia, she found herself smiling at her. Helen still had her beauty, but it was her warmth and charm that made it impossible to hate her. She had borne Paris two sons during the years they'd been besieged by the Achaeans, and her shape was just a little more matronly than before.

Myrina saw that Yildiz gaped in open-mouthed admiration at the Queen of Sparta.

"And who is this proud warrior-child?" Helen asked, stretching out her hand to stroke Yildiz' cheek.

"Yildiz, my sister's child. Her mother was killed by the Ant Men and now she calls me Mother."

Helen's eyes clouded over. "So much death," she murmured. "And I fear that you will hold me to blame."

260

"No." Yildiz spoke up at once. "The Ant Men are to blame."

Helen bent to kiss her. "Thank you for that, my darling."

Myrina sighed and shook her head. "You are just the excuse they use," she acknowledged. "We Mazagardi knew well enough that they would come sooner or later; my father always warned of it. They want our lands—they want to control the passage through to the Black Sea."

Paris came to join them and bowed politely to Myrina. He was thinner and his hair was flecked with gray; a lot of his swagger seemed to have gone and his cheek bore a long scar. "I remember the bareback rider," he said. "We are greatly indebted to you. My father begs that you will eat with us."

When Myrina entered the great feasting hall of the palace, she was again shaken by the changes that had taken place. The walls, once covered with gleaming brazen shields, were bare, the tables scrubbed clean, but worn and battered. Once gleaming with golden bowls and goblets, they were now laid with gray earthenware—though at least there were plenty of wholesome olives, bread, and cheese, which Myrina recognized as part of the supplies they had brought. She smiled with amusement as she saw that Bremusa had taken charge of the palace kitchen and was ordering servants back and forth.

"Thank goodness you are here." Bremusa came to clap her on the back, full of relief to see her. "We were worried that you'd get into trouble out there. Your charge of horses was a sight to see, Snake Lady. Like a rolling thunderstorm of dust and manes! We couldn't stop to cheer when we saw you take off, but by Maa we cheered once we were safe inside."

Myrina and Yildiz were invited to sit at the high table and Myrina was surprised to see that now the men mingled together with the women in a much more equal manner than before. Ragged women and children crammed together next to Thracian warriors on the lower tables. The hall thrummed with the babble of voices, all talking and arguing in many different languages, some with voices raised in frustration, others waving their hands about, trying to make themselves understood by using signs: it seemed that many boundaries had been removed by the sharing of bitter hardship and suffering.

Cassandra saw her taking it all in and smiled, and Myrina suddenly understood. "You have done this," she approved. "You have got rid of the separate tables for men."

"There are so few men left, it wasn't worth it," her

friend replied. "We women must now do much of the work the men once did, and the weaving slaves work all over the citadel. There's no time for producing fine fabrics—that's another reason why our clothes hang together by threads."

Myrina remembered the royal princes' table, crowded about with Priam's many offspring, Hector at their head. The warrior lord Aeneas, leader of the Dardanian allies, seemed to have taken charge of the defense of Troy; he sat at the head of the table in what had once been Hector's place. There was Paris there beside him, and his younger brother Deiphobus, whom she had never liked— but where were the others and their serving men, grooms, and armor-bearers? The chilling answer came to her as she remembered the dreadful stinking pit of ashes that she'd skirted outside the citadel walls.

CHAPTER THIRTY-FIVE

The Misery of Troy

MYRINA COULD EAT little as the meal progressed, her head so full of memories of musicians who strummed on lyres to accompany beautifully clad dancers. The diners were served now by slave women in worn smocks, rope anklets tied above their bare feet. Myrina could see that they had been brought in from the weaving sheds and dye tubs, for some of them had arms and feet tainted purple or blue.

Even before the war started, Myrina had hated the sight of the long low sheds where these women were tied up at their work. They had spent their days fastened to a bench, while they dyed and spun and wove the beautiful fabrics that had once contributed to the riches of Troy. At least now they were able to move about the citadel, instead of being fastened up all day.

She frowned at the sight. "Are the slave women still locked up at night?" she asked Cassandra.

The princess looked shamefaced, but she nodded. "I cannot manage to get them real freedom," she said. "My father insists that they are still slaves. He sees them as the last of the booty that is left to him, for he gave his gold to Achilles when he begged him to return Hector's body. You cannot know how terrible . . ."

"Oh yes, I do know." Myrina touched her friend's shoulder in compassion. All of Anatolia had heard how Achilles had not been satisfied by killing Troy's bravest warrior, but had abused Hector's battered body by dragging it behind his chariot in the dust, while his parents and sisters, watching from the tower, wept helplessly; how Priam had taken all the gold and jewels left to him and humiliated himself before the Achaean warrior, before he had at last been given his son's body.

But then Myrina's critical gaze went back to the slave women, who quietly served food with hands stained red and purple. Why should they suffer more than anyone else in this miserable place? Cassandra picked up on her thoughts. "It isn't simple," she said quietly. "I could go to the guards and order them to release the slaves, and even though it would be against my father's wishes, I would do it. But then where would they go? If we let them out of the city, they'd walk straight into the path of Achaean raiding gangs and Ant Men. That would be worse than anything."

"Yes," Myrina had to agree. "That would be worse than anything."

Cassandra looked more troubled than ever. "I know a little of that from my friend Chryseis," she whispered.

"Where is Chryseis?" Myrina asked, remembering with warmth the serene and gentle priestess of Apollo, who had always been a true friend to Cassandra.

Cassandra's mouth was grim. "I will take you to her after we have eaten," she said.

Yildiz could hardly eat for staring about her. For a child who until these last few weeks had known nothing but her home-tent, this palace and its wild mixture of people was astonishing. Still her admiring gaze kept going back to Helen. "Does Queen Helen have her mother with her?" she asked.

Myrina shook her head uncertainly and asked Cassandra, "Who is the old woman who sits at Helen's left side? She seems to help her as though she were her own mother, but I know it cannot be."

"No," Cassandra agreed. "Her name is Aethra. Have you never heard of her?"

Myrina frowned. "I've heard that name, yes . . . but I thought that Aethra was the mother of Theseus, the fierce warrior lord who stole away Antiope the Moon Rider?"

Cassandra nodded. "This war brings together many

strange people, and Theseus stole women wherever he went. Just like Antiope, he once stole Helen from her home, when she was naught but a child. Her brothers fought to get her back and they won. Part of the punishment they insisted on was that Theseus's queenly mother, Aethra, should be forced to work as handmaid to Helen for the rest of her life."

"That's not fair," Yildiz butted in. "Why should his mother have to suffer the blame?"

"Many things are not fair, Little Star," Myrina told her. "So that fragile old woman is the mother of Theseus?"

"Yes." Cassandra nodded. "She came here as Helen's servant, but . . ." She sighed. "You know Helen—she finds a way to get on with everyone—she truly has a gift for it—and over the years the two have become friends and Helen does indeed look after her as though she were her mother."

Myrina sighed. "It seems that you cannot be angry with Helen, no matter how hard you try."

"That's not all," Cassandra continued. "Aethra's two grandsons camp outside the walls and fight with the Achaeans. The old woman has seen them from the walls and Helen and I have begged my father to let the old one go free. I understand the confusion that those young men must struggle with: one of them is the son of your Moon Rider Antiope, the child she refused to leave. Those two

Achaean lords would sail away at once, were their grandmother freed, but my father can still be a very stubborn man."

Myrina shook her head, her own thoughts in confusion. Such a terrible muddle this war had brought.

After the meal Cassandra took a bowl of bread and olive oil for Chryseis and asked Myrina to go with her. Yildiz followed them, as ever, but Cassandra shook her head in concern. "Leave the child with Bremusa," she insisted. "This is not for her to see."

Myrina persuaded the girl to go with Bremusa to the stables to see that Isatis and Silene were well cared for, then followed her friend up to the sleeping chambers, feeling more troubled at every step. "What is it that Yildiz may not see?" she asked.

Cassandra stopped. "Chryseis was captured—did you know?"

Myrina shook her head. "In my mirror-visions I looked only for you."

"Well . . . she was taken from Apollo's temple on the island of Tenedos by Agamemnon himself and used by him as a concubine."

"Oh! Poor priestess," Myrina whispered. She remembered the quiet dignity that had always surrounded Chryseis.

"Well," Cassandra continued, "her father had taken refuge on the island of Sminthe, where he was building a new temple to Apollo. But he left the safety of that place and went bravely to the camp to demand her return—and surprisingly she was handed over. They say that the crazy priest Chalcis swore that all the Achaeans' troubles and the sickness in their camps were due to the taking of Chryseis; her capture had offended the sun god. So she was escorted back here by Odysseus and her father was allowed to return safely to Sminthe."

Myrina was amazed. "So this time Chalcis was of some use to us?"

Cassandra's blue and green eyes glinted with scorn. "We know that the sickness in the Achaeans' camp is due to the fact that their tents and huts are set up in the middle of a marsh, with mists and mosquitoes on every side. I cannot understand how that man thinks—but still, we got Chryseis, though she came back to us a different person. She was pregnant with Agamemnon's child and now she has a son, but the bitter humiliation of her treatment has changed her beyond recognition. Her father left her in my care, for he could do nothing to comfort her."

Myrina frowned and shook her head. "But none of this is blame to her."

"No," Cassandra agreed grimly, "but I cannot seem to

make her see it that way. She will barely eat or drink and never leaves her room, seeing none but me. I hoped that maybe your presence might take her back to a happier time, before all this trouble came. She always used to ask after you and remembered with pleasure the girl who danced on horseback."

Myrina was apprehensive, but she nodded. "Let us see her," she said.

Chryseis was indeed a shocking sight. Though Cassandra had kept her bedding clean and decent, she lay staring blankly at the bottom of her bed, her once silky hair falling all over her face in a wild, rumpled mess. Her bedgown was askew and her bony fingers constantly picked at her arms, so that raw, scaly wounds covered her skin. She was very thin.

Myrina was deeply shaken to see her in such a state, but went to sit on the bed beside her. "Priestess," she murmured. "Lady Priestess, do you know me—Myrina the Moon Rider?"

For a moment a look of recognition came, but then Chryseis turned her head away and would look only at the wall.

"I must try to feed her," Cassandra said.

Myrina watched uncomfortably as Cassandra put the bowl down beside the bed. Then, talking gently all the time, she forced a small piece of oil-soaked bread between her friend's lips; a few sips of wine followed. Myrina could think of nothing else to do but take Chryseis's scabby hand in hers and stroke it.

Cassandra nodded encouragement as the priestess's fierce glare began to soften and her eyelids drooped. At last she fell asleep and they went quietly from her room.

"It seems a small thing, but that was good," Cassandra told Myrina. "She rarely sleeps and I think it does at least bring her a little relief."

"Where is the child?" Myrina asked.

"One of the slave women is acting as wet nurse." Cassandra dropped her voice to a whisper. "Chryseis will not feed the child; she will not even look at him."

Myrina sank for a moment into deep despair. Seeing Chryseis brought so low was a terrible thing and she felt a heavy lump of pain dragging at her stomach. The joy at the success of the horse stampede had fled.

But Cassandra hadn't finished yet. "I have something else I wish to show you. Can you manage a short walk, or do you need to sleep? You must be exhausted."

"Is it more misery?" Myrina asked uncertainly.

Cassandra looked thoughtful. "Yes and no," she said, and for a moment Myrina remembered the irritation that she had once felt toward this strange princess who sometimes insisted on speaking in riddles.

Cassandra saw it and smiled. "Yes, there is misery," she explained. "But there is hope, too, and something that I am sure will interest you."

CHAPTER THIRTY-SIX

Those Who Howl at the Moon

CURIOSITY GOT THE better of exhaustion and Myrina followed Cassandra down through the citadel past once elegant palaces, now squatters' camps. Smoking fires were everywhere, and the smell of cooked salt fish from the Sea of Marmara. Around every corner they met with greetings and thanks to the Snake Lady. They turned away from the main route and went down toward the Southern Gate through a narrow back alley. As they walked Myrina became aware of a repetitive, rhythmic sound—the beat of a drum and women's voices rising in song. They came to the long, low weaving sheds, where once the women slaves had worked all day and which were still their sleeping quarters.

Myrina stopped, listening with wonder, for there was something familiar about the sound, though the melody and words were quite unknown to her.

"This happens every night," Cassandra whispered.

"They almost sound like . . ." Myrina murmured. "They almost sound like the Moon Riders."

"Yes," Cassandra agreed. "I think it is something very like."

As they moved closer to the sheds, a slight movement could be seen through the wooden slatted gateway. Two guards sat there, wearily playing knucklebones, ignoring the sounds that were so unexpected here in the back streets of war-torn Troy. Myrina went straight up to press her face against the wooden slats of the gates. The guards looked up at her a little uncertainly. "We ought to start to charge." One of them guffawed. "A coin or a kiss to see the bitches howling at the moon." But then they saw Cassandra and scrambled to their feet to bow.

"That is the Snake Lady who brought us food," another man whispered, roughly nudging his loud-mouthed companion.

The joker turned serious at once and bowed to Myrina respectfully. "Forgive me, Snake Lady. I would do anything to please you."

Myrina ignored them as she stared through the locked gates at the rows of women, the moonlight full on their faces. They were fastened to hard wooden sleeping boards by ropes tied around their ankles, which meant that they could move very little. But still the sense of movement was very powerful. They swung their hips from side to side as one, their feet shuffling to the left, then to the right. Each one held hands with the women next but one, so that a crisscross pattern of linked arms formed in front of their bodies. Heads swung to the right, then to the left, then rolled down toward their chests and up to the right again, following the shape of a crescent moon.

Myrina gasped. "They move and sing in perfect time," she whispered.

"Yes," Cassandra answered. "And look at their faces."

"Yes! What faces . . . rapt, serene . . . almost happy. Is this a sacred dance for them? Where do they come from?"

Cassandra shook her head. "They hail from distant regions and speak in different tongues. This singing and dancing is a patchwork of their many traditions, but I think it has indeed become a sacred dance for them."

Myrina turned back to watch them again, seeing that some were pale skinned, some dark and others black as obsidian.

"I often come down here to watch them," Cassandra told her. "There is some strange comfort in their music and their dance. I use them in my own service each day—as many as I can. It is my way of protecting them from warriors who think they may use them as they like. I have learned that each woman brings something of her own to the dance and their ritual grows more powerful with every step and turn."

"Yes." Myrina understood at once. As the Moon Riders drew power from their own dancing, so these desperate women had also found a way to give one another strength, enough to carry them through the hardships they must bear.

"There are children here," Cassandra whispered. "Trojan warriors and their allies use these women for their pleasure, but now the men's bones lie charred outside our gates and the children who have survived sleep over there in the shed."

"Why doesn't your father stop this?" Myrina asked sharply. "Can't you make him stop it?"

Cassandra flinched a little. "He thinks it is a warrior's right. He says, 'What else are slaves for?'"

Myrina sighed. She knew well enough the fate of women captured in war. Hadn't Antiope been just such a one, but she had lived with Theseus in comfort, as a captured queen, not chained to a bed board as these women were. She was filled with anger and sadness at their plight, but also with a wondering admiration at their resilience. Somehow they had found a way to survive, as Chryseis had not.

"They must be freed." She spoke with utter determination. "But you are right: not as prey to the Achaean wolves. We must think carefully and find a way to do it."

"One thing that I *can* do is to order one of these women to serve you as your maid," Cassandra ventured.

"Maid?" Myrina looked fiercely at her friend and spoke indignantly. "I have never needed a maid!"

Cassandra put her hand to her mouth to cover what was almost a giggle, the first truly happy sound that Myrina had heard from her since she had arrived in Troy. Suddenly the weary princess, burdened with practical cares and tragedy, was gone. "Fool!" she whispered, stamping her foot, but still laughing. "You can have her wait on you or not as you wish, but this will give you a means of communicating with them and finding out more. I will send you Akasya, an Egyptian who speaks the Luvvian tongue."

Myrina understood then and nodded. "My brain is full of raw cotton," she agreed. "There is so much to think about. Yes, send Akasya to me."

Cassandra's laughter vanished quickly and her voice shook a little. "I will help all I can, but . . . my mind is clouded with frightening visions. I thought that Troy couldn't suffer any more after Hector was killed, but now I see even greater sorrows to come."

"What greater sorrows?"

Cassandra shook her head violently from side to side.

Myrina sighed. Cassandra's gift of seeing had always

been a great and terrible gift. Sometimes she could put it to use, but more often the visions were unclear and her family simply thought her crazy when she tried to tell them what she saw. The shabby princess clenched her fists in frustration, then turned to rest her head against the once elegant façade of a Trojan house, a small trickle of blood running from her nose. She wiped it quickly away, but her words seemed to echo her body's response. "There's misery and terror in the very stone of our walls; I see our streets running with blood."

"Then you must escape," Myrina insisted, frowning.

Cassandra shook her head. "My fate is not important."

"Do you know it?" Myrina asked. "Can you see what is to happen to you?"

"No . . . it's not clear," Cassandra replied quietly. "But I am troubled with dreams of horses. Sometimes there's a great gray horse that gallops about our city and kicks wildly at our walls so that they begin to crumble; at other times I see a horse that is stiff like a statue and, though its legs are still, it comes toward us, moving steadily to the citadel."

"How can it move and be still?" Myrina's head was aching.

"I don't know, but it comes on and on and breaks through our walls."

Myrina was so tired that her patience was short, even

though she was glad to be with Cassandra again.

"Then there is the tiny firefly," Cassandra went on. "It flits around the Achaean tents, setting them aflame. And there is the other dream, and again it is full of horses and you, Myrina. You are riding Isatis and leading a great herd. So when you came to take the Mazagardi horses, I knew that my other dreams must speak some truth as well."

Myrina struggled to understand. "You always had the gift of true sight," she said. "And Atisha swore that we should listen to you. But . . . when we took the Mazagardi horses, it wasn't me who led them; it was Yildiz. I followed behind. Did you not see Yildiz in your dream?"

Cassandra shook her head firmly. "No. It was you who led the way and I fear there was a terrible feeling of loneliness all about you. You were leading a great herd and yet you were somehow terribly alone!"

Myrina shivered. "Send Akasya to me in the morning," she cut in sharply. She suddenly didn't want to hear any more. "Now I must rest before I fall asleep on my feet."

Myrina found Bremusa in her sleeping chamber, soothing Yildiz by stroking her brow. "She is in a strange, unsettled mood," Bremusa whispered as she left to find her own chamber.

Myrina lay down beside Yildiz and closed her eyes at last.

"I love you, Snake Mother," Yildiz whispered. "I will always love you."

Myrina smiled wearily. "And I you," she murmured. "Go to sleep, Little Star—it has been a very long day."

Myrina woke with a jolt, suddenly aware that there was an empty, cold space beside her, though the morning light was only just beginning to creep into the room. "Yildiz! Yildiz, where are you?" she called. She got up and stumbled sleepily about the room and out into the passageway. "Yildiz!" she called again.

Coronilla came tearing up the stairway toward her with a face like thunder. At the sight of her, a terrible lurch of sickness swung from one side of Myrina's stomach to the other.

"I think you had better come," Coronilla whispered.

"What is it? Tell me!" Myrina clenched her fists tightly.

"The princess says it is Odysseus, the Lord of Ithaca."

"Ah yes—he is their go-between. Has he come to talk?"

For all that she was so wiry and strong, Coronilla's chin trembled like a child's. "No. He walks toward the Southern Gate," she said. "And in his arms he bears . . . a burden."

"What burden?"

Coronilla shook her head. "We have seen them from the Southern Tower. His servant leads a bay mare; it is Silene."

"He carries a burden? You mean he carries Yildiz?"

Coronilla's face was grim as she nodded.

"No!" Myrina cried. "No!" She raised her hand and smashed her clenched fist against the limestone wall, grazing her knuckles so brutally that they started to bleed. "Yildiz! She said . . . Last night . . . Oh, how could she be so foolish?"

"Come quickly!" Coronilla grabbed her arm. "There may be hope! Do not waste your strength on anger."

Myrina unclenched her bleeding fist and they ran.

CHAPTER THIRTY-SEVEN

The Firefly

CASSANDRA HAD GIVEN orders for the huge wooden doors of the Southern Gate to be opened and now a group of Trojan guards escorted her through the streets of the lower town. A small crowd followed the princess, curious to see what was going on. This was not the usual way that Odysseus approached the city when he wished to issue threats or agree a brief truce for funerals.

He reached the first dusty, crumbling shacks and stood still, waiting. Cassandra went to him, Myrina and Coronilla racing after her. They caught up just as Cassandra reached the stocky figure. He hung his head, his face weary and lined, bent with concern over the small shape of Yildiz.

"We meet again, Princess." He bowed. "I do not think there is much hope for your brave little firefly, but I would not see her trampled beneath the feet of the Ant Men."

"Firefly?" Cassandra's face contorted in sudden torment and her hands flew up to rake at her cheeks. "Ah no!"

"She may be small, but she has the sting of a wasp. The little one snatched a brand from the watchmen's fire and sent a hail of burning arrows into Achilles' tents, so that half of them are burnt and his men stagger about in fury, trying to put them out."

Myrina pushed through the staring crowd and took Yildiz in her arms. A terrible pain constricted her throat. She tried to speak, but nothing would come, so she turned and marched immediately back to the citadel, leaving Cassandra to deal with the King of Ithaca.

Yildiz was bleeding profusely from what looked like a spear wound to her throat, her cheeks deathly white, eyes closed.

"Let me help carry her," Coronilla begged, striding along beside Myrina.

Myrina shook her head. "Run ahead!" she snapped. "Fetch water and binding cloths."

Coronilla said no more and broke into a run. Myrina could hear her shouting to the slaves as she leaped up the stairs.

Bremusa and Alcibie were waiting in Myrina's chamber with warm water and bindings and ointment, but as Myrina lowered Yildiz onto the bed she saw that her breathing was very shallow. Her eyelids fluttered and just for a moment a bright gleam of joy appeared on her face. "I got them, Snake Mother," she murmured. Then she closed her eyes and ceased to breathe.

"No!" Myrina gasped. "This cannot happen. No . . . it is too much." She slumped on the floor beside the bed, unable to get her own breath, her mind spinning. There was a moment of silent disbelief, but then Bremusa stooped to rub her back, whispering comforting words. Cassandra came in, her face white and strained, eyes swimming with tears as she looked down at Yildiz's still, small body, the worn linen sheet beneath her stained with blood.

Suddenly all Myrina could feel was a blazing anger that shot through her whole body. "Firefly!" she screamed, pointing a shaking finger at Cassandra. "Firefly! You saw it all and you didn't warn us. You let it happen, just let it happen!"

Cassandra's face became a frozen mask of horror, but she said nothing, just turned and fled the room.

Myrina's gang carefully cleaned the small body and prepared it for funeral rites. Myrina herself sat watching them in shocked silence, unable to move. Priam, Hecuba, Helen, and Paris all came to the chamber to pay their respects and offer sympathy. Coronilla answered them courteously through her tears, but Myrina still couldn't speak. Gradually the heated rage began to subside a little and at last a biting, painful tenderness flooded her whole being, as she looked across at Yildiz's white face. She got up and went to sit beside the bed, now draped in clean, worn linen, with bunches of bloodred poppies lovingly laid on the coverlet beside the dead girl. She took Yildiz's cold hand in hers and looked for a long time into the childlike face. "She is almost smiling," she murmured.

Bremusa touched her shoulder. "Yes, she is smiling; we must take some comfort from that. Our Little Star died like a true Moon Rider. Alcibie says they are calling her Young Amazon in the streets of Troy, just as they did in Athens when Hippolyta was killed."

Later that day the serious-faced Lord Aeneas came to visit Myrina. "This little one shall have a royal funeral," he told her. "Odysseus has sent a message that they will keep a truce while we hold our rites and build another funeral pyre."

Myrina shuddered with horror as she remembered the foul pit of ashes that she had seen outside the Eastern Gate. "No," she whispered. "We cannot build her pyre there by the upper gates."

Aeneas bowed his head, but looked puzzled. "What else would you wish for her?"

Myrina's thoughts swam around her head in muddled desperation, but then suddenly she had the answer clear: "The Tomb of Dancing Myrina." It was the mound of the ancient queen of the Moon Riders for whom she herself had been named. "That is the only place nearby that is right for Yildiz."

"Ah yes." Aeneas understood. "But it is far from the citadel gates, out in no-man's-land, close to where the warriors gather for battle. I do not know . . . but I will do my best." He turned and left the chamber.

The Tomb of Dancing Myrina brought thoughts of Cassandra back. Myrina remembered the princess's strange mystical stories of when she was a young child growing up in a happier Troy. "Where is Cassandra?" she asked, puzzled. "Why is she not here?"

The young women looked at one another, distressed and worried. Then Bremusa folded her arms and did not mince her words. "The princess fled and I'd not blame her if she never spoke to you again. You made it pretty clear, by Maa you did, that you blamed our Little Star's death on her!"

Myrina looked up into Bremusa's round face and a vague memory came back to her. "I did," she murmured, "and I was wrong; it is on my own shoulders that the blame must fall. You told me that she was in a strange mood, but . . . I was tired and wouldn't listen."

Coronilla crouched beside her and stroked her arm. "Nothing could have stopped Yildiz. Not Cassandra, not you—none of us. She was secretly determined to get her revenge, carrying burning anger within her all the way from the flames of her home-tent to Troy."

Wearily Myrina nodded, then stumbled to her feet. "But where is Cassandra? I must put things right with her."

"Nobody has seen her all day," Alcibie told her. "But there is a slave woman called Akasya who has been waiting in the passage, saying that Cassandra sent her to you."

"Ah yes." Myrina struggled to clear her mind. She went outside and sure enough there was a young woman, standing erect, rough rope links about her ankles.

"Akasya?"

"Yes . . . Snake Lady. I am your slave to do your bidding all through the day, but I must return to the huts at night, after the evening meal."

Myrina nodded. It seemed a lifetime ago that she had stood there with Cassandra watching the dancing slaves. "Where is the princess now?"

Akasya shook her head. "I do not know for sure, but when the princess is troubled she often goes to the temple of the Trojan sun god and talks to Theano the priestess."

"Can you take me there?"

"Yes, Snake Lady."

Akasya led the way and Myrina hurried after her. She found the princess white and trembling, deep in conversation with an older woman who wore a ragged saffron priestess's robe. Cassandra looked up and, when she saw that it was Myrina, turned her face away.

Myrina went to kneel before her. "Forgive me, my friend," she whispered.

Cassandra turned around at once and hugged her. The priestess quietly left them and they wept together for what seemed a long time. When at last they raised their heads, Myrina remembered her maid. Akasya stood obediently in the shadows by the doorway, her own face wet with silent tears.

Aeneas greeted Myrina the next morning. "The King of Ithaca has arranged a truce, Snake Lady," he said. "We may lead a funeral procession out to the Tomb of Dancing Myrina and there build a pyre. None of the Achaean warriors will attack until sunrise tomorrow."

The Moon Riders thanked him and at noon a procession headed out through the lower town, carrying the small body toward the sacred mound.

What was left of the Trojan royal family came with them to the Southern Gate, but Priam declined to go farther, offering his apologies, uncertain that the Achaean truce would respect him and his own. Myrina was glad to leave them behind, for she felt that they had little knowledge of Yildiz. Cassandra insisted on accompanying them, and as the smaller party walked farther out into no-man's-land Myrina saw that Akasya was there unbidden, moving determinedly behind her new mistress, keeping her distance but always there within call.

Myrina's gang and Cassandra performed the slow dance for the dead about the burning pyre.

"I was the first to hold her in my arms when she was born," Myrina whispered as the dance came to a quiet ending.

"And you were the last to hold her when she died," Bremusa agreed. "That was right and good."

CHAPTER THIRTY-EIGHT

The War God's Daughter

S THE FUNERAL pyre burned low, the sun began to set in the west. Myrina looked at the ragged fringe of dark shapes that were Agamemnon's huts and tents all along the dark peaceful blue of the Aegean Sea. The smoke from their campfires rose into the sky and small movements of carts and wagons made them look almost domestic. Each war leader's own small camp was set slightly separate from the others, as with any great meeting of the nomadic tribes. The thought came to Myrina that most of them were just ordinary men, who must wish desperately that they were at home. Why did they not pack up and go?

As she stood there, watching, two Trojan guards rode out from the Southern Gate and spoke to Coronilla. She came at once to Myrina. "We should go back within the city walls," she said. "The guards have seen dust rising in the east."

"They swore there would be no attack." Bremusa's hand went to her bow strap.

Cassandra turned her head toward Mount Ida. "This is no Achaean attack; the War God's Daughter comes," she said, pointing toward the distant peak, her blue and green eyes staring wildly. "She comes at the head of an army and they will fight for Troy."

They all looked at her with concern.

"Who comes?" Myrina asked, her mind still cloudy with sadness. But though Cassandra gave no answer, she suddenly knew. "Ah . . . it's Penthesilea. I should have known. She has looked in her mirror and seen Yildiz—she has seen it all."

"Of course," Bremusa agreed, suddenly animated. "She could not watch our firefly die and stand by. She'll lead the Thracians and the Phrygians to avenge the child, and I say she does right!"

"But have the Ethiopians come?" Myrina asked. "Has she got the allies all together at her back? I should have looked in my mirror. I should have looked for Tomi."

"I can see them," Bremusa cried, pointing in the direction of Ida.

Everyone turned to look and it wasn't long before they could all see the dust rising and the dark movement of riders.

"They are here!" Bremusa was shouting wildly and

waving. On the far eastern horizon the shapes of warriors on horseback with banners aloft, riding fast in full body armor, emerged from the cloud of dust that rose before them. They looked magnificent.

Myrina's gang leaped up and down, lifting their voices in the ululating Moon Riders' joy-cry. Myrina could not help but feel a surge of fierce pride at the sight of them as they galloped over the higher land above the plain of Troy.

The Achaeans had got wind of what was happening and the warning sound of horns could be heard all along the camps by the sea. Penthesilea rode at the head of the army, leading the warrior priestesses in their battle caps and leather greaves, racing toward the Mound of Dancing Myrina. Thracians, Phrygians, and Pelagian warriors followed, fierce Paeonian bowmen, muscular Cicones, Mysians, and Carians, all armed to the teeth. They slowed their horses as they approached and dismounted, gathering about the smoking pyre, falling on their knees to pay their respects to the lost firefly.

Myrina was deeply moved to see so many battle-hardened warriors honoring Yildiz, but she looked about, anxiously longing for a glimpse of Tomi's broad shoulders and square jaw. He was not to be seen and nowhere could she spy the dark skins of the Ethiopian warriors. "Where is King Memnon?" she cried.

Cassandra shook her head and her mouth was grim. "I fear our brave Penthesilea has come without the Ethiopians."

Myrina strode through the crowd toward Penthesilea. She grabbed her by the shoulder and shouted at her, "Where are the Ethiopians? Where is King Memnon?"

"A fine welcome!" Penthesilea's eyes flashed dangerously. "I swore that I would avenge your Little Star and so I shall. I will not wait for warriors from distant lands, who may never come!"

"You swore to wait for King Memnon," Myrina spat back at her. "You have come at half strength!"

Penthesilea rose to her full height, snarling with fury. "Half strength? I will show you what half strength can do! I shall blow the war horns and ride at once to Achilles' tents and challenge that foul murderer to fight. How dare you challenge my right?"

Myrina, half dazed, saw that Akasya had moved fast to her side, but then Cassandra stepped in front of them both.

"No, dear friend," the princess said calmly to Penthesilea. "The Achaeans have sworn a truce today so that we may lay Yildiz properly to rest. It would bring shame to her memory if that truce were broken. Tomorrow when the sun rises—that is the time for you to fight."

Cassandra's words cooled Penthesilea's anger, for the thought of acting dishonorably was terrible to the fierce Moon Rider.

Myrina's anger and disappointment also slipped away. Penthesilea had spoken fairly. What right had she to decide what should or should not be done? Surely her own carelessness had been partly to blame for the loss of Yildiz? "Forgive me," she said, catching Penthesilea by her shoulder in a more loving way. "My anger at Yildiz's fate makes me turn on those most dear to me. I should have protected the child and kept her safe—it is I whom you should challenge, for I have neglected her."

Penthesilea engulfed her at once in a fierce hug. "I saw her in my mirror," she whispered. "I watched as every flaming arrow flew to its target. None of us could have prevented it. Cassandra is right! Tomorrow we will rid the shores of Anatolia of these murdering invaders. Come, Snake Lady, you and I must not fall out."

"No—we will not," Myrina agreed.

Then the army of Trojan allies led their horses steadily toward the city, while lanterns and lights along the shoreline bobbed in the distance as great numbers of Achaean warriors watched them with swords drawn and spears at the ready.

King Priam stood at the Southern Gate to greet them,

along with Aeneas. Hecuba was there, dressed in her finest gown and looking cleaner, her face wreathed in smiles. "My son is coming home, my son is coming home," she whispered to all who would listen.

The arrival of Penthesilea had been seen from the high towers of the citadel and at once a feast had been prepared. There were so many horses to accommodate that corrals had to be set up again outside the walls, but this time with Trojan guards. Myrina could not help but feel that it was unwise to hold such a feast, as the food they had brought from the Isle of Marble was half consumed already.

"We couldn't persuade your father to hold back a little?" she asked Cassandra.

The princess looked as sad as ever. "My father is a stubborn man," she whispered. "He will rarely listen to advice and I suppose he believes that tomorrow will bring us victory at last."

"And what do you think?"

Cassandra shook her head. "I see a bloodred mist hanging over the Trojan plain," she murmured. "Nothing can be stopped. Nothing can be changed."

"We do not need this feast—it is foolishness," Myrina insisted. "Our food should be saved. Everything is going wrong—I can see that so clearly—and yet I have no power to make things different."

Cassandra looked at her sharply—a look of recognition, almost of joy.

Myrina understood. "This is how you feel, isn't it?"

"Yes," the princess replied. "All the time, all the time! But it is not in our power to change these things and somehow we must accept them. There is good there as well as evil. We will have a feast and perhaps it is only right that our firefly should have her funeral supper."

"Yes," Myrina agreed at last. "That is the only way that I can face it. This is a feast for Yildiz."

Akasya came forward with a clean gown for her to wear, one of Cassandra's, worn and mended but still beautiful. Myrina challenged the slave woman: "You were not afraid of the Moon Riders' fierce leader then?"

"No." Akasya shook her head. "In the streets of Troy they call her the War God's Daughter, but now I realize that she would not have hurt you, Snake Lady."

"I wouldn't be too sure of that!" Myrina smiled.

The feast was lavish by recent standards; wine was mixed and poured and all the Trojans raised their cups to Penthesilea. "To the War God's Daughter!" they cried.

Helen and Paris made a grand entrance in their finery and jewels, rarely seen in war-torn Troy, their two small children, led by their nurses, behind them.

The War God's Daughter eyed them both with suspicion, but Helen worked her charm even on such a one as Penthesilea, who was little impressed by jewels and fine clothes.

Later, flushed with wine and compliments, Penthesilea told Myrina that she could understand the prince's desire for the woman. "She's not as beautiful as I had heard," Penthesilea judged. "But still the woman has a warmth and a vulnerability that makes me want to protect her, and . . . despite her look of helplessness, she's no fool."

"You are right," Myrina agreed. Helen had pointed out to her that while Troy was rejoicing in the arrival of Penthesilea, on the shoreward side of the city three small boats had set sail from Agamemnon's camp over to the island of Tenedos.

"What do you think that means?" Myrina had asked.

Helen smiled her charming smile and her mouth twitched a little wryly at the corners. "Reinforcements?" she replied, shrugging her shoulders.

Myrina said nothing. Whether there were Achaean reinforcements coming or not, there would be no stopping Penthesilea from fighting in the morning, of that she was very sure.

CHAPTER THIRTY-NINE

Atonement

MYRINA COULD NOT sleep that night. Her mind was full of pictures of Yildiz, first a tiny baby in her arms, then riding like a wild firefly and setting Achilles' tents aflame. At last she got out of bed and went to look for water. Her stomach had recently been trained to accept only a small amount of food, and the unaccustomed feast and wine had left her feeling bloated. She wandered down the marble passageway to where the water ewer and its little beaker were kept, and saw that a torch still blazed in the chamber allotted to Penthesilea.

"Another one who cannot sleep?" she said as she saw her friend sitting on the balcony, looking down at the lights and fires of the distant Achaean camp.

Penthesilea turned to her and Myrina was shocked to see traces of tears on her cheeks. In all the years they had ridden together, she had never known Penthesilea to weep.

Myrina stood there uncertainly, feeling that she had intruded into something private, but Penthesilea held out her hand. "Come sit beside me, Snake Lady," she begged. "I have need of one who can bolster my courage."

"You?" Myrina was stunned. "Your courage has never failed."

Penthesilea laughed low. "But tonight it fails me. I have been waiting all my life for this moment and tomorrow I must face Achilles, the dreaded Ant Man himself. His followers swear that he is immortal, you know. They say his mother was a magical sea nymph and that she made him invincible."

Myrina went to sit close beside her. "But we do not believe in such a thing," she insisted. "All of us must return to the womb of Mother Earth and Achilles will not escape that fate."

"No, he will not," Penthesilea agreed. "But how many more will he send before him?"

Myrina sat in silence, Yildiz in her thoughts as well. At last she spoke. "You do not have to face Achilles tomorrow. Your fate is in your own hands. You can decide against a battle charge and we may dig in our heels and wait till winter sends many of the Achaeans searching for more comfortable sleeping quarters."

But Penthesilea shook her head sadly. "It is my fate to

ride tomorrow. It is more than that, it is my penance."

Myrina was puzzled but said nothing, sensing that she must be patient.

Penthesilea turned to her, smiling. "Did you know that I was once a princess—daughter of a king?"

"No!" Myrina tried to conceal her astonishment.

"Oh yes." Penthesilea laughed, but the sound was mirthless. "I was as royal as your Cassandra, but I did something that was unforgivable."

"I cannot believe that." Myrina put out her hand and gently stroked the leaping panther that Penthesilea bore on her forearm, the symbol of her wild spirit, scratched in when she was a child.

"Oh yes," Penthesilea insisted. "It was unforgivable. I had a young sister; her name was Hippolyta, after the famous Moon Rider. She rode like a centaur and we were inseparable; we wrestled and fought and hunted together."

Penthesilea paused, and it seemed that she could not utter the words, but at last she swallowed hard and went on. "I killed her."

"No!" Myrina cried involuntarily.

"Yes," Penthesilea insisted. "One day when we were out hunting I threw my spear into some bushes and instead of the deer I thought we stalked . . . I killed my own sister."

"But . . . that was an accident . . . a terrible accident," Myrina told her at once.

"Yes . . . it was an accident, but that does not make it any less true or any less dreadful. I killed my own sister. Can you imagine how my parents felt? They—they could not even look at me."

"How old were you?"

"I had seen eleven springs; the same as Yildiz. You see, when I saw your Little Star, so angry and vengeful, well . . . I knew what it was like to be so young and to feel such hurt inside."

"But it was not your fault," Myrina insisted, though she could imagine only too well the terrible guilt that must follow such a thing. "What happened to you?"

"My parents sent for Atisha and begged her to take me as a Moon Rider. It was agreed that the Old Woman would let me ride with her, but I was never to return to my home. I was banished."

Myrina frowned. It seemed a terrible punishment for one so young. She offered what comfort she could: "Atisha loves you as her own child," she said.

"Yes, and I love her as though she were both mother and father to me, but . . . I have always known that I must find the courage to do something great with my life— something that will atone."

"You have done it already," Myrina replied at once.

"You rescued Iphigenia from the evil priest; we could never have succeeded without your daring. That is atonement enough for any wrong! There is a life that you have truly saved!"

"No." Penthesilea shook her head. "That was not enough. What I do tomorrow . . . this is what matters. I have to face the warrior of warriors and bring him down."

Myrina was full of sadness and fear, but she knew that all the arguments in the world would make no difference to Penthesilea's resolve, so she simply wrapped her arms around her friend and they stayed like that, sitting close together, until the first glimmerings of light appeared in the east.

As dawn spread over the plain of Troy, Penthesilea stirred. She wiped all traces of tears from her cheeks, then turned to Myrina and planted a fierce kiss on her brow. "I have never told anyone else what I confided to you last night," she said. "Only Atisha knows. Remember, Snake Lady, whenever I bawl and shout at you, that I love you still."

Then suddenly she was her usual bossy, energetic self. She snatched up the torch and was soon striding about the citadel, ordering her disparate followers to feed and water the horses, then strap their armor on.

All was bustle and energy within the walls of Troy.

Myrina could feel the tension thrumming through the streets. Every warrior was preparing meticulously for this fight, tempers drawn tight as bowstrings. If ever the tide could be turned against the Achaeans, it must be now.

Back in her chamber Myrina joined her gang and fastened on her horse-skin body armor. She tied across her chest the strong leather strap that protected the right breast, so flattening it and giving the impression of being one-breasted. She smiled, remembering how Atisha laughed when their enemies called them Amazons: "breastless ones." "If they are stupid enough to think that we would do such a thing as cut off a breast—let them think it!" the Old Woman would say. "They may well fear us more if they think we are capable of such madness."

Myrina picked up her leg leathers, but found that other deft fingers at once set about strapping them into place. "Akasya—you are here again."

Akasya nodded and did the job with grim efficiency, while Myrina pulled the stiffened Phrygian cap over her ears, so that it protected her like a helmet. But then she suddenly stopped. Atisha's scathing words about the straps reminded her of other matters that the Old Woman had been very clear about, and much more recently: "Do not go out and fight with Penthesilea," she had warned. Myrina's mind had been so full of Yildiz that she had forgotten all about Atisha's last words to her.

After the closeness that she and Penthesilea had shared last night, such a thing was unthinkable. How could she refuse to follow Penthesilea onto the battlefield?

"What is it?" Bremusa asked, reaching over to help her fix the Moon Rider's quiver to her thigh, so that arrows could be drawn at great speed. "You look troubled."

Myrina shook her head. "No," she whispered. "She cannot have meant now."

"What is wrong?" Coronilla demanded.

Myrina struggled to explain, her face full of pain and shame that she should be voicing these words. "Atisha—" she said, "Atisha told me not to fight alongside Penthesilea—she made me swear it."

Akasya stopped her work at once; there was stillness in the chamber. All three Moon Riders stared at her, shocked. Atisha had never told anyone not to fight before—it was unheard of.

"But . . . when the black ships came, we all turned warrior and we swore to defend the traveling lands of the tribes." Alcibie spoke in a whisper.

"Yes," Myrina agreed. "And Atisha cannot have known that we would be fighting for the honor of Yildiz. She could not have meant me to stand by and see my Little Star slaughtered and take no revenge."

But Polymusa was troubled. "Atisha never speaks thoughtlessly."

"No," Coronilla agreed. "She does not."

"But we cannot fight without Myrina to lead us." Alcibie was distressed. "We are Myrina's gang."

They all stood there, looking uncertain, until Bremusa moved decisively. She reached out and pulled loose the straps of Myrina's helmet. "We are still Myrina's gang, whether Myrina fights or not."

At once Akasya began to untie Myrina's leg straps, a look of relief on her face.

Polymusa nodded. "Bremusa is right! You must not ignore Atisha's orders," she said.

Coronilla agreed. "The Old Woman has wisdom beyond our understanding."

Alcibie still looked lost, but then her courage flooded back. "We are Myrina's gang, with or without Myrina at our side," she said.

Myrina tore off her helmet, her face flushed. "I will have to face Penthesilea and tell her," she said. "Believe me, this is the hardest thing I've ever done."

Penthesilea was pacing impatiently back and forth on Fleetwind as the Thracians and the Phrygians assembled. She frowned and shook her head as Myrina shouted up at her that she wasn't going to fight. Penthesilea dismounted at once, her face full of disbelief. "Not fight?" she growled.

"I forgot; I was so angry about Yildiz that I could think of nothing else . . . and then last night I was so very sad for you. But I remembered as I was dressing: Atisha told me not to fight alongside you." Myrina felt that she sounded like a spoiled child.

Penthesilea's eyes flashed flinty gray and her mouth curled in disdain. "What is this? I never took you to be a coward, Snake Lady! The Old Woman is going crazy in her head! A Moon Rider not fight?"

Myrina gritted her teeth and stood her ground in silence, Akasya at her side, staring defiantly up at the War God's Daughter.

"Why? Did she say why? Tell me why!"

Myrina hung her head. It would only take a second to change her mind and fetch Isatis from the stable. It would be easier by far to do so. But suddenly Cassandra was there, facing Penthesilea with her. "Tell her why!" the princess urged quietly.

"Yes, tell me why!" Penthesilea looked from one to the other.

At last Myrina thrust up her chin, but it still trembled. "Because—if you are lost, there must be someone here to clear up the mess and lead the Moon Riders!"

Penthesilea's eyes glistened for just a moment, then suddenly her shoulders dropped and she clasped Myrina tight in her arms. "Remember what I said last night, Snake Lady: though I growl at you, I still love you. The Old Woman is not so crazy after all. Good-bye! Ride well! Lead well!"

CHAPTER FORTY

The Ride of the War God's Daughter

ENTHESILEA LEAPED ONTO Fleetwind's back and urged the powerful mare forward. "We ride," she yelled, raising her bow in salute to the gathered warriors. "We ride for the honor of Maa and the city of Troy."

A wild answering cheer went up from all the many gathered bands of allies.

Myrina's gang moved in behind Penthesilea. "For Maa and Myrina!" they yelled.

Myrina was touched, but she and Cassandra had to step back quickly as they all surged forward, Aeneas at the head of the Dardanians, Peiroos leading the Thracian tribes and Paris at the head of the remaining Trojans. They rode out across the plain toward the Tomb of Dancing Myrina, where the armies would face each other.

"Come to the Southern Tower," Cassandra said. "My

parents always watch from there."

Myrina caught the princess's arm sharply. "Do you know?" she asked. "Do you know what will come of it?"

Cassandra's voice was faint and her eyes avoided Myrina's. "No," she said. "There will be glory and sorrow—that is all I know. I wished to put on armor and fight with the Moon Riders, too, but the Dardanian Aeneas begged me not to. He swore that the Trojans still see me as the priestess of Apollo and think that their god will desert them if I am lost."

"Yes." Myrina felt sorry for her sharp words and she took hold of her friend's arm. "Sometimes it is very hard, not to fight."

They could hear the cheers from the walls of Troy as Penthesilea led her army forward. The allies looked wonderful; their different styles of armor made them a wild and colorful sight and their weapons glinted in the sun. They galloped on, giving voice to their various war cries as they rode: a wild, conflicting babble of sounds, but united in their determination to fight against this invasion of their lands. The Achaeans in the distance seemed dull and dusty, their chariots and armor rusted with rain and seawater. Agamemnon and the warlords led the way, strong horses pulling their chariots, with the great mass of foot fighters following behind. They looked squat, an army of ants indeed, in contrast to the swirling cloaks and wavelike motion of the allied riders, but they came on and on, more and more of them, until the whole of the seaboard horizon was filled end to end with the advancing black shapes of Achaean warriors.

Myrina saw with a sinking heart that as the valiant figure of Penthesilea rode into the distance, she looked smaller and smaller, while the sprawling Achaean advance grew wider. Priam and Hecuba could see it, too, and their pride in their allies faltered a little, so that a hush fell over the watchers up on the Southern Tower. Helen stood beside them, her face unreadable. The old lady who was Theseus's mother was given a stool and she and Helen exchanged glances from time to time.

Penthesilea did not hesitate, but led the Moon Riders at once in a great arc across the front of the closing Achaeans, giving the wild ululating cry that all the warrior women knew signified a bow charge. They rode across the face of the Achaean advance, sending a constant rain of arrows into the army, turning in the saddle as only they could, so that their backs were never exposed. Then they wheeled around in a great crescent, coming back at once, as the Achaeans turned tail in the face of this deadly rain and tried to retreat. Many had fallen, wounded, and were now trampled beneath the feet of Mazagardi horses.

Cheers rose from the city walls. Though smaller in

number, the new allies, it seemed, were not to be vanquished easily, so fierce and unexpected was their way of war.

Once again Penthesilea wheeled Fleetwind about and charged, this time with all the allies at her back. They found the Achaeans in disarray, fleeing back toward the boats that were anchored all along the shoreline. At last, when there was nowhere else for them to go but the sea, Agamemnon's warriors turned and made a stand. The Achaean war chariots closed in with their long spears and swords and the fighting began in deadly seriousness; horses reared and screamed in pain.

Myrina turned her face away. "I cannot just stand here and watch," she growled.

Cassandra took her arm. "Come with me. We will go down to the gate where they bring back the wounded. I find it best to busy myself easing pain if I can, then my head will not thunder so with anger and sorrow."

Myrina followed her, wondering how she who was so sensitive could also be so calm. Akasya as ever marched three paces behind them. "I suppose you have got used to this," Myrina whispered to her friend.

Cassandra shook her head. "No. One can never get used to it. I have learned how to survive, that is all. We women of Troy have had to learn this."

The wounded were already being dragged away from

the fighting by the slave women. Some of them would be wounded and slaughtered themselves as they carried out the work. The injured were laid on boards inside the protective walls, while other slaves brought water and binding cloths and set about patching them up if it was possible. The ground was awash with blood and vomit and there was a stink that came from those who were wounded in the bowels. The air was filled with the sounds of groans and chattering teeth, though screams were rare. The slave women went calmly about their work and Myrina saw that they often made a small downward hand-sign that called Cassandra to their side. The princess went to a man whose stomach had been deeply pierced: he convulsed and whimpered with pain as his guts spilled out. Cassandra took a small vial from her belt and forced a few drops between his lips. She stroked his cheek and in a moment the convulsions ceased. He lay back, white and still.

When she saw this, Myrina understood at once why the Trojans sometimes called Cassandra the Priestess of Sleep. She glanced down at her own collection of potions that swung from her belt; some of Atisha's medicines could also bring merciful death. She must set about the same terrible job of work.

All through the morning she worked to bring peace to those who could never recover, and there were many.

The most dreadful, heartbreaking moment was when she bent to find that the wounded one was Bremusa, her chest pierced deeply with a spear, a sword slash across her head. The strong woman still breathed and her eyelids fluttered. She saw Myrina's white face hovering above her and reached for the vial herself.

"Sleep well, brave Bremusa," Myrina choked out. She smoothed her hair and gently closed her eyes. Then she took a vial of the same poppy juice that hung from Bremusa's belt. They would need every drop they could get.

The priestess Theano came down from the temple of Apollo to help them and it was her sudden cry of concern that made Cassandra look up and see a gang of Trojan women marching down through the streets toward the Southern Gate, all dressed in leather armor. They had stuck knives into their belts and they carried their husbands' spears.

"Stop at once!" Theano shouted, leaving the sick and racing toward them.

Cassandra and Myrina both followed.

"What are you doing?" Theano asked.

The women stopped. Some of them were very young, but most of them were middle-aged and they all wore the black veil that marked them out as widows.

The younger girls at the front looked frightened at the

challenge, but one of the older women pushed forward. "We are going to fight," she said. "Penthesilea is fighting for us and she is a woman. All the Moon Riders are women, and they are so young and brave. It is shameful that we Trojan women hang back and let the warrior priestesses fight for us."

"No," Theano cried. "This is madness."

Cassandra strode forward and bowed to them. "I honor you," she said. "I honor your courage, but you are not battle-trained as Penthesilea and the Moon Riders are. You would be slaughtered like calves if you went out there."

The women hesitated, but then another older woman spoke. "What do we care if we die? Our husbands and fathers are dead and gone. What is there left for us if Troy should fall? We will be dragged away to act as slaves to the very men who've killed our menfolk. We'll be forced into their beds and made to bear Achaean children. How can being slaughtered be worse than that?"

There was silence for a moment—this reasoning was hard to counter. Then Cassandra drew herself up very tall and lifted her chin. "I am your princess," she said. "I order you to stay."

The women looked at one another uncertainly, then Myrina spoke up. "Look at me," she said. "You know me as the Snake Lady. I brought you food and drink. I am no coward, I hope you will not call me so, but I do not bear arms today. There are many ways of fighting and many ways of resisting the Achaeans. Put down your weapons and come with us to help the wounded. The sight of death is even harsher than the wielding of weapons and you will prove your bravery by looking it in the face."

After a moment one of the younger girls threw her spear aside and went to stand by Myrina. "I will tend the sick," she agreed. "It's true that the sight of death is worse than fighting, but I will do it."

Then slowly the others followed. Cassandra and Theano heaved a sigh of relief. "You did well," Cassandra told Myrina. "I couldn't see them killed like lambs, but there is some truth in what they say. They are all lost among the bloodred mist."

They returned to their dismal work with more helpers, unsure whether they'd done right to stop the women joining battle.

As the sun rose high in the sky there seemed to be a small lull in the numbers of wounded arriving and Akasya rushed to shake Myrina's shoulder. "The allies have returned to the lower town to regroup, and the Ant Man has followed them, shouting at the Panther Lady," she said. "She leaps from her horse to fight him. You should come up to the tower again."

"Ah no!" Myrina left her terrible work and followed her at once.

315

CHAPTER FORTY-ONE

The Warrior of Warriors

MYRINA STUMBLED UP the steps of the Southern Tower in her bloodstained smock and leggings to find a hushed silence and great tension among the royal watchers. "What has happened?" She panted.

"Your brave leader has dismounted," Helen told her, shaking her head. "She should not have done that."

"Why?" Myrina gasped.

Helen frowned. "The Moon Riders have done well with their swift battle charges, proving that on horseback they are more than equal to these armored warriors. But Achilles followed her back to the gates, bellowing and taunting her that she would not be so brave on her feet."

Myrina's stomach lurched. She knew only too well that Penthesilea would rise at once to such a challenge. She pushed through to the front and stood there between

Priam and his wife, forgetting the normal courtesies.

They did not take offense and Priam even made room for her, but the old man shook his head. "I do not understand. We have seen what that man can do. Why has the War God's Daughter made herself so vulnerable to him?"

Myrina explained, "You do not know our Penthesilea. She cannot bear to have her courage doubted. Why are the other warriors backing away from her?"

"She has agreed to fight Achilles in single combat," Priam said, his hands trembling. "Not good! Not good!"

Andromache, Hector's young widow, stood beside them looking troubled. "How can Penthesilea dream that she can win against that bear of a man, when my valiant husband couldn't?"

"No, dear. Hector will soon come to rescue us all." Hecuba's voice wavered, but she smiled happily at all who stood around her. "My son will soon be here, do not fear. You'll soon have your husband back!"

Andromache bit her lips and swallowed hard. Myrina felt bitterly sorry for the young widow, for she could see that living with Hecuba and constantly hearing such things must be painful.

Then she turned back to watch Penthesilea and remembered how they had talked all through the night and how her friend had insisted that she must face up to this warrior of warriors. What Helen said was true: on

Fleetwind's back, with bow in hand and a quiverful of arrows, Penthesilea was unreachable, but on the ground she was just a tall young woman, facing up to a giant of a man whose greatest skill lay in spear-throwing.

The combat was taking place inside a clear circle of space. Agamemnon, gloomy but resplendent in his magnificent gold armor, removed his helmet, confident that he was safe until this fight was over. His brother Menelaus, red-haired and stocky, did the same, but his eyes wandered from the fight at hand to search the faces that looked down from the Southern Tower. Myrina could not help but turn to where Helen stood, and saw that the Spartan queen looked down with cheerful curiosity at the man who was once her husband.

There was a ripple of excitement as Penthesilea took a spear offered by Aeneas and advanced toward her opponent.

Myrina bent her head and clapped her hands over her eyes as Penthesilea circled Achilles. But seeing nothing and hearing only silence was even worse, so she gritted her teeth to watch again. Even though she was so tall, Penthesilea looked like an elegant deer advancing on a lion. Achilles laughed and refused even to brace himself for the onslaught, but suddenly the War God's Daughter set her spear twirling around and around above her head and then swishing down close to the Ant Man's shoulder, so that he was forced to duck. There was a sudden gasp from the watchers as Achilles stumbled heavily to the side, while Penthesilea leaped pantherlike toward him. Perhaps after all there was a chance for Penthesilea, who was lighter and more sure-footed. She did not wait for her opponent to retaliate but went forward bravely again and caught his armored shoulder, though the spear fell away, leaving him undamaged.

Myrina stared down from the tower. The man was so heavily armored that no glimpse of flesh could be seen. How could Penthesilea, even with all her skill, find a chink in his protective shell?

Achilles, annoyed at last, drew his sword and swung at her with all his might, his teasing humor suddenly changed. Penthesilea ducked easily beneath his clumsy lunges. Now she took a sword from her own belt and swung it with force, but it clashed heavily and swerved uselessly aside.

The fight was bitter and determined and it went on and on, each dealing sword blow after sword blow that stunned and sliced, until blood seeped out from beneath the beaten horse-skin armor that Penthesilea wore. Achilles' armor kept him safe, but the blows that he received must have battered and bruised.

The sun moved across the sky and still Penthesilea swung her sword at Achilles. Once the huge man crashed down to the ground as she feinted to the side. It must have been a painful fall, and he rose up, growling with anger, and snatched up his spear again. It flew with the full force of his huge strength, right through Penthesilea's throat.

Cries of despair came from the Southern Tower of Troy. Myrina pushed through the crowd and went tearing down the steps, out through the Southern Gate toward her friend, who lay pinned to the ground.

There was a terrible silence on the battlefield as Myrina ran, her heart pounding and her throat constricting so that she could hardly breathe. She slowed up as she came close to the circle where they had fought and saw that Penthesilea was dead. Death must have been instantaneous; at least there had been no pain for her.

As Myrina stood there watching, Achilles removed his helmet then bent over Penthesilea, gently removing the spear. His very gentleness made Myrina more furious than ever; what was the point of gentleness now?

He went down on one knee and carefully removed the Moon Rider's polished horsehide helmet, revealing Penthesilea's young face and beautiful panther-patterned cheeks. Her long brown hair fell all about her head, gleaming as though with life and health.

From many of the Achaean warriors there came astonished gasps and murmurs:

"Look at her!"

"She's so young!"

"Beautiful!"

"To fight so fiercely and look like that!"

Battle-hardened warriors stood still, heads bowed. Just for a moment shame was there on their faces. Myrina trembled with sorrow and hatred, her hands making tight fists, tears rolling down her cheeks. Suddenly, a sneering Achaean foot soldier approached them, leering at the fallen warrior priestess. He bent over Penthesilea. "Give us a kiss before y' go, darling."

"Do not you dare to touch her—I'll have your guts on a plate," Myrina hissed, whipping her knife out from her belt.

Achilles took a step back and swore. He brought his armored forearm swiftly down on the man's head. "She had more courage in her little finger than you have in all your evil frame," he growled.

But there was no reply. The man had dropped at once and lay there as still as Penthesilea.

Myrina moved slowly forward and kneeled to cradle Penthesilea's head in her arms, heedless of the blood that flooded over her already stained smock. She sat there gently rocking back and forth, ignoring the huge bulk of Achilles, who towered above her so that she could see the sweat that ran down his face, and smell the animal warmth of his body.

Again there was a moment of silence; then Achilles looked over to where Aeneas stood, his cheeks lined and gray. "My Lord Aeneas, let us have a three-day truce to see our dead honored. Though there will be no honor for this fellow." He turned once more and kicked the body of the fallen Achaean. The man would not be getting up to return to his tent.

Aeneas bowed courteously and then all the warriors, Trojans and Achaeans alike, bowed again to one another and turned, wandering wearily back to their own tents and lodgings.

"What is this?" Myrina muttered through gritted teeth. "What deadly polite, jolly sport?" She hated them even more for their courtesy.

She stayed there for a long while, nursing Penthesilea in her arms, until at last she looked up and saw that Akasya stood at Penthesilea's feet, with Cassandra beside her. They had brought a litter draped with clean silk and bearers to carry it.

"Let us take her now," Cassandra said.

Carefully they lifted Penthesilea's muscular body between them and carried her back to the citadel.

More sorrow waited there in the city walls. Myrina found that Alcibie and Polymusa were laid out beside Bremusa; Coronilla was wounded, the only survivor from

Myrina's gang. Many of the Moon Riders who had followed Penthesilea lay beside them. The losses among the Trojan allies had been great, though many Achaeans had been killed, too.

Again the Trojan royal family tried to offer elaborate funeral rites, but Myrina shook her head. "We Moon Riders return our dead to the earth simply. I wish another pyre to be built beside the Mound of Dancing Myrina, and then we few who are left may dance alone to honor our dead."

The courteous Aeneas once again made all arrangements for them, and while the Achaeans held their funeral rites in the distance, the Moon Riders and Cassandra danced quietly to a slow beating drum. The Trojans built another funeral pyre above the stinking ash pit, while their king wept pitifully. Queen Hecuba smiled and nodded her head to everyone, saying that she must not stay long for she was preparing rooms for Hector.

CHAPTER FORTY-TWO

Honor and Dignity

I N THE DAYS that followed Myrina spent all her time nursing Coronilla, who, to her great relief, recovered slowly. She used all her knowledge of herbs and healing and was constantly helped by the faithful Akasya. Slowly as they worked together, while Coronilla slept soundly under the healing influence of Atisha's herb lore, they got to know each other better. Akasya had been captured as a child after a Hittite raid on her homeland. The Hittites were in dispute with the Egyptian pharaoh over the land where she had once lived. Prince Paris had ridden in the service of the great Hittite king and led the raiding party. He'd been awarded both goods and slaves in return for his services.

"Terrible." Myrina shook her head. "To be dragged away from your home and family."

"My parents and sisters were killed," Akasya told her. "I was the lucky one."

Myrina nodded, her head full of images of burning Mazagardi huts and her own parents lying together in the dust. "I know how that feels," she told Akasya. "But at least I was not captured and forced to live as a slave. Do you hate Prince Paris?"

"There could be worse for us than this," Akasya replied.

Although Myrina thought that she knew the answer, she asked, "What could be worse?"

Akasya took a deep breath. "If Troy should fall, as I swear it must, it is to those men who camp outside these walls that we shall be given. Their anger grows with each month and year they are forced to stay away from their homes. They live a barren fighting life here in the marshes; they will treat us like animals when Troy falls. The Trojan women will be dragged away as slaves and concubines to the Achaean lords—but what of us, who are slaves already? They'll let the battle-hardened lowest ranks loose on us. Those who've been deprived of all decency and lived like beasts out there for nine long years."

Myrina nodded in silence. So the slave women understood well enough what their fate would be.

Akasya's face was grim with fear. "I'd rather die," she whispered. "We slaves know well that we might rush the guards at the upper gate. But what then? Where could we go? The hills are full of prowling raiding bands. Even if we managed to get away, we'd fall into the hands of those we dread most."

Myrina nodded. "Would you join us as a Moon Rider?" she asked.

For a moment there was disbelief on Akasya's face, then suddenly joy. "Yes," she whispered. "I would give anything to join the honored priestesses."

"And are there others who would come?"

Akasya laughed. "Which of us would not? But . . . I thought that such a thing was impossible. Don't you have to train from childhood and ride like a centaur? Most of us slaves have never sat astride a horse."

"Desperate times mean changes." Myrina was thinking fast. "Atisha, our Old Woman, made me swear not to fight. She knew Penthesilea like a mother, and I think she guessed what might happen. I must now take the lead and somehow find a way for the Moon Riders to survive. Our numbers are small—so many are dead—we need brave women to swell our ranks, and in those sleeping sheds I see what I need."

Akasya was suddenly trembling, her eyes filled with tears.

"What is it?" Myrina demanded.

"To be a Moon Rider . . . it would give us more than freedom; it would give us back our dignity."

"Some of you may die in the struggle," Myrina warned.

"We will die anyway, whatever comes."

Myrina was convinced that she must find a way to free them. "Speak to the other women, but do not let a word of this be heard by the Trojans. King Priam would not allow it; only the Princess Cassandra can be trusted."

Akasya nodded, but her face was full of hope. "The princess has always been our friend," she agreed.

So, as the hottest days of the Month of Burning Heat wore on, Myrina's mind was busy with plans. Another one that occupied her thoughts much was Chryseis. Whenever there was time she would visit the priestess, but there was little response from her. Myrina would sit beside her bed and stroke her hand, murmuring soft words, so that the troubled woman sometimes drifted off to sleep. Cassandra insisted she could see that Chryseis benefited from this concern. At least the priestess's skin was looking a little better and she allowed herself to be fed.

Myrina asked Cassandra whether it might be possible to take the priestess away with them, if they could only find a way of getting the slave women out of Troy.

Cassandra looked thoughtful and sighed, shaking her head. "I cannot get her even to leave her bed," she said. "At night I have her little son brought to my chamber so that at least he may know something like a mother's love."

"Does he thrive?"

"Few babes thrive these days in Troy, but at least he does survive."

The sadness of it all touched Myrina and she thought often of the joy she'd left behind her on the Isle of Marble. She wished that she could somehow find a way to help Chryseis.

Between her plans and the work that must be done to keep the Trojans fed and their spirits up she found a few moments to seek out her mirror-visions.

One evening, when the sun was setting, she retired to her chamber and took out her looking glass. First she looked for Tomi, and was reassured to see that he was alive and well but struggling through a mountainous region, surrounded by strong-looking fighting men whose skins gleamed black as ebony.

Then she looked for her grandmother and her young niece Phoebe. The little girl looked strong and happy as Grandmother Hati led her along on the back of a fine, dappled mare. The glimpses that she got of Atisha troubled her, for the Old Woman looked ill, but she was being nursed devotedly by Iphigenia. It was while she gazed on this gentle image that an idea came to her. She let the vision fade at once and put her precious mirror away carefully; then she got up and went to Cassandra's chamber.

"Where is Chryseis' baby?" she demanded.

Cassandra looked surprised. "Why? The wet nurse should be bringing him here at any moment."

Myrina sat down to wait, but was very impatient.

"What is it that you want with the child?" her friend asked.

"A thought has come to me; it is just a different way of looking at things. It may not work, but it is worth trying. May I take the child to Chryseis and speak to her?"

Cassandra sighed. "Of course you may. Try anything that you can, but I doubt . . ."

The nurse arrived and Myrina could see at once that the child was fretful and thin. She took the little struggling bundle into her arms and went at once into Chryseis's chamber.

Chryseis looked puzzled for a moment to see her there with a child in her arms, but then she clearly understood that this was her child and turned her head at once to the wall. Cassandra followed Myrina quietly into the room, looking a little concerned as Myrina approached with the baby to sit unbidden on the bed.

The little boy fretted and weak cries filled the room, but Myrina ignored the small sounds and began to talk.

"I was looking in my mirror today," she said, "and I saw in my vision the Princess Iphigenia. I saw that she is on the banks of the River Thermodon and is taking good care of the Moon Riders' Old Woman, who is sick. Do you remember the Princess Iphigenia?"

Chryseis made no reply, but a small movement of her head told them that she was listening. Myrina looked up at Cassandra, who nodded her encouragement.

"Do you remember the young princess who came to Troy with her mother? The little girl who delighted in the beautiful gowns that were brought for her, and who followed you and Cassandra about like a faithful, loving shadow?"

Still no word passed the priestess's lips, but they both saw that a tear trickled slowly down her cheek. She did remember the little girl, that was certain, and the sadness that went with that memory told them that she remembered the terrible plight that Iphigenia had found herself in when her father had agreed to sacrifice his daughter.

"You must remember how we rode down through Thrace," Myrina went on insistently, as though she were telling a story. "We were led by our dear Penthesilea and we saved the princess. We snatched her away from Chalcis's knife."

There was silence for a moment and then once again the baby mewed his tiny cry. "Well." Myrina took a deep breath and plunged in again. "Have you ever thought, Priestess, that this little one you bore is Iphigenia's brother? Never mind who his father is, we care naught for that man, but his sister matters very much to us!"

The silence that followed was very tense. Both Myrina and Cassandra held their breaths and once again the child whimpered pitifully, breaking into the quiet with his pathetic sounds.

As he cried on, Chryseis at last turned slowly around and looked at her child. She looked at him properly as he struggled in Myrina's arms, and at last she spoke. "But . . . he's so thin!"

"He needs his mother." Myrina tried to make the words sound free of any judgment.

"Then give him to me!" Chryseis held out her arms.

Myrina passed him over at once and she and Cassandra, with tears in their eyes, watched the priestess awkwardly cradling her child, concern showing in her face at last. "Iphigenia's little brother," she murmured.

Cassandra put her hands on Myrina's shoulders. "You are a very clever Snake," she whispered in her ear.

Chryseis looked up at them. "What is his name?" she asked.

Cassandra shook her head. "It is his mother's right to name him."

"Well, then . . . I shall call him Chryse, after my father, priest of Sminthean Apollo," she told them.

"A good name," Myrina agreed.

Chryseis swung her feet around and got up from the bed. She stood there, wobbly-legged, and Myrina reached out to steady her. "I must find food for him," the priestess told them with motherly concern.

Cassandra opened her mouth to say that she would have some sent up to the room, but then, as she saw Chryseis's shaky but determined progress toward the door, she held the words back.

Chryseis turned back to Myrina. "Thank you," she said quietly. "I shall try to be a good mother to him. You have made me see how I may regain my honor."

CHAPTER FORTY-THREE

Snake Venom

I T WAS NOT long before Chryseis was to be seen striding about Troy as she used to, giving help and encouragement to all who needed it. She met with concern and kindness in return and was touched to find that the people still referred to her respectfully as Priestess. She was never without the now thriving baby strapped to her back.

Myrina confided her plans for the slave women to Chryseis and begged her to join them. She was quite surprised when the priestess shook her head. "My father has taken refuge on the isle of Sminthe," she said. "Whatever happens to Troy, I shall do my best to return to him and take his grandson home to the sanctuary there."

Questions and plans whirled through Myrina's head and she could get little sleep. One moment she was miserable and hopeless, the next full of wild excitement and a belief that she could succeed.

One night she woke from a troubled dream. She had seen herself nursing Penthesilea in her arms once again, while Achilles stood above them, huge and terrible, and a small brown viper coiled itself unnoticed around his ankle. She got up too disturbed to sleep, leaving the chamber that she shared with Coronilla and went out of the slumbering palace. The quiet streets of the citadel were bathed in moonlight.

A few guards stepped out to challenge her, but when they saw that it was the Snake Lady, they bowed and let her pass. She made her way to the Southern Tower and crept up the stairway to the lookout point. She stood there for a while, looking down across the quiet plain. All along the distant seaboard torches burned where the tents and huts of the Achaeans lay. It was hard to believe in the silver moonlight that so much terror and destruction could be wrought here, in this beautiful landscape.

There was a sigh and a scuffling sound behind her and a voice that she knew: "I see the Snake Lady cannot sleep either!"

She turned sharply and saw a silhouette of broad shoulders and a glint of golden silver hair above. She recognized the shape and voice of Paris. Though he was not her favorite person, he seemed very subdued and unthreatening here in the dark. "You are right, I could not sleep," she agreed.

"Such a beautiful site for so much pain and misery," he said, and his words so closely echoed Myrina's own thoughts that she was startled and couldn't think how to reply. "And so much of it must be borne here, on these shoulders," he went on.

Myrina still could not think what to say. She had never imagined that he cared or was bothered by the responsibility that he should indeed feel.

Paris sighed. "Do you know what the worst thing is? If I could go back in time and change it all, I know that I would still do the same. I would do anything to be with Helen, however high the cost."

Myrina was touched by his honest words. This was not the boastful favorite prince whom she remembered from long ago. This was a man worn by harsh experience, who had grown to know himself and face his faults, however bad they were.

"Helen wins everyone's heart," she told him gently. "Somehow she makes you love her even if you do not want to."

"Even the fierce Moon Riders?" Paris teased.

"Even them," Myrina agreed.

Then Paris's voice became serious again. "I am so sorry for the loss of your brave Penthesilea."

Myrina nodded. "You should not think yourself responsible for that. Penthesilea always did exactly what she wanted. Nothing could have stopped her riding out that day."

Paris moved to stand beside her, and they both stared out toward the farthest end of the shore, where Achilles' tents and huts were sited.

"How can we defeat him?" Paris murmured. "A man like a bear, who leads his poisoned ants so that they swarm around us in every direction. It seems that no one can defeat him, not Penthesilea, not even my brave brother Hector."

"Of course they can't; the man is protected like a tortoise," Myrina agreed. "That gleaming armor covers him from head to toe."

Then suddenly she remembered something from her dream: the small brown snake around Achilles' ankle. She saw herself sitting on the ground, rocking Penthesilea once again, with the great warrior towering above her so close that she could smell his sweat. She also remembered that in that moment she'd seen bare, brown flesh and muscle showing beneath his highly polished leg armor.

"Except . . . for his heels," she said, frowning and trying to recall them to her mind carefully. "His heels are vulnerable. The heavy armor doesn't cover there."

"His heels?" Paris was puzzled. "But even a direct sword cut there would do little to harm such a man."

"That's true," Myrina agreed, then she suddenly

laughed. "But we horsewomen see our greatest weapon as the bow. An arrow might bury itself deep in a man's heel, and, were that arrow tipped with snake venom, I doubt he'd live."

Paris was thoughtful and interested. "And would a snake lady have such a thing as snake venom?" he asked.

Myrina hesitated for a moment, but Penthesilea's white face rose before her. Would it be dishonorable to kill a man so? Then she remembered with fury the bowing and courtesy of the three-day truce. The anger that it had brought rose in her again. "We Moon Riders do not fight for honor or gain," she said grimly, "but for freedom." She unfastened one of the smallest vials that swung from her belt, the stopper sealed well in place. It was Atisha's most deadly weapon and she had never used it. "Here is your snake venom," she said, holding it out to Paris. "The one who uses it must make a very accurate shot."

"It shall be so," said Paris.

Myrina turned to go, but then remembered a question that had been there in her mind since her talks with Akasya. "Why does not the great Hittite king send his warriors to rescue you?"

"Ah." Paris smiled. "The Snake Lady knows everything. I had hoped that it would be so. When I stole Helen away from her home, I did it with confidence that such support would be given me, but . . . times have changed. The Hittite king has sent his armies to defend his lands in the south and in the east. The great Hittite empire itself must now fight off invasion. They have no warriors to spare for little, struggling Troy."

Myrina sighed. It seemed that loyalty was as changeable as the wind these days.

"Those slave women who languish in the old weaving sheds—are they not your slaves? Did you not bring them back to Troy as your reward? Might you spare them and set them free?"

Paris shook his head. "Alas, they are my father's slaves now, not mine. And though he is very old, my father is still the king of Troy."

"Well . . . I have given you the means to take a great and powerful life. Might you not pay me back in kind? What I wish is to save many humble lives."

Paris looked at her thoughtfully. "You make strange requests, Snake Lady, but if I am successful with my snake venom, then I swear that I will do all I can to help you."

Myrina nodded her head. That sounded fair. It gave her a rather shivery feeling to be in league with the handsome cause of all the trouble.

Then at last as she went to leave he bowed and kissed her hand. "I have still never seen anyone dance on horseback like you," he whispered.

Myrina wandered back to her chamber, her mind spinning with new possibilities.

The next day at noon Myrina was in her chamber when she heard the Trojans in the streets below cheering wildly. "What is that?" Coronilla murmured.

Cassandra came running up the palace stairs. "Achilles is dead," she cried. "I can't believe it! My brother Paris has shot him in the heel and he struggled for a while to get up, but then suddenly fell down dead."

Wild singing and cheering was heard all about the citadel.

"They carry Paris through Troy shoulder high. He was never so popular before!"

Myrina nodded, unsurprised.

Cassandra came close to look at her face. "You knew!"

Myrina smiled up at her. "You are not the only one whose visions may speak the truth," she said.

The joy inside the walls did not last for long, for it was only a few days afterward that Paris himself was brought back wounded by a deadly sword thrust. He lingered for a while but then died in Helen's arms.

Myrina saw the terrible constriction there on the beautiful face, just for a moment, but very quickly the Queen of Sparta seemed to master her feelings and regain her composure. She retained her dignity throughout the prince's funeral rites, but as the pyre burnt low, Deiphobus, Paris's younger brother, stood up before the whole gathering and claimed the right to take Helen as his wife now that his brother was gone.

Helen's composure slipped at last and an expression of terrified loathing was there for all to see. But then the queenly manner returned and Helen declined politely, saying that she must spend time in mourning for Paris.

But Deiphobus would not let it be: he was on his feet again, insisting that it was the tradition in Troy that a younger brother might claim his older brother's widow.

King Priam bowed his head in agreement and declared that it was indeed the Trojan custom to take a dead brother's wife if a man so wished, and he added sharply that the mourning must not last too long.

Helen bowed her acquiescence, but Cassandra and Myrina exchanged a troubled glance. They could not believe that Helen intended to spend the rest of her life in Deiphobus's arms—indeed neither of them could blame her. The man was pushy and boastful and had an unpleasant, leering manner toward women. Myrina knew that she herself would do anything rather than be married to such a one.

Myrina found herself truly sad that the handsome prince of Troy was dead, but much worse was the knowledge that her new hopes of an easy rescue for the slaves had gone with him.

* * *

The fighting continued every day, though since the deaths of Penthesilea and Paris, the heart had gone out of the Trojan allies, who'd left their homelands to fight for this strategic city. Aeneas struggled dutifully to command them, but it was clear that many of them longed for their own hearthside and could see that there was little chance of Anatolia ever ridding itself of the huge Achaean force. It was more a question of how long it could hold out.

Food was diminishing and desperation grew, until the day when once again the sound of cheering was heard from the lookouts on the towers. Dust was rising in the east and a large band of warriors appeared over the horizon, coming from the direction of Mount Ida.

Coronilla was now able to walk again and, supported by Myrina and Akasya, she managed to struggle up the steps to the top of the Southern Tower.

The ragged people beneath them in the lower town waved and screamed out their joy. "The Ethiopians—the Ethiopians!"

Myrina's heart thundered. Why had she not looked in her mirror of late? How could she have been so busy that she could forget to look for Tomi?

She stared wildly among the huge crowd of advancing riders, who were now making for the Southern Gate, unimpeded by the Achaeans, who sent out scouts to watch but did not interfere. She narrowed her eyes, trying to make out who was who. King Memnon was not difficult to spot for he rode at the head of his warriors, and his neck and arms were covered in rich gold jewelry, a cloth of gold cloak floating out behind him, a broad gold circlet on his brow. His warriors were tall, with skin like gleaming obsidian, and many of them were also ornamented with gold.

Then suddenly she saw him. She should have looked for him in the place of honor, not among the following ranks. Tomi rode at the front, a Mazagardi warrior, in his tribal horsehide body armor, a full quiver at his back and bow strapped across his shoulders. He rode beside King Memnon on his light gray stallion, Moon Silver, and looked as brave and handsome as she remembered him.

Myrina's hands were suddenly trembling; her knees seemed to turn to water. Did Tomi remember her? Had he kept his promise to wait for her? What would he think of her—a ragged, sorrow-worn warrior woman, whom life had battered hard since he last saw her?

CHAPTER FORTY-FOUR

We Have Waited Long Enough

As Tomi rode in glory through the Southern Gate, Myrina did what she had never done; she left Coronilla and Akasya and ran to her chamber to hide. Once there she took up her mirror and stared critically at her reflection, searching not for visions but to see herself as he would see her. Her hair was dull with the dust that seemed to constantly swirl about the once elegant streets and her cheeks sunburnt, her sharp arrow pictures faded a little with every year that passed. Her smock was ragged about the neck; there had been no time for mending or self-adornment. Still her face was young and her eyes bright.

She remembered the day that she and Tomi had promised to stay unmarried and wait for each other. That was more than ten long years ago and she and Tomi were now adults; she was well past the age when a Moon Rider should return to her tribe and choose her husband. But now there were no Mazagardi home-tents to return to.

Cassandra came into her chamber, surprised to find her there. "They are here," she cried. "The Ethiopians! What are you doing hiding away here?"

Myrina turned away from her mirror, self-doubt showing clearly in her eyes.

"He is looking for you," Cassandra told her. "Your Tomi. He asks everyone for the Snake Lady and they direct him here and there, but he doesn't know his way about. You must come and rescue him."

"I wish . . . I wish I had the jewelry that I once had and a fine silk smock." Myrina was suddenly stumbling over the words.

But Cassandra smiled and hugged her. "You forget one thing," she said. "He is Mazagardi, same as you. When did Mazagardi look for a painted, delicate woman?"

Myrina laughed nervously. "I suppose you are right. But . . . when he sees Helen?"

"You have the strength that he needs," Cassandra insisted. "You are a powerful survivor, Myrina; that's the beauty of Mazagardi women. He would not want a painted butterfly like Helen. Put away your mirror and save it for its truest purpose. Come and find him, or you'll regret it all your life."

Myrina smiled at last. "Yes, Princess, I do your bidding,

as ever." She gave a mock bow and followed Cassandra downstairs.

Tomi saw her with the Trojan princess and pushed his way determinedly through the crowd toward her. Her fears were soon forgotten for, as soon as they could reach each other, he held his arms wide and hugged her tightly. He kissed her on the lips, then gently rested his cheek against hers, sighing deeply. "I have longed for this," he whispered.

Myrina sighed, too, and with that sigh all the hardness and struggle of the last few months vanished. "I, too," she replied, realizing only now how much she had longed for this loving intimacy.

"Do you still wait for a husband?" he whispered, throwing aside any formality or shyness, pulling back to look her straight in the face.

She looked back at him. This was her Tomi and yet he was not; he was a strong, confident man, matured by years in the saddle, honored by the Ethiopian king, and yet she still felt completely comfortable with him. "I wait for you," she whispered.

"Well, here I am." He laughed and swung her around. "Why should we wait any longer? Let us have our wedding now—at once."

"Yes, yes." Coronilla was beside them, picking up on his words. She looked flushed and well, better than she'd seemed at any time since Penthesilea's battle. "Let us have a wedding! Oh, do let us have a wedding! It is just what we all need!"

Myrina's face clouded over. "But, Tomi . . . you know what happened . . . at the Lake of Kus?"

Tomi nodded solemnly.

"Your mother and father, too!" she spoke gently.

"Yes." His voice shook a little. "I know it all. Such terrible news travels far and fast."

"And little Yildiz?"

Tomi bowed his head. "Cassandra has told me of her courage." Then he looked her full in the face again. "There is great sorrow all about us, but the sadness only makes you more dear and precious to me. I am more certain than ever that we should not waste any time. We must wed now, while we still have the chance."

"But . . ." She hesitated, remembering her plans for the slave women and determined to be truthful. "I have plans that I must carry out and I fear that I am not yet ready to melt down my mirror to make a marriage bangle, as a good Mazagardi woman should."

"I do not ask it. In these strange times we have to change. I do not want a marriage bangle; I want you, Myrina the Snake Lady."

She looked up at him, laughing. "Very well then, Tomi of the Mazagardi tribe, I choose you to be my husband."

* * *

Coronilla could not contain her excitement and Cassandra spoke at once to her father, who declared the feast a double celebration: to honor King Memnon and to celebrate the Snake Lady's marriage.

"Now you must deck yourself out with finery," Coronilla cried, and even Cassandra would not allow her to object. They snatched her away from Tomi and dragged her upstairs into her chamber. They had been there only a few moments before Helen and her waiting women appeared carrying silken gowns and jewelry and little pots of paint.

Helen came and kissed Myrina on both cheeks and insisted on giving her a gown. "Yes, yes," she said. "A marriage celebration is very much needed here in Troy and if it's yours, my dear, then at least I can put off Deiphobus for a little while longer."

The waiting women exchanged glances. Helen's revulsion for the younger prince of Troy was shared by all of them.

So Myrina allowed them to paint her face and decorate her neck and hair with Helen's jewels. She chose a simple linen gown the color of fresh goat's milk, and by the time the feast was ready the Moon Riders had come to her chamber to lead her down.

The feasting hall was crowded with hosts and guests. King Memnon had brought his own contribution to the food stocks, for a herd of goats and sheep had been driven in the wake of the warriors. The Trojans were cheered enormously by the sight of so much food and raised their beakers to the Snake Lady, who through her warrior husband had brought them fresh supplies of food once again. King Memnon was given the seat of honor next to Priam, while Helen spoke charmingly to everyone and acted capably as hostess. Hecuba wandered vaguely among the guests, looking for her son. Andromache sat quietly in the corner with her little boy Astyanax. There were amused murmurings and whisperings that Helen might prefer the old man to the young prince Deiphobus, and general agreement that marriage to anyone else would be better.

Myrina suddenly felt that something was missing; she looked about her for Akasya and saw that she was serving food with the other slave women, who had been kept late in the palace to wait on the guests. Myrina marched over to her, apologized to the elderly Trojan warrior whom Akasya was serving and made her come to stand beside her as witness to the Mazagardi hand-fasting ceremony. There were small gasps of shock that the Snake Lady should want a slave to take that role, but Akasya rose to the moment and conducted herself as though she'd acted as witness many times before.

The remaining Moon Riders, only thirty in number, danced in a circle about the couple. They moved to the sound of cymbals, bringing the blessings of Mother Maa to their union. Tomi could not wipe the huge smile from his face and Myrina fell into a happy daze, unsure whether this was a dream or not, but as it seemed a wonderful dream she allowed it to lead her where it would.

King Memnon stooped from his great height and kissed her; then he handed her a round box of scented cedarwood with a crescent moon carved on its lid. "I have heard nothing but praise of the fierce and beautiful Snake Lady," he told her, laughing as he imitated a lovesick Tomi. "So I decided to have a fine present made for this famous one."

Myrina opened the box and found inside a most beautifully crafted golden bangle in the shape of a coiled snake. Tomi pushed it into place on her arm, where it curled magnificently from wrist to elbow, echoing the dark, fading pattern of her body picture.

"There. You have your marriage bangle after all," Tomi whispered.

Myrina didn't know how to thank King Memnon, but he laughed loudly and brushed her thanks aside. "Were it not for your Tomi, we'd still be lost in the mountains," he said. "And though this night be joyful, we must not forget that we fight in the morning and go early to our beds."

They went, obedient and exhausted, Myrina leading

Tomi up to her chamber, after Coronilla had tactfully whispered that she'd be sleeping in Cassandra's quarters from now on.

Coronilla and Akasya had found time secretly to strew Myrina's bed with sharp-scented lavender. For a while she and Tomi lay contentedly together in each other's arms, but then she sat up. "This is not for us," she whispered.

Tomi sat up quickly, distressed.

"No, no!" Myrina laughed. "I mean that a bed enclosed by thick walls is not the place for Mazagardi lovers. I want to be outside beneath the silver moonlight, with the warm earth beneath us and the scent of poppies in the air."

Tomi smiled at her again.

They slipped out of the palace and up to the hidden gate. The guards there grinned at them but said nothing, so they climbed a little way up the slope and found a place of soft grass, sheltered by olive trees. They lay down together with the hillside at their back and the dark blue Aegean in the distance before them.

"You do not regret this, Snake Lady?" Tomi asked.

"No," she said firmly. "You and I have waited long enough."

CHAPTER FORTY-FIVE

Secret Plans

T HEY WERE SO comfortable and sheltered beneath the olive trees that the bright morning sun did not wake them. Myrina slept deeply, warm and restful as she snuggled close to Tomi. She had not slept so thoroughly since long before this land had been troubled by war. It was the distant sound of horns and trumpets that eventually woke them. They sat up, knuckling the sleep from their bleary eyes, to see that the sun was well up in the sky and King Memnon was leading his warriors out through the Southern Gate to face the Achaeans. The gold of their weapons and jewelry glinted in the morning sun and they looked magnificent.

Tomi leaped to his feet. "I should be there, I should be with them!"

Myrina struggled up, brushing grass and flowers from her hair. All the joy of last night was ebbing fast away. "Do you have to fight alongside them?" she asked.

Tomi stared at her in surprise. "I never thought to hear you say such a thing! You cannot want a coward for a husband."

"I know that you are no coward," she answered him quickly. "But . . . I have a different fight on my hands and I need you to help me. The fight that I prepare for may be just as bitter, I fear."

Tomi looked back again at the battle lines that were forming down on the plain below. King Memnon's warriors were strong and muscular; moving lightly on their feet, they jogged toward the Achaean battle ranks like loping gazelles. They ran fearlessly to the fight, spears at the ready, but the Achaean lines, as ever, grew and grew. Achilles' Ant Men, now led by his son, were smaller in number, but still Agamemnon's forces sprawled right across the southern horizon. Up there on the hillside Myrina and Tomi could see only too well that it was once more to be an uneven fight.

Tomi clenched his jaw. "By Maa!" he swore. "What chance have they got? I have led them to their deaths!"

Myrina took him by the shoulders. "They have come of their own accord. Listen to me—you can make little difference in that fight down there, but a very big difference in the struggle that I plan."

He still looked over to the plain, but then shook his head. "What you say is true—I can do little to help them now. I will do whatever you want of me."

Then they turned to watch as the two sides approached each other.

"Your brave king should have turned about and gone straight home," Myrina whispered.

"He could never do that." Tomi shook his head. "He has the biggest heart of any man I know and his honor is all to him. If only I could have got him here earlier."

"You are not to blame for that!" Myrina told him almost angrily. "Penthesilea should have waited! Though you know I loved her with all my heart, I can still say that—she should have waited!"

They turned and headed back to the hidden gate, walking slowly hand in hand.

"Tell me then, what is this plan of yours?" Tomi asked.

The battle raged all day and once again the Trojan royal family watched from the top of the Southern Tower. Tomi listened to Myrina's plan to release the slave women and take them to safety.

When she had finished he laughed and applauded. "So you will save their lives and find your new recruits all at once. Only my clever Snake Lady could think of that."

"But will you help?" she asked urgently.

"Of course I will," he agreed.

"Come speak to Akasya," Myrina told him. "She is my

maid and my go-between."

Akasya boldly scolded Myrina for taking the risk of leaving the safety of the walls.

Tomi laughed again. "I understand things better and better," he said. "This woman is no slave but a Moon Rider through and through."

"And so are all the others," Myrina said. "But there is one great problem. Most of them cannot ride a horse!"

Tomi tried to listen but he could not help but be distracted by his concern for his Ethiopian friends and the battle that raged outside the city walls. By the time the sun had begun to sink in the west, Myrina was once again down at the Southern Gate with Cassandra, ministering to the wounded. Tomi joined those who went out to carry the injured back.

King Memnon had fought fiercely, but that evening he was among the dead. King Priam wearily ordered funeral rites to be held once more, and among the miserable Trojans there was, at last, talk of giving Helen back.

"We have failed yet again! Now Paris is dead, why should we fight on?"

"Perhaps they will spare us if she is handed back!"

"Will they go at last, in return for Deiphobus's unwilling bride?"

There were no more allies to ride to the rescue and

even Aeneas, who had so bravely led the forces after Hector's death, was voicing doubts about the sense in carrying on the fight.

Cassandra took his side and begged her father to give Helen up. "She will go willingly enough." Cassandra was sure.

But her father was adamant. "To fight for ten long years and now give in—never!"

Cassandra wept and pleaded, but he wouldn't listen and threatened to have her locked up if she didn't keep quiet. Myrina comforted her and begged her to help set the slaves free and ride away with them.

Cassandra still shook her head at that suggestion. "These Trojans who are left have known me all my life; they still see me as the priestess of Trojan Apollo. I must stay here to the bitter end."

Myrina shook her head. "But when the Achaeans batter their way inside, as it seems they must, what will happen to you?"

Cassandra pressed her lips together in determination. "I have plans, too, my friend. The Priestess Theano is planning to slip away to Thrace and wait in hiding there, taking Chryseis and the child along with her. Once Troy has fallen, as we know it must, the Achaeans will desert our shores for a while."

"But what of you, Princess?" Myrina demanded.

"I will do my best to join my friends and travel southeast with them to the little island of Sminthe, where Chryseis's father, Chryse, still holds out in the temple of Smintheon Apollo. At least, that is where we will try to meet up and find peace together."

Myrina clicked her tongue in frustration. "But you are a princess of the royal Trojan blood. You would be a great prize to Agamemnon or his brother. I fear that they may drag you away with them and humiliate you to show what great victors they are."

Cassandra smiled. "But you have forgotten something. You and I carry a secret that Agamemnon might value even beyond such pride."

"Ahh." Myrina began to understand.

"I can tell him that despite his great cruelty, Iphigenia is still safe. I could bear witness to his wife, Clytemnestra, and tell her that her daughter surely lives. Do you not think that he will put some value on that?"

Myrina remembered the dark, moody face of Agamemnon as he had watched Penthesilea fight. The man certainly looked as though he bore a terrible burden. Was he eaten up with guilt? So he should be!

Myrina had learned to take note of what Cassandra said, though she despised Agamemnon. "Will he believe you?"

Cassandra nodded. "He will grasp at the knowledge as

a drowning man grasps for a rope."

Myrina took her hand. "You know this?"

"Yes, I do."

That night Myrina and Tomi took Isatis and Moon Silver quietly out through the hidden upper gate. They led their horses onto the hillside and then mounted, riding steadily around the jutting scars and grassland that surrounded Troy, making soft whispering horse calls. They returned before the morning light, leading six Mazagardi mares that they had found wandering, lost since Penthesilea's battle. Some of the horses were scarred and others bore an arrow tip or a gash, but the surviving Moon Riders set to work to feed them and heal their wounds, helped willingly by the slave women.

The next night they set out again and this time Coronilla came with them. They returned with ten horses; with the thirty they already had, they began to fill up the depleted royal stables.

Early one morning, when Myrina was returning to her chamber still under cover of darkness, having put three fresh horses in the stable, she passed a man walking quietly through the streets. There was something about him that made her look twice: something about the thickset shoulders and stocky build was familiar. She caught her breath, then turned and followed him quietly, sure that he bore the broad-shouldered stoop and crafty face of the King of Ithaca.

From the sure and silent way that he moved, she knew that this was not the first time that Odysseus had made a night visit to Troy. He stopped beneath an archway that was shrouded in thick climbing plants, as though waiting for something or someone. Myrina stood still, too, and watched as from the shadows of a sweet-smelling jasmine emerged the Queen of Sparta and her elderly slave woman, Aethra. They whispered together for a few moments, and then Helen kissed the old woman and slipped away. The King of Ithaca led Aethra back down through the streets, walking slowly, matching his pace to hers. Myrina shrank into a covered alleyway as they went past. She could hear Odysseus speaking in a low voice to reassure the old woman.

After they had gone Myrina remained hidden in the shadows, her mind racing. She could go at once and call the Trojan guards or report to King Priam, but what good would that do? Was not she herself about secret business that would not please the King of Troy, had he known of it? She was desperate to save the slave women and ensure that the Moon Riders survived. In just the same way, perhaps Helen had a right to see an old woman safely back into the care of her grandsons.

The affair was intriguing. How many more secret plots

were stirring within the walls of Troy? The war leader Aeneas seemed to have withdrawn his energy from the fight, and Myrina could not believe that such a clever man as he would stay within the walls, awaiting his fate.

The following morning she went to Helen's chamber, courteously asking after the queen's health as cover for her curiosity. As she'd expected, she found Helen on her balcony, watching a good-sized Achaean ship moving out to the deeper water, where the crew set about hauling up the sails.

"A fair wind for Athens?" Myrina whispered.

Helen turned to look at her sharply.

"Don't be afraid," Myrina assured her. "The time is coming for us all to think how best we may survive."

CHAPTER FORTY-SIX

The Earth Shaker

O VER THE NEXT days Cassandra sent small groups of slave women out through the upper gate under the direction of Myrina and Tomi. They took baskets and jars with them, which they were supposed to be filling with olives, apples, and berries. The excuse was believed, as food stocks were now lower than ever. When they returned in the evening with their baskets, the guards did not look closely to see what they had brought back, and nobody guessed that they'd spent most of the day learning to ride.

It wasn't possible to teach the women the skills of the Mazagardi, but at least they could sit astride and hold on, while the horses would obey the cries of those who were more able.

Once or twice they wandered into the path of solitary Achaeans, who like them seemed to be busy scavenging. They usually saw them from afar and kept their distance.

Once Tomi swore that he had watched a gang of them cutting down apple trees and dragging the wood away.

As the Month of Falling Leaves came close, Priam began to look hopefully toward the colder weather. Each year the Achaean lords would withdraw and sail south to make camp on warmer, more comfortable islands, leaving only a small force of weather-hardened warriors to watch the high-walled city. Winter brought a little more liberty to Troy and the possibility of fresh supplies of fish from the Sea of Marmara and olives and grain from those small Phrygian towns that could spare it.

But this year as the weary Achaean lords made preparations to leave, another disaster befell the city on the hill, and this one was not man-made.

Tomi and Myrina were fast asleep when it began. The first sign was that the wooden door to the chamber started to bang, as though someone were slamming it back and forth. They woke up with a start and found that the very bed they slept in was slithering across the room. Then all at once they were rolling together across the floor. They clutched at each other. "Earth tremor," Tomi whispered. "Are you hurt?"

"No." Myrina shook her head, dizzy. "Don't think so—just a bit battered."

They got up, still shaken, and went at once to see that Cassandra and Chryseis were unharmed. The palace stood solidly enough, but great cracks had appeared in the walls and cries of distress could be heard echoing through the corridors.

"The Earth Shaker!"

"The sea god is angry!"

"Poseidon attacks us now?"

They were in Cassandra's chamber when they heard a terrible, heartbreaking wail. All four of them ran out into the passageway to find that the dreadful sounds came from Helen's bedchamber. Helen clutched her head and screamed repeatedly in an agony of despair. Two nurses covered in dust kneeled before her, and laid out on the floor were the bodies of the two little sons that Helen had borne to Paris. They had been sleeping with their nurses in the children's quarters.

"Ah no," Cassandra cried.

"The walls fell down . . . the walls fell down on top of them!" the nurses cried. "We could not get in to them fast enough! It's not our fault! It's not!"

Suddenly Cassandra backed away, pale and trembling, clapping her hands to her ears.

"What is it?" Myrina caught her arm.

"The horse . . . the horse that gallops around and around the walls," she muttered, shaking from head to toe. "Can't you hear it? It kicks down the walls of Troy!" Suddenly blood streamed from her nose and down her gown.

"Get her out of here! Get her out!" Helen began screaming and pointing at Cassandra. "She brings disaster wherever she goes. She's a witch! I swear it! She is to blame for this. Get her out!"

Myrina grabbed Cassandra and she and Tomi pulled her away, down the passageway to her room. They made her lie down and Chryseis washed her face.

The bleeding stopped almost at once and Cassandra quickly became calm again. Suddenly she was getting up and seemed quite in control, her voice deep and strong. "This is the moment," she told Myrina as she struggled to her feet. "You must wait no longer, you must go."

Myrina hesitated for a moment, but Chryseis agreed. "This is your moment," she said.

Tomi frowned in uncertainty, but Cassandra took Myrina by the hand and led them all onto her balcony, which overlooked the south of the city. "Can you see it?" She pointed. "Look down there! Can you see it? By the fig tree."

They stared down to where she seemed to be pointing, but all they could see was a group of guards standing on top of the tower looking down at the wall. They seemed to be pointing and shouting, quite agitated about something.

"What is it?" Myrina asked.

"The wall is cracked from top to bottom," Cassandra told her. "Just a little rain and a little sun and it will fall apart and crumble like a castle made of sand when they return."

Myrina and Tomi looked at each other, puzzled. "When they return?"

Then Cassandra pointed out to sea, and as they turned to look they saw at once that it was dotted with Achaean ships sailing fast away from the Trojan shore, leaving behind them few tents and no cooking fires.

"What are they doing?" Tomi asked.

"Do they leave for the Bitter Months?" Myrina wondered.

"Perhaps they think themselves safer out at sea than on the shaking land," said Tomi.

Myrina turned back to the cracked wall. It was hard to think; everything seemed to be happening at once. She could see no crack, but the guards down there were certainly disturbed and looking at something and Myrina knew better than to disregard Cassandra's warnings. It would be hard to leave her friend, but perhaps the moment had indeed come.

She turned to her and gripped her shoulders. "Come with us—please come with us!"

Cassandra simply shook her head.

"We are like the rats that sailors say will always leave a

sinking ship." Myrina couldn't stop tears from rolling down her cheeks.

But now Cassandra took hold of her, smiling. "How right you are! How right you are, my lovely Snake Lady. But why do rats leave a sinking ship? Because then they will not be dragged down; they will swim and have a chance to survive! Get your women and your horses and go—I shall order the guards to let them out under your direction."

"The princess speaks truth." Chryseis was convinced. "Now is the moment. Priam has too many other things to worry about."

"Yes!" Myrina assented and Tomi nodded.

"Will you travel to Iphigenia's place of safety?" Chryseis asked.

"Yes; will you come?"

Chryseis shook her head. "No, but if you are willing, Theano and I will ride out with you, but then we will head for the safety of Thrace."

"Of course," Myrina agreed.

"But . . . please tell Iphigenia about my little Chryse. I plan to make us a home on Sminthe Island with my father as soon as I can, and Iphigenia will always be welcome to join us there—please tell her that! There will be a home for her on Sminthe once the Achaeans have left our ruined land."

"I will tell her," Myrina promised. Then she hurried away, shouting for Coronilla. "Go at once to gather the other Moon Riders and then to the stables! Prepare the horses!"

"Is this it?" Coronilla was wildly excited. They had longed for this moment and she was eager to put their plans into action.

Tomi, Myrina, and Cassandra set off at once down the passageway, toward the southern entrance to the palace. They passed Helen's room again. The door stood wide open and Myrina could not help but pause for a moment in her stride, for the sight there shocked her deeply. The nurses and waiting women were carefully washing the two poor dead children, laying out fresh garments to dress them in, but Helen sat in front of her mirror, smoothing rose oil into her cheeks. The scent of the precious oil filled the whole room and drifted out into the passage.

The Queen of Sparta picked up a pot of rouge and a small brush and began carefully to paint her lips. She stopped for a moment and turned, aware of Myrina standing white-faced in her doorway. All trace of tears had gone and already the skillful work that she had done made her face look radiant.

"There is nothing left here for me now," she said calmly. "Menelaus always liked this shade of rouge and he loved the scent of roses on my skin."

Myrina just stared at her. "We are all rats," she murmured.

Helen shook her head vaguely and smiled. She looked serene and beautiful, despite her silver graying hair—more beautiful at that moment, thought Myrina, than at any time before. There was certainly strong metal hidden beneath all that softness and charm; Helen would survive. Myrina shook her head, remembering that she must hurry. She turned and ran after Cassandra and Tomi.

There was wailing as they ran through the streets, and dust and disorder everywhere. In the slaves' sleeping quarters, part of the roof of the shed where the children slept had come down. Myrina marched up to the gate and Cassandra drew herself up very tall and imperiously told the guards that all the women were to be put under her command to clear up the stones and bricks that had fallen in the night.

They obeyed her willingly enough.

Myrina made the agreed sign to Akasya, flicking out her fingers from a closed fist; it meant "freedom." The sign spread like fire from woman to woman and from hand to hand, but never a word was spoken. The guards untied the ropes and the women marched out in an orderly way. Some had small babies strapped to their chests; others had the more difficult role of leading toddlers, but each child was quiet and obedient, glad to get away from the walls that had threatened to crush them in the night.

Akasya whispered low that two children had died like Helen's little ones and their mothers were refusing to leave. Myrina stooped to enter the low building that was now half filled with rubble. The mothers sat together, each with her own dead child in her arms. There was no keening from them, just a terrible, staring silence, as they rocked gently back and forth as though soothing their children to sleep. Myrina made the "freedom" sign to them, but both shook their heads. Myrina nodded.

"We cannot make them come," she said to Cassandra. "We all have our own choices to make."

"I will take them as my waiting women," Cassandra told her. "Two I can try to save; all of them I cannot."

Myrina turned to her with the terrible realization that the time had come to say good-bye. Who could tell whether they would ever meet again? She could not make a display of this moment for fear that the guards would become suspicious. This leave-taking was more painful than she had ever imagined it could be. "I pray to Maa that you will save yourself," she whispered.

But Cassandra for once was fearless. "I will save myself," she insisted. "Helen has her means and I have mine. Look in your mirror, Snake Lady, and you shall see!"

"I will," Myrina told her.

"I go to the upper gate now," Cassandra told her coolly. "I'll make sure that it is open. Then, whatever happens, do not stop or turn back, just ride, ride, ride! Snake Lady . . . I will always think of you!"

CHAPTER FORTY-SEVEN

Apples and Freedom

A S CASSANDRA HAD promised, the upper gates were open, with only a small number of guards, who were distracted enough with all the difficulties that the earth tremor had brought. The slave women mounted the horses as they had planned, two to each mare. Each Moon Rider took a woman who had never ridden and many of those also had a child perched in front. Akasya and the other women who had recently had lessons from Myrina took a mare for themselves. Chryseis and Theano joined them, little Chryse strapped snugly to his mother's back. The two priestesses gave the large party of riders even more of an air of authority. They ambled quietly through the upper streets with Myrina at their head. Tomi brought up the rear.

Cassandra issued more orders to the guards as the horses began to pass steadily out through the hidden gateway. All seemed well, but as more and more rode through, the guards became suspicious.

"What is this? Why so many?"

"But the princess has ordered it!"

"Never mind the princess—what of her father? We have never let so many out before!"

"Why are these children going? These babies never go outside!"

"You will do as you are told!" Cassandra ordered. "Do you wish the wrath of Trojan Apollo on your head? Has not the Earth Shaker shown enough anger to this city in the night?"

The captain of the guard would have no more. "Stop them!" he bellowed.

But by then every last woman was out and Tomi, bringing up the rear, wheeled his horse about. "Ride!" he bellowed, taking his bow from his shoulder. "Ride!"

All the riders heard his cry—even Myrina on Isatis at the front. Instinctively she urged her mare onward, but at the same time her heart sank to her boots.

"Ride!" Tomi cried, as he notched an arrow to his bow, and sent it flying toward the angry guards, who knew at once that they had been tricked.

Tomi's arrows flew fast and furious and he shot down each guard that came at him, trying to follow the women. It was a short but bitter battle and at the end of it every one of the small group of men lay dead, but so did Tomi.

Myrina and the women galloped on and vanished over the hilltop.

Cassandra stood by the gates, her hands trembling, but then she made herself walk quietly out to where Tomi lay, his horse still snuffling at his bloodstained cheek. "Ya, ya yush!" she whispered, tears flooding down her cheeks.

Moon Silver reared his head. "Ya, ya yush!" Cassandra repeated.

The silver stallion turned obediently and headed up the hillside, following in Myrina's wake.

Cassandra sat beside Tomi for a while, but then she got up and carefully pulled his body back inside the hidden gate. She closed the great wooden doors, knuckled the tears from her eyes and calmly called for a servant to see the bodies taken away. "A band of Achaean warriors have captured our slaves," she announced.

"All of them, Princess?"

Cassandra looked at him sternly; her blue and green eyes did not waver.

"Yes, Princess." The man said no more; there was far too much else to concern both lords and servants in Troy than this.

"Take the Mazagardi warrior to my chamber," she ordered. "I myself will lay him out and prepare him for the pyre. He was a very brave man."

"Yes, Princess." He did her bidding at once.

As Myrina breasted the hilltop, an astonishing sight lay before her. There, crossing their pathway, was a great gang of Achaeans, led by Odysseus. They moved steadily toward the downward path leading to the plain below. They dragged and pushed a heavy wooden battle engine with a great pointed head, the whole thing on wheels. Ropes were fastened to it on all sides and those at the front hauled away, while others pushed from the back. Myrina thought at once of Cassandra's words: "A horse that moves toward the walls."

The Achaeans were absorbed in their task, so that they did not immediately see the gang of women who appeared over the hilltop to the side of them. Myrina almost stopped at the sight of them, but Cassandra's last words came to her: "Do not stop, or turn back, just ride, ride, ride!"

She whipped her bow from her shoulder and had an arrow notched before any of the men had noticed. Then, as she rode on and more Moon Riders appeared over the hilltop with bows instantly at the ready, she knew that they must simply charge their way through.

The Achaeans were not armed with bows, but some had spears and swords. As soon as they saw the Snake Lady charging toward them, they snatched up their weapons, but Myrina could see fear in their eyes as memories of Penthesilea came to their minds. Then suddenly there was a shout from their leader. "Hold!" Odysseus bellowed.

Myrina slowed Isatis for just a moment, wondering if he would recognize her as the friend of Yildiz and Penthesilea.

"Hold!" he repeated, his eyes wide with surprise as he looked at the strange mixture of women who followed Myrina: Moon Riders in full armor and helmets, weary ragged slaves with children in their arms, and even two priestesses.

Then he spoke quietly. "Our quarrel is not with such as you. Do not interfere with us and you may ride on!"

Myrina lowered her bow and gave a sharp little nod; she rode on fast.

All through the day she rode on and on. She remembered the words that Cassandra had used to describe her dream: "You were leading a great herd, and yet you were somehow terribly alone!" The words echoed through her head. No Yildiz! No Tomi! Gone . . . all gone. Alone.

Then she forced those thoughts away. She was not alone, not on Isatis's back. She could never be alone, not while she still had Isatis. She made herself chant under her breath, "Just ride, ride, ride! I am not alone!"

She led the women through the high mountainous lands that she knew so well, heading north toward the coast of the Sea of Marmara. She did not stop for anything; she did not stop to look for Tomi or ask about him. She knew the price that she had paid for freedom—it was a high price indeed.

Chryseis and Theano separated from them when the sun was high in the sky. They did not stop to say goodbye, just gave the priestess's salute and turned their horses' heads to the west. Myrina understood from their sorrowful looks that they understood only too well the sacrifice that had been made.

As the sun sank, Myrina slowed her pace at last. They came to a stream with a dark silhouette of sheltering trees that she recognized would make a good resting place for the night. Coronilla and Akasya came to her at once, leading the riderless Moon Silver, their faces grim.

Myrina slipped down from Isatis's back, bone-weary and numb. "Do not say it!" she warned them angrily. "I do not want to hear the words!"

They obeyed her and all the women moved quietly in sympathy, hushing their children in respect for her feelings. They lit a fire with flint and the dried fennel twigs that Coronilla had brought and drank the clean fresh water of the stream. Though there had been little time to think of food—and little food left in Troy to bring—Coronilla had managed to snatch up a bag of grain so that they could make flat bread cakes. The Moon Riders showed the children that many of the trees were apple trees and still bore fruit. Myrina heard small voices whispering joyfully in the Luvvian language, "We have apples and freedom!"

"Tomorrow you will have fish from the Sea of Marmara," she promised. "My friend the King of Marble Island will help us in every way he can."

Tears came at last to her and she wandered away from the others and sat down beside the stream. The women allowed her to weep in peace, but when at last she was so weary that no more tears would come, she began to dry her eyes, hearing a gentle rhythmical sound in the distance. She got up and wandered back toward the camp. All the women—Moon Riders, those who had once been slaves, and even their children—were dancing about the fire, arms linked, turning their heads to the north, to the south, and then up to the moon. There beneath the apple trees they moved together, singing the strange song that had sustained them through all their years of hardship in Troy.

Myrina approached, but they still sang on, more gently than ever. A powerful wave of comfort flooded out to her from each and every one of them. As she came close they slowed and stopped, uncertain whether they caused more pain.

"No," she said. "Don't stop. You must always do this

dance. You must never forget it. It is a dance of great power and it will carry you through all you have to face."

"We won't forget it." Akasya held out her hand to Myrina. "Come and join us. Tonight we dance to honor Tomi and after this day, whenever we do this dance, we will always think of him."

Myrina went to her, smiling shakily. "Thank you," she whispered.

They made a space for her and then started to sing and move together again in harmony, turning their heads from side to side like rippling waves, and then up to the silver moon.

It was the Month of New Leaves and five women, mounted on horseback, reined in their mares at the top of the highest hill above the thickly wooded valley of the River Thermodon. They looked confidently to the south, for six months had passed since the city of Troy had fallen and most of the raiding Achaeans had returned to their homes. The tribal traveling lands were slowly becoming safe again.

Atisha and Hati were both very old and slow-moving, but they had insisted on riding out that afternoon. Iphigenia and Centaurea moved a little way ahead, but the most eager of all was four-year-old Phoebe, who rode her mare as confidently and straight-backed as the adults.

"Snake Lady, Snake Lady, come to us!" she whispered impatiently.

At last they thought they could see movement in the distance. They strained their eyes. "Is it them?" Phoebe shrilled.

"Yes, my little cistus flower, I think so." Atisha's voice cracked with emotion.

They urged their horses forward. Atisha and Hati slowed their mounts so that they could take in the sight and wonder at it. Myrina rode toward them on Isatis at the head of a huge party of horsewomen; Akasya and Coronilla galloped at her side. Behind them followed the great mass of riders, their steeds well fed, with gleaming coats. They rode as though they had spent their lives in the saddle and every one of them was equipped with leather body armor, strung bows and quivers full of arrows fastened to their thighs. Little children sat confidently in front of their mothers; the older children who rode with them managed their own mounts with confidence. The Moon Riders were a strong and potent force once again.

"Snake Lady." Hati's voice broke. Tears spilled down her withered cheeks as she welcomed Myrina, hugging her tight. "I can't believe it," she whispered. "A whole new band of Moon Riders at your back."

"Grandmother," Myrina scolded, "you never cry!"

"On such a day as this I do." Hati had no shame in the tears.

"We have seen all your joys and sorrows," Atisha told Myrina sadly. "We know the rash courage of Penthesilea, and those that you have had to leave behind."

Hati wiped her eyes. "I am so sorrowful that when I go there will be only you and little Phoebe left of our once great Mazagardi tribe."

"No, that is not quite true, Grandmother," Myrina told her, smiling, "for I will be needing your help as a midwife soon."

Then Atisha and Hati laughed with joy as they saw that her hand rested protectively on her swollen belly.

"It seems that Phoebe and I will not be the last of the Mazagardi after all!"

Epilogue

M YRINA AND IPHIGENIA sat together beside a
waterfall on a hot day in the Month of
Burning Heat. Myrina's tiny daughter,
Tamsin, lay beside them in the shade, kicking her legs,
but for once both the women were ignoring her, each
one gazing into her own mirror, but sharing the vision
they saw.

Suddenly Iphigenia cried out, shocked, "He is dead.
My father is dead!"

Myrina reached out and clasped her hand, but neither
of them dared to take her eyes from her mirror, for
Cassandra, the one they were most concerned about,
stood face to face with Iphigenia's mother, Clytemnestra.
They could see the terrible anger that was written there
in the aging queen's face; she was a bitter, dark-haired
version of her sister Helen.

As they watched, Clytemnestra reached accusingly to

Cassandra with a bloodstained hand, but the Princess of Troy did not flinch. She stood her ground and spoke. Though Myrina and Iphigenia could not hear the words clearly, they understood very well what was being said. Suddenly Clytemnestra put her head down and sobbed. It was Cassandra's own arms that reached out to comfort the woman.

"She knows," Myrina said. "Your mother knows at last that you are safe."

Iphigenia heaved a great sigh. "Of this at least I am glad."

Then they watched as Clytemnestra led the way, hand in hand with Cassandra, down steep steps to a waiting boat. Hurriedly she ushered the princess on board and then stood back on the harborside, watching as the boat was rowed away and the sails were unfurled.

Cassandra sat there on the deck as the wind caught the sails and the captain gave the order to draw in the oars. The watchers both smiled as they saw her expression; it was one of great peace.

"She is safe." Iphigenia breathed with relief. "But where will she go?"

Myrina smiled and did not hesitate. "To the island of Sminthe," she said. "Perhaps one day you and I will go there, too."

Cast of Characters

Moon Riders:

Myrina—the Snake Lady, daughter of Aben and Gul, granddaughter of Hati, sister of Reseda, member of the Mazagardi tribe; an imaginary character.

Cassandra—Princess of Troy, daughter of Priam; a character from Greek mythology, portrayed in Homer's *Iliad*.

Atisha—Leader of the Moon Riders, old friend of Hati; an imaginary character.

Penthesilea—Moon Rider, Atisha's second-in-command; she is based on Penthesilea the Amazon Queen, a character from Greek mythology, portrayed in "The Fall of Troy," a heroic poem by Quintus of Smyrna.

Hati, Gul, and Reseda—female family members of Myrina who were Moon Riders before her; imaginary characters.

Yildiz and Phoebe—daughters of Reseda; imaginary characters.

Trojans:

Priam—King of Troy; a character from Greek mythology, portrayed in Homer's *Iliad*.

Hecuba—Queen of Troy; a character from Greek mythology, portrayed in Homer's *Iliad*.

Paris—Prince of Troy, son of Priam, Helen's lover; a character from Greek mythology, portrayed in Homer's *Iliad*.

Hector—Prince of Troy, eldest son of Priam; a character from Greek mythology, portrayed in Homer's *Iliad*.

Chryseis—friend of Cassandra, daughter of Chryse, priest of Apollo; based on a character from Greek mythology, portrayed in Homer's *Iliad*.

Achaeans:

Agamemnon—King of Mycenae, powerful overlord of the Achaean lands; a character from Greek mythology, portrayed in Homer's *Iliad*.

Clytemnestra—Queen of Mycenae, wife of Agamemnon, mother of Iphigenia and also Helen's sister; character from Greek mythology, portrayed in Homer's *Iliad*.

Iphigenia—Princess of Mycenae, daughter of Clytemnestra and Agamemnon, friend to Cassandra; a character from Greek mythology, *not* mentioned in the *Iliad* but in Aeschylus's *The Libation Bearers* and Euripides' *Iphigenia at Aulis* and *Iphigenia at Tauris*.

Menelaus—King of Sparta; a character from Greek mythology portrayed in Homer's *Iliad*.

Helen—Queen of Sparta, wife of Menelaus, Paris's lover, and Clytemnestra's sister; a character from Greek mythology, portrayed in Homer's *Iliad*.

Achilles—Leader of the Myrmidon warriors who fight on behalf of Agamemnon; a character from Greek mythology, portrayed in Homer's *Iliad*.

Author's Note

As a child I struggled to learn Latin for about six months, but eventually the teacher gave up in despair and I was sent down the corridor to join the "Greek Literature in Translation" class instead. I felt this to be a terrible disgrace but was soon cheered as, with a broad-minded, humorous nun as a teacher, I discovered an exciting and rather shocking world of adventure, magic, love, and tragedy. We read *The Odyssey*, *The Iliad*, *The Oedipus Trilogy* and *The Histories* of Herodotus. It was here that I first came across fabulous stories of the warlike women known as the Amazons.

Many years later, in 1997, I watched a BBC 2 "Horizon" television program called *The Ice Maiden*. An archaeologist, Natalia Polasmak, had discovered the frozen mummified body of a young woman buried with great honor and respect in the Altai Mountains, her shoulders, arms, and hands covered in beautiful tattoos. I found the whole program very moving, and was fascinated to hear the women archaeologists relating this find and other burials of women with weapons to *The Histories* of Herodotus. It seemed that the fabulous stories of Amazons might after all have been based on real nomadic tribeswomen, who lived, rode, and fought long ago in the area to the north and surrounding the Black Sea.

My interest in this subject was taken much further when I found Lyn Webster Wilde's fascinating and thoroughly researched book *On the Trail of the Women Warriors*. I felt inspired to try to write a novel for young people based on the legends of the Amazons, but the more I discovered about Amazon mythology and history, the more vast and overwhelming the subject became. Remembering my Greek Literature school studies once again brought me to focus on the ever appealing, tragic story of Troy.

More research followed: Michael Wood's *In Search of the Trojan War* was full of clear, practical, down-to-earth information and ideas, making the Trojan War only too real and believable. Neal Ascherson's wonderfully human and readable book *Black Sea* helped to build a picture of the people and landscape to the north of Troy. *The Fall of Troy*, an epic poem by Quintus of Smyrna, 400 BC, told the story of Penthesilea's fight with Achilles.

Despite these excellent sources of information, I still felt that there was something lacking. I could not get a clear picture in my mind of the colors, plants, and landscape. In the end there was nothing for it but to go to have a look at the ruins of Troy myself. On a cold, windy day in early May 2000, my husband and I walked around the ruins on the hillside at Hisarlik with the local guide and author, Mustafa Askin. Mustafa was full of information about the ruins and the history of Troy. His enthusiasm for the place was infectious as he patiently answered all our questions.

Later that day the sun came out. As I stood among the broken, but still sturdy, golden limestone walls of Troy, gazing down at the deep blue Aegean Sea, with the Hellespont to the right and Mount Ida behind to the left, I felt that somehow I'd come full circle, and that perhaps being sent out of the Latin class was one of the best things that had ever happened to me.

THERESA TOMLINSON, 2002
www.theresatomlinson.com